SINFUL LOVE

LAUREN BLAKELY

ALSO BY LAUREN BLAKELY

Standalone Male-POV books

Big Rock

Mister O

Well Hung

Full Package

Joy Ride

Hard Wood

One Love Series dual-POV Standalones

The Sexy One

The Only One

The Hot One

Standalones

The Knocked Up Plan

Most Valuable Playboy

Stud Finder

The V Card

Most Likely to Score (January 2018)

Wanderlust (February 2018)

Come As You Are (April 2018)

Part-Time Lover (June 2018)

The Real Deal (Summer 2018)

Far Too Tempting

21 Stolen Kisses

Playing With Her Heart

Out of Bounds

The Caught Up in Love Series

Caught Up In Us

Pretending He's Mine

Trophy Husband

Stars in Their Eyes

The No Regrets Series

The Thrill of It

The Start of Us

Every Second With You

The Seductive Nights Series

First Night (Julia and Clay, prequel novella)

Night After Night (Julia and Clay, book one)

After This Night (Julia and Clay, book two)

One More Night (Julia and Clay, book three)

A Wildly Seductive Night (Julia and Clay novella, book 3.5)

Nights With Him (A standalone novel about Michelle and Jack)

Forbidden Nights (A standalone novel about Nate and Casey)

The Sinful Nights Series

Sweet Sinful Nights

Sinful Desire

Sinful Longing

Sinful Love

The Fighting Fire Series

Burn For Me (Smith and Jamie)

Melt for Him (Megan and Becker)

Consumed By You (Travis and Cara)

The Jewel Series

A two-book sexy contemporary romance series

The Sapphire Affair

The Sapphire Heist

ABOUT

Intense. Devoted. Protective.

Michael Sloan is all of the above, with a hard tough edge to boot. He's not the guy he used to be. Years ago, before all the s&%t went down, he was laidback, carefree, and even happy-go-lucky.

Life changed him. Hardened him.

There's one woman though who can break down his walls. Someone who knew him then. Who can reach inside to that heart he protects fiercely...because she's the only one he ever gave it to. When they collide, it's tender and savage, gentle and rough, and makes them both hungry for more of this electric, once-in-a-blue moon kind of sexual chemistry. But it's a battle of wills between Michael and the woman he loves, with words and emotions held close to the vest.

She doesn't believe she can ever move on from her own heartbreak, but when Michael makes her feel for the first time in years, it's both thrilling and scares the hell out of her, setting off all her flight instincts. He's determined not to lose her again, but he'll have to learn to let her in if he ever wants to fully heal from the past...

The problem is, she knows something about the night his family shattered. She has the missing puzzle piece...but neither one of them realizes it.

YET.

DEDICATION

This book is dedicated to the women who helped shape and refine the Sinful Nights series – Jen McCoy, Kim Bias, Lauren McKellar, Crystal Perkins, Trish Mint, and Candy's amazing editor. And, as always, to my dear friend Cynthia.

1

The letter smelled like her. Like rain.

He ran his thumb over the corner of the paper and closed his eyes briefly. Memories rose to the surface, bringing with them feelings of hope and possibility.

Things that were far too risky when it came to her.

Michael shut them down, opened his eyes, and stared out the floor-to-ceiling windows of his penthouse on the Strip, trying to focus on the here and now, not the enticing lure of *what if*. Tonight the lights of Vegas would blink like a carnival unfolding below him, from the miniature Eiffel Tower, to the pyramid, to the blazing signs adorning the Cosmopolitan. Neon, glitz, and billboards ten stories high whispered of the *best nights ever*.

But he had to stay fixed on the minute details of the present, not be seduced by the past and how good it was, or of how much he'd longed for a future with her.

He wasn't having the easiest time of that. From his vantage point, twenty stories above the concrete ribbon that beckoned millions of tourists, he brought the letter to his nose for one final inhale.

The scent of falling rain.

Try as he might to fight it, a reel of sensory images rushed back to him from years ago, like the *snap, snap, snap* of old film. How many times had he kissed Annalise in the rain? Brushed her wild red hair off her cheeks and touched her soft skin? Listened to her laugh?

Countless. Just like the times his mind had lingered on her over the last eighteen years, including that heart-breaking day in Marseilles, which had damn near slaughtered all his hopes in the world.

Carefully, he folded up the letter, slid it back into the tiny envelope postmarked from France, and stuffed it into his wallet next to a crinkled, faded, threadbare note from his father that he'd carried with him always. Her letter had arrived two weeks ago, and he'd read it a thousand times already. He could read it a thousand more, but it wouldn't change his answer—the same one he'd emailed back to her.

Yes.

It was always yes with her.

Dear Michael,

I hope this note finds you well. I will be in Las Vegas for business in a few weeks. I would love to see you again. Would you like to have a coffee with me? Come to think of it, do you drink coffee now? If memory serves, you were never fond of it. Perhaps a tea, or water, or martinis at midday? Any, all, or some would be lovely.

My information is below so you can respond. I would have emailed, but a letter seemed more fitting. And, truth be told, easier to ignore, should that be your preference.

Though I will be wishing to see your name pop up in my email soon.

xoxo

Annalise

As if he stood a chance of *not* emailing her. As if there were any universe, parallel, perpendicular, or otherwise, where he wouldn't take her up on her offer for coffee, tea, liquor, or a few minutes in a café.

Any, all, or some.

He turned away from the midday view of the city he loved and headed to the stereo system above his flat-screen, which piped music through his home. Thank Christ for the soundproof walls—they allowed him to blast his tunes. This Sunday afternoon, following a long, hard run and an even longer workout at the gym, he'd cued up his favorite playlist as he got ready to see her, methodically picking music he'd discovered in the last year, rather than the music he'd shared with her when they were younger.

Not that he didn't still love his late 90s tunes. He just knew he'd be a goner if he let himself trip that far back in time.

He turned off the fading guitar riff from The Foals, and silence descended on his home.

He grabbed his keys and his phone from the entryway table, locked the door behind him, and headed down the hall, wishing his pulse wasn't already competing in a race.

The ride down the elevator was both interminable and not long enough. Anticipation curled through him as he left his high-rise building, crossed the big intersection, and headed toward Las Vegas Boulevard. The air had cooled; late October had rolled into his hometown. This brief walk in the crisp air would surely quell the nerves that bounced in his chest.

He didn't fucking want to feel them. Nor did he want to experience this wild sense of hope rattling in him like a marble sliding down a chute. Dragging a hand through his dark hair, he tried to focus on anything but what might happen when he saw her.

Later this afternoon he had a meeting with a client, then this evening he'd review some new contracts for work. Sometime this week he'd meet with the detective working his father's case, touching base with him before he left for a trip. He also needed to check in with the private—

His phone bleated from his back pocket, and he grabbed it quickly. His friend Mindy's name flashed across the screen. "Hey there," he said, while winding his way through the throngs of visitors on the sidewalk.

"Whatcha wearing?" she singsonged. "Wait. Don't tell me. You went for your favorite jeans and a lucky T-shirt."

He laughed. "I assure you I don't have a lucky T-shirt."

"Well, you should. I would get on that right away."

"Duly noted. I'll order up one lucky T-shirt after this meeting."

"*Meeting.* You make it sound so businesslike."

"How should I make it sound?"

"Like you've been counting down the hours for this since you received the *letter*," she said, making the note sound ominous. An information Hoover, Mindy had a way of wheedling details out of him, ever since they'd graduated from professional colleagues to good friends over the summer when they'd paired up on a moon-lighting project.

"Speaking of counting down the hours, I'll see you early evening still?" he asked, sidestepping her far too accurate assessment of how he'd measured the time since Annalise's missive had arrived.

"Yup. I'll be there at five. I fully expect you to tell me every dirty detail."

"There won't be any dirty details."

She scoffed. "Oh, I bet there will, and I plan on extracting them all."

"Good-bye, Mindy," he said.

The thought of seeing Annalise Delacroix had pretty much played on a loop in Michael's mind since he'd flipped through the mail on his desk two weeks ago, the lavender envelope sliding from the top of the pile into his palm, the past thundering into the present. He had a shoebox full of her letters from years ago. He hadn't looked at the others in ages. He couldn't bring himself to chuck them, but he also wasn't interested in inflicting the kind of self-torture that reading them would bring.

He threaded through the crowds outside the Bellagio as sprays of water from the fountains arced in their daytime ballet, his shoes clicking against the stone pathway that curved around the man-made lake. He stepped into a wedge of the revolving door, which whisked him into the hotel lobby with its polished marble floors, glass sculptures, and grand archways.

As he cut a path toward the casino floor, he tried to pretend he was here at this hotel for business. Meeting a potential client. Seeing an old friend. But the way his heart tried to torpedo out of his skin, he was going to need some much better tricks to fool himself.

When he reached the hostess stand at the upscale Petrossian Bar, he simply resigned himself to the storm brewing inside of him. Besides, how else was he supposed to feel right before he was about to see—as his brother Colin had so aptly called her—his "what if" girl?

"Like this," he muttered to himself. Like a case of *what if* bombs had exploded inside his chest.

"May I help you?"

The even-toned, sweet-sounding voice jarred him because it was so normal. How could anyone feel fine this second? He felt the opposite of fine. *He* felt a mixed-up, jumbled mess of emotions that boiled down to two warring ones—a fervent wish that this *meeting* would not be a repeat of the airport in Marseilles, and the hope that all his ex-girlfriends were incorrect in their diagnosis of his heart trouble.

He was *not* hung up on her. No matter what they had said to the contrary.

The hostess in her trim gray suit cocked her head, waiting for him to answer.

"I'm looking for...someone," Michael said, his voice gravelly, as if words were new to him.

"Would you like to have a look around and see if..." She trailed off, letting him fill in the blank.

"Yeah. I'll take a look."

The pianist in the bar tapped out an old Cole Porter song. Michael turned the corner, scanning the lounge-style seating for a tall, willowy woman.

Briefly, he wondered if he'd recognize her. He'd first known her when they were teenagers, then he saw her again at age twenty-four in Marseilles. That was ten years ago, and surely he didn't look the same. He had crinkles at the corners of his blue eyes, and his hair, inexplicably, had darkened. His sister Shannon joked that it was turning black, like his heart.

He was also sturdier than he had been before. His shoulders were broader, arms more defined. At twenty-four, he'd been in the army, working in intelligence; now, he was a twice-daily fixture at the gym and had the bigger muscles to show for it.

But whether Annalise Delacroix had dyed her hair or shaved it all off, he was pretty confident he'd find her easily without having seen a photo of her recently. He hadn't stalked her on social media, but he *had* researched the most important detail before he'd emailed her back.

He'd found the obit.

The one that gave him permission to have a cup of coffee. He shuddered. He still didn't like coffee. But coffee was the only path to her. Follow the roadmap, turn this corner, and see the first woman he'd ever loved. It had taken him forever to fall out of love with her, but he was there. He was absolutely there.

He hummed to distract himself as his eyes roamed over the crowd at the upscale establishment. He spotted auburn hair swept high in a twist, long elegant fingers, and the cut of her jawline. Her right collarbone was exposed; her black top had sloped down one shoulder, revealing soft flesh.

His heart thundered, and his blood roared.

Trying desperately to tamp down the riot inside of him, he inhaled, exhaled, then walked the final feet to her side. Her back was to him. When he reached her, she turned fully, and her green eyes lit up.

Gorgeous green eyes, like gems.

Carved cheekbones.

Lips, so red and lush.

She held a cup of espresso and had just brought it to her lips.

That lucky fucking mug.

She finished the gulp and laughed lightly. "Some habits never fade."

Truer words...

2

Annalise hadn't been in Las Vegas since she was a foreign exchange student during her junior year of high school, living with a host family and perfecting her English on American soil.

Odd, in some ways, that her job hadn't taken her back to this town even once in all the years—but perhaps that wasn't so strange, considering business was plentiful in Europe. For now, for a few days at least, business was here, and so was the man she'd fallen madly in love with as that teenage foreign exchange student.

He was more handsome than ever.

Imagine that.

The prettiest boy in America was now the hottest man she'd laid eyes on in a long, long time. But lusty admiration wasn't all she felt as she drank in the sight of Michael Sloan. A myriad of emotions she wasn't prepared for swam through her, and it was as if she'd become a host for a chemical concoction of regret, loneliness, and wistfulness, topped with excitement.

She zeroed in on that one, shoving all the others aside.

She stood, set down the cup, and dusted a barely-there kiss on his right cheek. His five-o'clock shadow stubble—even though it was only one o'clock on a Sunday—scratched her in a whiskery, sandpaper way. She pressed a kiss to his left cheek. The slightest whoosh of air escaped his lips.

Lips she'd known well. Lips she had spent years wanting to touch again.

"Cheek kisses. You haven't forgotten how the French do it." She sounded breathless, even to her own ears.

"How could I forget?" He said it lightly, as if he were talking only about the kisses, but there was so much more she hadn't forgotten. Was it that way for him, too?

"You look…" She let her voice trail off as a lump rose in her throat, and that storm of emotions stirred up again, churning inside her. It wasn't his looks that had knocked the wind out of her. Though seriously, there was nothing whatsoever to complain about in that regard, as she surveyed him in his black pants and crisp gray shirt, taking in his trim waist, strong shoulders, and tall frame. Nor was it his dark black hair, his cool blue eyes, or the cut of his jaw, dusted with that faint stubble.

The tumult was courtesy of the past, hurtling itself headfirst into her present. Yes, it was her choice to be here. Still, she hadn't expected to be walloped by the mere sight of him. She swallowed harshly, trying to dislodge that hitch, wanting to feel some semblance of cool and calm. Her shoulders rose and fell, and she tried desperately to breathe in such a way that didn't require her to relearn how to take in oxygen. She dug her four-inch black stilettos into the plush carpet, seeking purchase as she attempted to reconnect with her ability to form words.

"You look good," she said, the understatement of the year. Wait. Make that a lifetime.

"And you look...lovely."

Lovely.

That was *so* him.

He'd never been one for hot, smoking, gorgeous, babe, or any of those sayings of the moment. There was something in him that spiraled deeper, and leaned on words that had more heft. Like *lovely.*

What to say next? She should have scripted this rendezvous. Wrote out talking points. But she didn't know which direction in the conversational path to turn, so she went for the obvious.

"We finally made it to the Bellagio," she said, gesturing to the crowds clicking by outside the bar. God, this was hard. How do you just have a drink with someone you once thought you'd marry? Someone who was your everything? She'd been his rock; he'd been her hope.

"Yeah. We finally did," he echoed.

It had only taken eighteen years, an ocean, countless letters, two broken hearts, and a lengthy online search for him, which had taken time and research, since he'd changed his name and was absent from social media. The Bellagio was the symbol of all their promises. Young, foolish, and wildly in love, they'd been together when this hotel was under construction nearly two decades ago. They'd said they would check it out when it opened, even though they'd both known at the time it was an empty promise.

The hotel was slated to be finished months after she left town. By the time the doors finally opened, Michael's life had shattered, and she'd been thousands of miles away.

But the promise had been made anyway. It was a promise to reunite. One of many promises they'd made.

Some kept.

Some impossible to keep.

"Join me. *S'il vous plait*." She patted the back of the sofa as she sat down again.

"*Merci*." He took a seat next to her, and at last she felt like she could breathe. Her warring emotions settled, and now she was simply out with this man. Someone she'd been thinking about more and more lately.

"So," she said.

"So..." He rubbed his palms against his thighs.

"How are you?" she asked, stepping into the shallow end. "Are you well?"

"Good, good," he answered quickly. "And you?"

"Great. Everything is great," she said, as chipper as she could be, even though she'd hardly use *great* to describe the tundra that her heart had become during the last two years. "I'm glad you made it," she said to keep going, lest any silence turn this reunion more awkward.

"And I'm glad you asked me to meet you," he said, as if he were waiting for her to tell him *why* she'd wanted to meet. She didn't, though, because when he looked at her like that, the breath fled her lungs. He was so handsome, and his eyes were soulful, something she'd rarely use to describe blue eyes. His seemed to reveal a depth, forged by years of heartache and tragedy.

She parted her lips to speak, but she wasn't even sure what to say next. Did she go for lightness? For more catching-up-with-you chit-chat? Or plunge straight into the heart of why she'd wanted to see him? She was so accustomed to charging into situations fearlessly, to chasing after what she wanted, but all those skills escaped her in this moment, and she was a teabag steeping in a pot of awkward.

Fortunately, the waitress arrived and asked Michael if he wanted anything. "Club soda," he said, and when the woman left Annalise tilted her head.

"So, you still detest coffee?" she asked, because that was a far easier conversation entrée than all the other things they could talk about.

"Evidently, I still do."

"I never understood that about you," she said, shaking her head in disbelief. Funny that she and Michael had gotten on so well when they were younger—except on this. Their one bone of contention was over her passionate love of the deliciously addictive substance, and his disdain of it.

"It vexed you, I know."

"I tried to get you to like coffee. I even tried to make espresso for you."

"You were relentless," he said, and the corners of his lips quirked up. That smile, that lopsided grin she'd loved... Okay, this was better. This was a slow and steady slide back into the zone.

"Remember when I hunted all over Vegas trying to find something like what they'd serve in a café in Paris?" she said, reminiscing, slipping back into the time they were together years ago.

Like it was yesterday, he picked up the conversational baton. "You even used your babysitting money to buy an old espresso machine at a garage sale," he said, and the memory of her determination and his resistance made her laugh. "Remember that?"

Her eyes widened. "I do! It was a Saturday morning. I scoured the papers for garage sales, and hunted all around the neighborhood till I located the only one I could afford."

"Found one for ten dollars."

Annalise held up an index finger. "Ten dollars and twenty-five cents."

"Ah, well. The quarter made all the difference," he said, as the waitress brought his drink and he thanked her.

"I took it back to Becky and Sanders's home that afternoon, and I thought I'd win you over. That if you had a proper coffee, made like we do back home, you'd be converted." It was only coffee, but it was a thread that connected them to the distant past, when their lives were so much simpler. It was a far easier topic than the present, and certainly less painful than the words said the last time they saw each other, on that heartbreaking day in Marseilles after he'd sent her that letter that had torn her to pieces.

"Alas, I was non-convertible." He took a swallow of the club soda. "So what brings you to town?"

"Work."

He frowned and glanced from side to side, like he was sweeping the bar for trouble. "There's a war in Vegas I'm not aware of?"

She laughed and shook her head. "I'm not a photojournalist any longer. Now I shoot fashion—lingerie and boudoir. I'm here doing the high-end catalogue for Veronica's," she said, naming the famous lingerie chain with which she'd nabbed a plum gig. "Some of the shoots are at the Cosmopolitan and around town. We did the Venetian Canals earlier today. Caesars Palace is tomorrow."

"So this is you now," he said, waving a hand at her.

"Shooting barely dressed women in silk and lace instead of racing across the desert in a Humvee?"

She nodded. "From shrapnel to strapless."

"What happened to make you leave?"

"Death happened."

So did heartbreak and unfinished love.

He nodded in agreement, his expression turning somber. He cleared his throat. "I'm sorry to hear about Julien."

Her throat hitched, but she fought past that goddamn lump. She'd cried enough to end California's drought. "Thank you."

More quickly than she'd expected—and she was eminently grateful not to linger on talk of Julien with this man—Michael led them out of this conversation, returning to safer ground. "You like fashion better?"

She glanced up at the ceiling, considering. That was a tough question. She'd loved the adrenaline rush of photojournalism, the thrill of chasing a story that didn't want to be found, the chance to capture an image that would show her nation the truth of what was happening in the world, whether during her days in the Middle East, or covering breaking news across Europe for a French news agency. But the job became too risky and the costs too high, so she'd pivoted.

She had no regrets.

She met his eyes to answer. "Yes. I like fashion better now. I love what I do."

They chatted more as she told him tales of the models and their over-the-top requests at shoots—from the imperious blonde who required celery sticks chilled to a crisp 65 degrees, to the willowy brunette who would only drink artesian water—and how it compared to the bare-bones style of hunting images in her combat boots, cargo pants, and photographer's vest, in one of the most dangerous areas of the world.

"What about you, Michael? You're not fronting a band. I didn't see your guitar in any of your company photos," she said, nudging his arm gently. His strong, toned arm. So firm. She was going to need a reason to nudge him again.

He shrugged. "That was high school. I was just messing around in the garage with friends. I don't play much anymore."

"What happened to going to Seattle and becoming the next Eddie Vedder?" she asked, then her stomach dropped. "*Merde.* I'm sorry," she said, heat flaming across her cheeks. How could she have been so foolish? She knew the answer. She brought her hand to her face, embarrassed, and lowered her chin.

His hand touched hers. Her breath caught the instant he made contact. "It's okay. It was just a teenage dream."

Just a teenage dream. They'd had so many. They'd felt so real at the time.

"We had a lot of those," she said, softly.

"We did." He looked away. His jaw was set hard, but when he returned his gaze to her, he simply said, "I barely think about all those crazy dreams. I like my life now. I like running the security business. That's why I work on a Sunday. Speaking of work, how long are you in town for?"

"A few days," she said, and her voice rose higher, as it did when she was nervous. Because the first thing she'd thought when she landed this assignment was—*Michael.* Like a big, blaring sign. Like a flashing light at the end of a road. She had to see him, had to find him, had to connect with him. "I'm glad you're happy now...Michael

Sloan." She paused, his new last name rolling around strangely on her tongue. "I'm trying to get used to it. *Sloan.*"

"Took me a while, too."

"When did you change it?"

His eyes darkened. She'd touched a nerve. "Ten years ago," he said, his tone gruff.

The journalist in her didn't want to back down. "After I saw you in Marseilles?" she asked, nerves tightening her throat as she mentioned that day. That wonderful, horrible day.

He stared up at the ceiling, his brow knit together. "I suppose that'd be about right. But that wasn't the reason," he added.

"Why, then?" she pressed. "It made it harder to find you. I had to ask Becky."

He heaved a sigh. "Made it easier for me to live."

Unsure how to respond, she swallowed, then reached for her cup. Her fingers felt slippery. She gripped the ceramic more tightly as she brought it to her lips and took a sip.

He rubbed a hand across his jawline, silence sneaking between them, but not for long. "Tell me. Why did you look me up?"

"Because I was coming to town," she said, stating the simplest answer first, avoiding the tougher topic.

He stared at her, his blue eyes hooked into hers, telling her he didn't buy it.

"Because I was seeing Sanders and Becky," she said, mentioning her host family from when she was an exchange student.

"Did you see them?"

"I'm going to. Tomorrow."

"So then this," he said, pointing from her to him, "This is...?"

She looked at his mouth, blinked her eyes back up to his, and dropped her voice even more. They were surrounded by noise, the clink of silverware, the slip of ice cubes against glass, and the chatter of nearby patrons ordering smoked salmon and vodka samplers. She spoke the truest words. "This is because I wanted to."

———

There were things he wanted, as well. More time with her. More talking. Mostly, he didn't want for this to end. She was like sugary sand crystals in his hand, slipping through. He wanted to clutch his fist closed, hold them tight for just a few more moments. A few more days.

He went for it. "What are you doing tonight?"

3

The dealer slapped a card on the table.

"Wait. I want to write this down." Mindy shook her head in amusement as she reached for the card. "I want to record this moment. You, asking me for dating advice."

Michael narrowed his eyes. "I know how to date," he grumbled.

She held up a finger. "Correction. You know how to date women you just met. You don't know how to date the woman you were—"

"Do I see if she wants to meet for a drink?"

He cut her off because he didn't want the reminder. He knew how he felt.

As Mindy checked out her cards at the poker table at the Luxe, her favorite gambling spot, she said, "Yes, you want to have a drink with her, because you definitely need some lubricant."

He laughed. Mindy was unfiltered, and that was one of the reasons he enjoyed their friendship. The woman didn't mince words. "Noted. Use liquor for lube. Any other advice?"

She slid some chips to the center of the green felt, staying in. "Yes. You used to like music? Went to concerts together, right?"

He nodded. "Yeah, we did. Lots of local and indie bands. That was one of our things."

She shrugged, as if to say *duh*. "There you go. Brent said there's some new band at his nightclub tonight. A hot young indie-rock band. Take her to that. It'll be like old times."

"Is that what I want? Old times?"

"Yes. That's what you want," she said as she set down her cards, winning the hand with a trio of sixes.

"Nice," he said, with a low whistle of admiration.

She dragged a handful of chips closer. "So what was it like? Seeing her?"

That was the question of the day, one he'd been weighing since leaving the Petrossian Bar a few hours ago.

How could he even begin to describe seeing Annalise? It was like resistance meets infatuation. The whole time, he'd reined in his desire to kiss her, touch her, taste her lips. Because, well, that would be wholly inappropriate, and he had no fucking clue if she wanted it. A wild, delirious thought popped into his brain. Had she looked him up for the same reason he'd tried to find her ten years ago?

Ah, hell. No. He couldn't go there. Couldn't linger on the biggest heartbreak of his life. On the absolutely epic shellacking he'd walked right into, like a fool who thought the past could be resurrected. The past was best left buried. Tonight would just be...fun.

"It was awkward, but easy at the same time," he said, after much consideration. "If that makes sense."

Mindy nodded thoughtfully, her blue eyes serious. "Yeah, it does."

"We sort of slid right back into conversation about work and memories. It was good, even though I still feel like there are a million things I want to ask her."

Mindy patted his arm. "I know. But perhaps it's best to save 'Do you ever think about me?' for another time."

"Yeah. Good point."

"Keep it light and fun," she advised, then tipped her chin to his phone. "And maybe let her know the plan for tonight."

He texted Annalise the details, lingering to appreciate the ease with which he communicated with the woman he'd once had the hardest time in the world staying in touch with. So much had changed over the years. Even things like...text messaging. They hadn't had this luxury when they were younger.

When Mindy finished the round ahead, she thanked the dealer, collected her winnings, and walked away from the table. She was a measured player, always knowing when to stop. They wandered through the casino, then down the hall toward the restrooms, stopping outside the ladies room where it was quiet so they could catch up on other matters.

"Did you see the report from Morris?" she asked, mentioning the private detective he'd hired. Mindy had worked with the guy, so when Michael was looking for a solid recommendation, he'd taken hers.

"Yeah. Not much there. The guy goes to the grocery store, and to buy sheet music at the piano shop. Doesn't even take his girls to school. I swear I don't get it. How can he be head of a street gang?" Michael dragged a hand through his hair in frustration. He'd hired the detective to gather some intel on Luke Carlton, the mild-mannered local piano teacher by day, leader of the notorious street gang the Royal Sinners by night. The cops were trying to gather enough evidence to bring him in, and Michael wanted to do everything he could to help take down the fucker he was sure had played a role in plotting his father's death.

"But that's how it's always been," Mindy said. "This guy has supposedly been running the Royal Sinners for years, so he damn well knows how to be inconspicuous."

"That's the trouble," Michael said, as his phone buzzed.

Annalise.

A concert! Sounds great. I will be there.

He promptly forgot about Luke and zoned in on those last four words. She would be there.

His Annalise.

———

She peered in the mirror, considering the skinny jeans and boots she wore as the phone trilled in her ear and she waited for her sister to pick up.

"It's two in the morning," Noelle grumbled, sleep thick in her voice.

"I know," Annalise said, checking out the side view. *Not bad.* "But you instructed me to call you the second I had a report."

Her older sister groaned, then Annalise heard sheets rustle, and she assumed Noelle was dragging herself out of her tiny bed in her tiny flat in the Fifteenth Arrondissement. "Fine. Report."

"I'm seeing him again. Tonight," she said, a grin tugging at her lips.

"You've already seen him once?"

"Yes. This afternoon."

"And you didn't think to give me a report then?"

"I wanted to wait until I knew for certain another time would be happening. He just texted me details a few minutes ago."

"*Mon petite papillon*," Noelle said in a playful huff, using the nickname she'd bestowed on Annalise many moons ago. Annalise froze, not because it bothered her, but because it reminded her of what Michael used to call her. Not a butterfly, but he had given her an affectionate little name, and she hadn't thought about it in ages. She thought about it now, though, and how much she'd liked it. "Tell me more about tonight."

Annalise gave her the details of their coffee conversation, because it was Noelle who had encouraged her to see him in the first place. "*Time to move on,* mon petite papillon. *No more crying in the croissants,*" Noelle had said a few months ago.

Annalise wasn't crying in the croissants, or her pillow, anymore, thank you very much. She hadn't for many months. Still, was she truly ready? And ready for what?

"To love again," Noelle had said, and Annalise had scoffed and shaken her head.

"That won't happen."

"Then just go on a date."

Fine, a date seemed reasonable, if she could call it that. Finding Michael had been no easy task, but persistence had paid off, and she'd tracked him down, then sent the letter to his office.

He'd seemed a safe bet for her first time out with a

man in two years. Comforting, even. High school sweet-hearts, and all that.

Falling for Michael Sloan—back when he was Michael Paige-Prince—had been the easiest thing in the world when she was sixteen and living far, far away from home. He ran the radio station at their school, and played guitar in a band with some friends in the afternoons. He was laidback, easy-going, and quick with a joke. She was the arty French girl who liked the same indie music, and who took pictures of him and the other guys playing their instruments in the garage. They were late-90s teens in love, bonding over Pearl Jam and Nirvana, grunge and flannel, American jargon, and kisses that lasted well past midnight. Endless kisses, the kind that made her feel like her skin was humming.

"Call me when you're done with the concert," Noelle said from the other end of the line.

"So you do like my report at any time of day," Annalise teased.

"I'm a glutton for punishment when it comes to you. Just make sure it's a good report."

"What would make for a good report?"

"You know precisely what would make for a good report."

Yes. Yes, she did. Was it so wrong to hope he'd kiss her tonight? The flutter in her chest said a kiss would only be right; the spate of nerves flying across her skin told her the opposite.

She inched closer to the mirror, pursing her lips, studying them, wondering what it would feel like.... It had been so long since she'd felt anything. She ran her index finger over her top lip, both wanting something desperately from Michael, and terrified of how she'd feel if anything happened.

Anything at all.

A few hours later, she entered the dark, pulsing night-club and found him at the far end of the steel bar, his eyes on her the whole time she walked toward him.

The way he looked at her told her this night had the potential to take her breath away.

4

He'd changed his clothes.

She wasn't sure why this detail mattered, but she liked the chance to see him in a different outfit than earlier. Maybe because she'd changed, too. Or maybe because he looked so damn good in those dark jeans and the untucked navy blue button-down. He'd been so put-together and crisp earlier, and now he was a touch more casual. Still sharp, though, and still so fucking beautiful.

She wanted to photograph him. She imagined raising the lens to her eye so she could capture the cut of his jaw, the determination in his gaze, and the tiniest twinkle of a grin tugging at the corner of his lips.

Framing him in her mind's eye, she snapped the shot. There—she'd have it later to linger on.

"You look handsome in your navy shirt," she said when she reached him. She lifted her hand as if to run a finger across the collar or down the buttons. Then she scolded herself and dropped her hand to her side. That was muscle memory, an echo of the past.

She had no more permission to touch his clothes than she did to kiss him.

His eyes raked over her, as if he, too, was recording all the details. A flush crept across her neck from the intensity of his gaze, and then from his words as he spoke. "And you look as stunning in dark green as you did in black."

Stunning.

He'd never failed to compliment her when they were younger, and he excelled at the pursuit as an adult, too. "Even in this dark club you can tell the color of my top? And that it's different than earlier? I'm so impressed, Mr. Sloan. I never knew your color-matching skills were so top-notch."

He shrugged casually. "Impressive, I know. I've been working on it for some time. Can I get you a drink?"

"A drink sounds fantastic," she said, and he gestured to the bar, then placed his hand on the small of her back to guide her through the press of people waiting to get service. A spark zipped through her from the possessive touch, his palm pressed lightly against the silk of her top. The hum of music surrounded them, the low thump of the nightclub, though the band hadn't started yet.

At the bar Michael raised a finger, and the bartender at the far end nodded, indicating he'd be on his way.

"That was quick. Do they know you?" she asked.

"No. Brent just has really good bartenders. They're fast with all customers. Which is one of the reasons this place does so well."

"I'm glad to hear that. And he's married to Shan now?"

Michael nodded. "They *eloped* this summer. Translation: Got back together and went to a twenty-four-hour chapel to tie the knot."

She laughed. "Perfect for them. And congratulations to the happy couple. How is your sister doing?"

Michael made an arc with his hand over his belly.

A morsel of glee spread through Annalise. "How exciting! When is she due?"

"Five months," he said as the bartender arrived, a young man with a goatee who asked what he could get for them.

Michael turned to Annalise, letting her go first. "Champagne," she said to the man behind the bar.

"Make that two," Michael added.

"I wouldn't have pegged you for a champagne fan," she mused as the bartender set to work.

He arched a brow. "Why not? Do I seem like I have a dislike for drinks that are delicious?"

She shook her head. "No. I'd just have figured beer, or scotch, or something strong and manly."

He held up a hand. "Wait. Now I'm not manly? Because I ordered champagne?"

She laughed, shaking her head. "This is coming out all wrong. You're very manly. And champagne is very good. I'm glad we didn't have to sneak around to find some. Do you remember the time on New Year's Eve when we tried to figure out how to steal some from Becky and Sanders's collection?"

"Never found that damn champagne," he said, but the sparkle in his eyes as they latched onto hers told her he remembered the *other* way they'd rang in that new year— a long, lingering kiss at midnight that didn't stop at the lips. It went on and on, and led to hands under shirts, and below belts, and low, muffled groans, heated sighs, and their names falling off each other's lips.

The memory moved through her, heating her up. Or maybe it was just being near him now that did that.

"And now we don't have to track it down like thieves," he said.

"We have permission to drink it," she said. "I suppose that's a benefit of being older."

He nodded. "One of them."

"And, now it turns out champagne is good for you. Did you know that?"

"I read that recently. What's the story there?"

She tapped the side of her temple. "Supposedly, it helps improve memory."

"Ah," he said with a nod. "Sometimes, that's not my strongest suit. But that's what Post-It notes are for."

———

Post-It notes. Champagne. Jokes about the color of clothes.

He couldn't believe these were their discussion points.

But this was all he could handle. His pulse hammered in his neck, and he hoped she couldn't tell how goddamn hard it was to stand this close to her, to be so near to her, and not talk about the things he most wanted to know. The *why*.

Why she was here?

What did she want?

Did she ever think of him?

And how the hell was she doing, after everything that had happened to her?

But he couldn't go there. Not yet. He couldn't handle that kind of conversation. It would remind him too much of why he had loved her like crazy. Because he had talked to her about all those sorts of things once. Real things. Life, and death, and love, and hope, and dreams.

If they dared tread on that territory, he'd be lost.

Instead there were Post-It notes.

"Do you have them all over your home?" she asked, teasing him as the band began to set up on the low stage. "Little reminders of what to do? Put socks on before shoes? Insert key in lock before opening door?"

"Don't forget things like where my office is located. Or what floor I live on, too. That's another one."

Yeah, this was so much easier, and as she laughed, he started to relax, and give in to this...date.

She leaned against the bar, and he stood facing her. The club hummed, even on a Sunday night, and the press of bodies warmed the air. Annalise's green eyes seemed to know him intimately still; her voice was the sound he'd longed to hear those nights when he needed it most; and her lips were the ones he'd craved all the days they were apart. Now she was so close he could grab the hem of her shirt, tug her to him, and kiss her. He could run his hands along her arms, thread his fingers into her hair. He wondered if his thoughts were written in the air, or his wishes in his eyes.

He had to clench his fists to remember Mindy's advice. *Don't ask her if she ever thinks about you.*

"Which floor *do* you live on?" she asked, and he startled, her words knocking him back to the present.

"Hmm?"

"Floor? Which floor?" Her lips curved up, soft and naughty.

"Why do you ask? Are you planning to surprise me later?"

"Perhaps, I will."

Flirting.

Fucking flirting.

Just like they'd done in high school. When he was a teenager, he'd had a reputation as a complete flirt, and the girls had loved it. He'd always had an ease with the opposite sex, with talking to women, laughing with them, saying something laden with innuendo. Then, the beautiful, willowy redhead from Paris had arrived at his dad's best friend's home to stay with them for the year. His first thought had been that he had to see more of her.

"Want me to show you around town?" he'd asked her the day they'd met in Becky's kitchen.

"I would love that."

"Is there anything you want to see in Las Vegas?"

"Surprise me," she'd said, with a curve of her lips, the hint of a smile.

"I will," he'd said, and that had been the beginning of the love affair of his fucking life.

He blinked back to the present as she leaned in closer to him at the bar. "Would you like that?"

He knit his brows together, trying to stay rooted to the present instead of tripping back and forth between then and now like a time traveler caught in a slip. "Would I like what?"

"For me to surprise you?"

God, yes. So much. Surprise me. Come over. Knock on my door, dim the light, and kiss me like it's the thing you've been dreaming about all day.

Before he could answer, the bartender returned with their champagne. He thanked him then raised his glass, clinking it with hers. "To..." he began, but he didn't finish.

———

A flicker of sadness passed through his blue eyes as she lifted the glass. In that bare second, everything that had unfurled between eighteen years ago and today jabbed at her, like sharp little needles prickling her skin. Her fingers itched to run through his hair, to offer a reassuring touch, something that showed she understood what was unsaid. She resisted the impulse, not knowing how it would be taken, and afraid, too, of how it would feel. Good or bad.

"*À la présente*," she said in her native language, then quickly translated, "To the present."

"To the present," he repeated.

As he took a long swallow of his drink, she studied him. By nature she was an observer, and she catalogued the details—his lips on the glass, full, curved, and kissable; his Adam's apple bobbing in his throat as he drank; his strong, sturdy fingers on the stemware. Then, the bend of his wrist, the cuffs of his sleeves rolled up twice, revealing his forearms.

Muscular and corded.

Hot as fuck.

God, why were forearms so delicious? But she knew the answer. They spelled strength and power, and the ability for a man to anchor himself over a woman as he took her.

She slid her eyes away from him, trying to chase off her own dirty thoughts.

He set down his glass on the counter. "You said work brought you to town, that you're shooting the catalogue all over the city. Are you enjoying it?"

"Immensely," she said with a nod. "The models are beautiful, the locations are playful, and the lingerie is, as you say, *to die for.*"

His eyes flashed with mischief as he made a noise of approval. "Big fan of lingerie myself."

"That so? Something you want to tell me?" she said, coyness coloring her tone as they bantered, so much that it filled her with an effervescence that rivaled the champagne's effect.

"Very funny." He dropped his voice to a whisper. "I meant...on women."

That buzzing intensified. This was chemistry. This was the electricity in the air before a storm. She was wrong about him being a safe choice for her first time out in years.

Now that she was centimeters rather than an ocean away, she was intensely aware of how *not-safe* he was.

She threw caution to the wind. "Anything in particular when it comes to lingerie? Baby-dolls? Corsets? Garters? Hip-huggers? Bikinis? Cheektinis? Stockings? Bikini briefs? Boy-cut shorts? Thongs?" she said with the speed of a freight train, rattling off anything and everything silky that hugged a woman's bare flesh.

His lips quirked up as he took a drink. "That one," he said dryly, tapping the air with his index finger.

"Which one, Michael?"

He made a rolling gesture with his hand. "All of them. Every. Single. One." Then he scratched his chin. "Question, though. What on earth is a cheektini?"

Annalise lowered her arm to her hip, shifted her pose, and drew a line mid-cheek across the denim of her jeans. "They go right here."

Heat flashed in his gaze as he stared at her ass. "Right there, you say?"

"Yes." She traced the line once more across her rear.

"The panties cut across, so your cheeks..." She paused, searching for the right words in English. "They hang out?"

He nodded his understanding, his eyes on her the whole time, darkening. She hadn't expected the intensity of his stare. Nor had she expected the rush it sent through her. It had been so long since she'd felt like this. "Yes. And the one I'm wearing right now is red with lace trim."

She shocked herself when she said that. She hadn't expected to be so bold. But it felt easy, and right, and so damn good.

Perhaps she'd surprised him, too, because he licked his lips, then groaned softly as he uttered, "*Red*."

Like it had six syllables. Like it was the sexiest word in the world.

Before the conversation could turn naughtier, the music shifted, and the lead singer tapped the microphone, said hello, and launched into the first song.

"More champagne and then we go stage-dive?"

"Absolutely. Let's start a mosh pit."

They did neither, but a few minutes later, they were watching the band, listening to the music, and drinking another round. Someone bumped into Annalise, and she moved closer to Michael. Before she knew it, they were shoulder-to-shoulder, hip-to-hip, swaying to the music.

By the time the band finished, they'd polished off another glass or two. The buzz was headier, and so was the intoxication from the music, the low lights, the energy, and this whole night that felt like a cocoon of possibility.

She wiped a hand over her brow. The club was hot.

"Let's step outside," he said. "Where it's cooler."

She nodded, and once again, his hand was on her back. He guided her to the tall glass doors that spilled onto a terrace attached to the club. As he opened the door, he reached for her hand, holding it as they walked to a bench and sat down. Groups of club-goers were scattered at nearby tables.

He traced her palm lightly with the pad of his thumb, and her heart sped up. That barest touch was bursting with heat. Electricity flared between them. They could power the lights at this club, the billboards down the street. She barely understood how it was possible to *be* like this with someone she hadn't seen since that unexpected and heartbreaking day when they were both twenty-four. She'd been going one way in life; he'd been heading in another. Seeing him then had been as close as she'd ever come to the fire of temptation. She hadn't given in.

Now, they were both thirty-four, and her heart stuttered just from being near him. This torch might have flickered to a soft, ashen glow in years past, but it could be turned fiery and bright in an instant. "I'm glad you were free tonight," she said. "I'm glad you asked me to the show. I've had an amazing time. Most of all, I'm glad you said yes. I've been thinking of you."

"You have?" His voice sounded stretched full of hope, like he was holding all the world in that two-word question.

Like her answer to it had more power than she would have ever suspected.

5

This was what he'd wanted, but knowing she'd been thinking of him barely scratched the surface of his curiosity. His throat was parched, and he was so damn thirsty for more.

His voice was low, rough. "What do you think about?"

"How you are," she said, her gaze locked on his. "What you're doing. What your life is like now."

He licked his lips. "And that's why you wanted to see me?"

"Yes."

His skin was hot. His bones vibrated. *Want* sounded damn good to him. After feeling like she'd slipped through his fingers in Marseilles—his head had understood, but his heart had fucking rebelled when she'd walked away from him—he liked being wanted by her.

"So, were you wondering if I'd gone gray? Or bald, maybe?" he teased, running his hand through his thick hair. Now that she'd revealed a modicum of truth about tonight, he could return to this zone, where the terrain wasn't rocky and fraught with so many jagged ridges.

She laughed with her mouth wide open, her white teeth straight and gleaming. How he'd adored that smile of hers, the way she quirked up the corner of her lips when something was particularly funny. "I see you've held onto it all," she said.

"And you're redder." He gestured to her long, lush locks. Then he figured, *fuck it*. She'd said the words he most wanted to hear—she was thinking of him. He touched the end of a wave of hair—it had been auburn before. Now it was almost a dark cherry red, and so soft.

He let go.

"So is that what you wanted? To check out my hair color? Maybe to see if I grew a paunch?" he said, patting his flat stomach.

"Seems you've maintained your boyish figure," she said.

He was worn thin with wanting something, *anything* from her, and he wasn't even sure why. This was only one night, only drinks. He was the one who was investing this moment with too much importance. Hunting for a deep, meaningful reason—one like *Michael, I had to tell you I never stopped loving you.*

He scoffed. She wasn't here to say that, even if she had been thinking of him. Thinking was nothing. She was here for the class reunion effect. To say hello, to check him out, and to breeze back out of town when she was done shooting skinny models in skimpy clothes. He needed to get the fuck over her. More importantly, he needed to get out of his own head, and stop thinking that a letter that smelled like rain meant Annalise Delacroix wanted to curl up on his lap and tell him she hadn't forgotten him, either.

They'd been torn apart by time and distance, not by hurt, or anger, or falling out of love. No one had cheated.

No one had said unforgivable words. No invectives were lobbed, and no terrible secret had come between them. Their biggest foe when they were younger was miles. Thousands and thousands of uncrossable miles. They'd tried to fight it with letters, a seemingly endless stream of them. But after a few years of letters and phone calls, they were in college and too far away from each other. It wasn't going to happen. It wasn't meant to be. He didn't have enough money to fly to see her, nor did she have the funds or her family's permission to return to see her beau. The flames turned to blue flickers, then to low embers in the ash.

But the fire burned again tonight.

He couldn't resist. "And you look as beautiful as I remember."

Music from inside the club seeped out to the terrace. She lowered her forehead and whispered thanks at the same time a lock of hair slid over her eyes. His opportunity. He slipped his index finger under those strands and brushed them off her forehead.

She raised her lashes and looked up at him. "So..."

He ran his finger along the side of her temple. His pulse thundered in his throat. "Ask me what else I haven't forgotten."

Her green eyes shone with a hint of something, a flash of desire. She tilted her head curiously, taking the bait. "What else haven't you forgotten?"

The music seemed to emanate from another dimension. The waitress walking past them to a nearby table operated in a parallel universe. All the world around him slowed and stilled to this moment. He threaded his fingers into her soft hair, letting it fall like silk over his skin.

One more taste and he could stop longing for her.

Stop lingering. He could finally put to rest the arguments his ex-girlfriends had waged over the years, insisting he was stuck on someone else. Michael Sloan was going to take the one thing that had strung him up over the years and get it out of his system. One kiss and he could say good-bye to his first love.

"How you like to be kissed," he said, his fingers curling around her head. She gasped quietly, arching her back, her gorgeous breasts pushing closer. His bones thrummed with lust for her.

"You do?" Her voice was soft as the question ghosted across her lips. It was chased by a small smile, and that felt like an invitation.

"Yes. Yes, I do."

She swallowed, the next word so low it was merely an imprint on the air. "How?"

"Like this."

Gently at first, he pressed his lips to hers. His heart stopped, and his blood stilled, as if it simply had to make sense of this new input before it could reengage. *Kissing Annalise again.* It was as if a new map were being written, a new route sketched out. So this was what it was like to kiss her once more.

Sublime.

His heart ticked again, catching up as he swept his tongue over her lower lip. She murmured. Soft, like a purr. That sound was new from her. She'd always been quiet.

And she'd once liked lingering kisses that were like melting chocolate, like the rising sun. Their kisses had been easy and carefree. They'd turned him on, riled him up, and made him want so much more of her. They were tongues, and lips, and mouths, and heat.

But now, there were teeth.

Hers.

She pressed her teeth against his lower lip and drew it into her mouth like she was trying to suck on it, and with that, whatever wisp of apprehension she'd seemed to feel moments ago must have evaporated. His thoughts spun out of control, slipping into darker, more urgent territory. He moved his hand from her hair, held her face, and angled his mouth over hers, resuming control of the kiss and devouring her lips.

He drew the corner of her mouth into his and nipped her. Her murmurs intensified. Louder. Hotter.

She'd never been like this before, but now she demanded more. Her own hungry lips slanted over his, saying *mark me.*

"Oh God," she gasped, her eyes squeezed closed. "Oh my God."

He broke the kiss, whispering, "You okay?"

She nodded against him. "Yes. *So* okay."

"Good." He quickly moved his mouth to her jawline, kissing a trail there as he traveled along her skin. Each press brought out a tiny little growl from Annalise, a sexy sigh, a needy gasp. It made him want to rip off her clothes, push her against the wall and see how rough she liked it. He bent his head to her collarbone and grazed the exposed flesh with his teeth. Her hands shot up, roping through his hair as she moaned. Annalise was under some kind of spell, her body moving and flowing against his. She clutched his skull tighter, her nails digging in as he kissed her shoulder then returned to her mouth. That gorgeous red mouth. The lips he'd been obsessed with. The ones he'd memorized.

The lips he'd missed for so many years.

Like a persistent, aching hole in his chest, the missing

had defined him. Propelled him. Given him a focus when he'd needed one. Now, the missing disintegrated, and turned into a white-hot desire to have her. To have all of her, as he'd never had before. Now. Tonight. No more goddamn waiting. He pressed his forehead to hers, and ran his thumb over her mouth. "It's different now."

She nodded. "Yes. But so good," she said, breathless.

"Not good. It's better."

"It is," she said, her eyes wild.

"Think everyone's watching?"

She shook her head against him. "It's Vegas. No one cares."

"Do you care?" he whispered as he traced her lips, the sweetness of her breath on his fingertips.

"That you're kissing me like crazy on the terrace of a nightclub in a hotel?"

"Yes." He dragged his thumb along her teeth.

"No. I don't care where we are," she said, darting out the tip of her tongue to meet his thumb. She bit down. "I want more."

His mouth twitched in a knowing grin. "No, you don't care at all," he said, then crushed his lips to hers, wrapping his arms around her shoulders and kissing her with everything he had. Greedy kisses that promised red, swollen lips tomorrow.

This kiss was dizzying. It was a rush of blood to the head, then everywhere else. When they were younger, they'd held back because they were sixteen and foolish romantics. They'd done plenty below the belt with hands, but hadn't come close to going all the way. Tonight, they seemed to be charging in that direction. Good. He was no fool anymore, and he was hardly romantic. He had the distinct impression life had hardened her, too.

And that tonight she wanted hardness from him.

The sound of clinking glasses echoed from many feet away. The noise jarred him, and he pulled apart from her briefly. He swept her hair away from her face then bent his head to her ear. "Where are you staying?"

"Across the street. The Cosmopolitan," she said, her voice like a torch song.

"Do you want to leave? With me?"

Her lips parted, and he felt her soft breath on his neck. He pulled back to look into her green eyes. In them, he saw a lust that matched his, but a fear, too.

"Yes," she said, but in a second she shook her head. Then she nodded and said, "No."

Opposites. Okay, maybe she didn't want the same thing.

She sighed. "I mean..."

He pressed his finger to her lips. No way was he pushing her into this. He wanted Annalise with a fierceness he hadn't felt in ages, but she was either in it all the way or not at all. "It's okay. It's good to see you."

"Is that it? You're just leaving?" she said, her voice angry.

He pretended to look around. "Did I say I was leaving? Did I get up to go? I'm still here."

"I'm sorry. This is just..."

"You don't have to explain anything."

"I know. But I don't want you to think I don't want to."

"Do you want to?"

"Yes, but it's been a..." She didn't finish her thought, and he didn't push. Changing gears, she said, "It's late. I'm shooting tomorrow. Do you want to come by?"

"Visit you at a lingerie shoot?"

"You always used to come by my shoots."

"You shot bands. The soccer team. The pep rallies," he said, reminding her of her days as a yearbook photographer.

"And now I shoot beautiful women. Do you like beautiful women?"

His lips twitched, and he eyed her from head to toe. "Very much."

"Come by," she said, her fingers darting out quickly to touch his cheek for a moment. "I want to see you again before I go."

He swallowed dryly, but didn't ask when she was leaving. He'd rather linger on the feeling of her hand on his face instead.

"Give me the time and place."

She told him where, then added, "Tomorrow at one. You can see the end of the shoot, and maybe we can..."

Her words went unfinished.

Whatever she meant, he wasn't in the business of filling in her thoughts. All he knew was one taste wasn't nearly enough to forget her.

6

The elevator was too loud, too bright, too full of people.

As the couple in the far corner waxed on about their dinner of small plates and the fratty guys by the number pad debated how many more shots they could plow through, Annalise asked herself how long she could wait.

She'd been on ice, cryogenically frozen in a state of suspended animation for two years. Her body was still working, going through the motions. One foot in front of the other.

But inside? Beneath her skin?

All those parts had been dormant.

Turned off.

Now, she was turned all the way on. She was like one of those blow-up balloons in an old cartoon, shooting through the air, ready to pop. She was sure everyone in the elevator saw the desire written all over her skin. But as the car shot up past the tenth, eleventh, and twelfth floors, they continued in their own worlds.

She wanted her own world now. She wanted to live in the bubble of lust.

The elevator stopped on the fourteenth floor, and the couple exited. The trio of guys remained, and the tall one in the crew once again stabbed the silver button for the penthouse. "They'll be here soon. C'mon."

Hookers?

She almost breathed it aloud.

Instead, she covered her mouth with her hand, her fingers touching her greedy lips. But that was stupid. Because that only made her want to touch herself more. She couldn't help it. She dragged her index finger once across her top lip.

Like a match to a flame, it reignited her. My God, those kisses. Her lips were bruised with Michael's mouth. He'd imprinted himself on her, and she felt him everywhere— on her skin, inside her organs, and deep in the dark, protected corners of her heart.

And yes, most exquisitely, between her legs.

"*Vite, vite*," she muttered to herself.

If she'd stayed a moment longer at the club, she'd have grabbed his hand and dragged him to the restroom. Even the return to her hotel had felt terribly long, a new and cruel sort of torture as she'd walked with a wet, needy ache between her thighs.

For so long, she hadn't let herself feel a thing. Now, she was nothing but nerve endings rubbed raw, cells crying out for relief.

The elevator dinged at the seventeenth floor. She practically vaulted out the open doors and quickstepped down the hall in a mad dash for her room. She reached it, fumbled for her key card from the back pocket of her jeans, slid open the door, and stepped inside.

Her room was dark, cool, and the lights from the Strip

winked through the windows. The door shut with a heavy groan.

Her breath was hot and fast, her hands even faster. She dropped her purse to the floor, unbuttoned her jeans, and dipped her hand into her panties.

"Oh God," she groaned, fingertips slipping through her wetness, hot, fevered, and so fucking delirious.

This was what happened when you banished sex, what happened when you extradited it from your life, your heart, your bed. When you told yourself you weren't ready. You're better off without it. She hadn't wanted anyone to touch her, and she hadn't even touched herself in a long time, as if the mere act of masturbation would have sullied the memories of her husband and said something to the universe about her not loving him enough. Everything had conflated in the last two grief-filled years —sex, and love, and moving on, and hope, and even touching herself.

She couldn't stop now. She was a rocket, flying to the atmosphere, hell-bent on a jet-fueled trip to the stars. The floodgates were unleashed, and she stroked herself, riding her own hand urgently as a flash of images sparked before her closed eyes. Michael's kisses. Michael's lips. His voice in her ear. His teeth. He hadn't kissed like that before. Like he wanted to consume her. Bite her. Fuck her hard.

"*Michael.*"

She moaned his name, feeling its familiarity yet utter newness on her tongue as her fingers flew faster between her legs. There, standing against her hotel room door, shoulders rising and falling, breath tumbling rapidly from her lungs, sex on her brain, Annalise made herself come for the first time in two years.

Her orgasm slammed into her, fast and sharp as a hot

knife. Seizing her body. Lighting her up. Racing across every inch of her skin. It was everywhere, rapid and furious, pulsing, and over far too soon. She was left panting, and not nearly sated enough.

His name fell from her lips once more.

She didn't feel cold tonight.

She was burning up.

Her body was alive again, and she feared she would become addicted to this feeling before her heart was ready.

———

The dog's legs flew, like a flip-book at high speed, as Michael cruised down the trail.

No one ever beat the dog. Not even Colin, and he'd recently finished the Badass Triathlon. But today Michael was a few footfalls behind Johnny Cash, and his brothers Colin and Ryan, were eating his dust.

Pent-up lust could do that to a man. Desire could drive him to finish faster, push harder, focus more intensely.

With sweat slicking down his chest and his heart pounding, Michael ran as the sun peeked over the hills at Red Rock Canyon. His thoughts cycled between the bare-bones *one-foot-in-front-of-the-other* adrenaline and sheer, unrepentant want.

Last night was intense, sure. But it was only physical. It had to be that way. His ex-girlfriends had simply been wrong. As he whipped around a switchback, the black and white border collie in his crosshairs, Michael felt more confident than ever that his past relationship woes were never about Annalise. He wasn't a player. He didn't have a string of three-and-out dates trailing behind him. He'd had plenty of serious girlfriends over the years. He hadn't settled down with any of them because he simply hadn't met the right woman.

Not because he was hung up on *her*.

That was so not the case.

As the dust churned up beneath his sneakers, his mind flashed back to his ex-girlfriend Katrina's comments from a year ago. He'd been with her for ten solid months —so long Colin had placed bets on him getting down on one knee. Funny that the proposal possibility had crossed Colin's mind but never Michael's. Katrina was a massage therapist, and he'd met her working out at his gym, his home away from home. They'd had a good time together. At least, it had felt that way to him.

They'd done dinners and movies, and had fun trading gym playlists. Their favorite activity after a late-night gym visit was getting sweaty in another way. They'd fucked well, and often. But apparently that hadn't been enough for Katrina.

When she'd ended it, she simply shook her head in frustration and said, "You're in love with the past."

He'd scoffed, doubtful. "What does that mean?"

"Ask yourself. I'm done trying to figure you out."

"There's nothing to figure out. What you see is what you get."

"Well, what I'm getting isn't enough. You're stuck someplace else, Michael."

His quads burned from the fast pace on the dusty trail. Stuck. Ha. He was fine. Work and family were all he needed. Besides, he had too much going on. Business was booming, and the investigation into his father's death had gotten its first big break in ages last month when the police had arrested the getaway driver.

Michael was stuck on absolutely nothing.

Seeing Annalise had proved that, hadn't it? He wanted her, but he wasn't caught up in her. He'd be a stone-cold idiot to be hung up on someone who'd moved on more than a decade ago.

That kiss had proved it, he reasoned, as he neared the trailhead.

That was enough to get her out of his system.

Except he couldn't stop thinking about that kiss.

That intoxicating kiss.

That fucking kiss, which had ignited all his fantasies last night. She'd felt like fire in his arms, and just as hard to contain. But he'd craved the danger, the risk of touching her. Of what it might do to him to have her.

It would either free him or wreck him.

Those thoughts powered him the final feet to the end of the trail, where he caught up quickly to Ryan's four-legged best friend. Johnny Cash panted hard, tongue lolling from his snout. Michael's heart beat furiously as he pressed the spigot on the water fountain. "Here boy," he called, giving the dog first dibs on the water as Colin's relentless pace boomed closer.

"You bastard. You on the juice now?" he shouted as he caught up.

"No. Ryan is. That's the only way he can manage to finish within a minute of us," Michael said, panting.

Colin laughed as Michael took a drink of the water, then stepped away from the fountain for Colin to get his shot. When Ryan arrived, wiping his palm across his brow, Michael adopted a look of feigned disgust. "I see your almost-married life is slowing you down," he said, teasing his brother, who'd recently gotten engaged.

"Nothing slows me down. Not ever," Ryan said. "I let you win."

"You wish."

Michael wandered over to the wooden fence that edged the lot, parking his foot on a post to stretch. Colin and Ryan joined him, and Johnny Cash trotted behind, slumping in a furry black-and-white heap at Ryan's feet.

"Listen. We've got some things to figure out," Michael said, diving into a conversation he'd told his brothers they needed to have on their run today. "I was thinking we need to take care of Marcus when shit starts going down. Probably even sooner."

Colin nodded, shoving a hand through his dark hair. "Definitely. I've been talking to him about what to expect."

"What does he say? What does John say?" Ryan asked, his blue eyes shifting from Colin to Michael. Ryan was engaged to Detective John Winston's sister Sophie, but John kept most of the details of the reopened investigation into their father's murder two decades ago close to the vest, understandably. However, with their half-brother Marcus spending more time at Colin's home, and acting as an informant in some ways for the detective, the three of them had a sense that matters might heat up soon.

One of the accomplices in the murder had been arrested several weeks ago. Kenny Nelson, the getaway driver, was behind bars for several smaller crimes, and was likely going to be tried for accessory to murder, too. With the revelation that by night Marcus's father was the leader of the notorious street gang the Royal Sinners, John and his colleagues were even busier. Presumably, the cops were working to devise the best way to dismantle the gang and connect Luke to the murder. Michael reasoned that any sort of sting operation to take down the group's head, who'd successfully operated as the clandestine leader for more than two decades, would put Luke's son Marcus square in the face of danger.

"He's already working on transferring to another college out of state," Colin said, breathing hard as he stretched his quads after their five-mile run. "That way he has a real reason to get out of town without his dad knowing he's been giving key details to the detectives. He's looking to go to school in Florida."

"Smart kid. And that's where we come in," Michael said. "We need to pay for his school, his new home, and make sure he's got round-the-clock security for a while, even if he's clear on the other side of the country."

"Absolutely," Ryan quickly agreed.

"No question about it." Colin nodded.

Michael pointed at Colin. "You see him the most. You let him know we got his back on this, all right? He's our brother, and we'll take care of him. Without him, we might not have a chance at taking down the other men who killed our father. I want them all behind bars. Every last one of them."

One man—the gunman—was already in prison and had been for eighteen years. So was their mother, who'd plotted the murder. Now, Kenny Nelson was likely on his way to the big house, but Michael wouldn't rest until T.J. Nelson, the alleged mastermind of the gunman's hits, joined him there, along with the head of the gang. Michael had a hunch that Luke had been pulling the strings all along, hiding behind his harmless piano-teacher persona as he operated a gang of thieves, thugs, and murderers. The brothers were sure he was part of it, and that was why Michael had hired the private detective, with Mindy's help, to conduct his own recon, do his part to push things along.

"I've got to hit the road. Lots to do in the office," Michael said, then turned to Ryan. "I'm taking the afternoon off."

Ryan stopped in his tracks. "Whoa. You never take off. You prepping for your New York trip?"

Michael was slated to meet with some clients in Manhattan at the end of the week. "Nope. Just a meeting locally."

"With who?" Ryan asked, and the question was perfectly reasonable because he and Ryan ran Sloan Protection Resources together.

Michael didn't answer. He didn't like lying, but he didn't want to get into the details. He reached for his door handle, trying to ignore the question.

"Wait." Colin's hand came down on his shoulder. "You're seeing *her*."

He spun around. "What?"

Colin wagged his finger and grinned like he'd caught Michael red-handed. "Yep. I knew it. You told me she wrote to you, and I fucking *knew* you were going to see her."

Michael shrugged, trying to make light of it. "Big deal. So I saw her."

"And now you're playing hooky to see her again," Ryan teased, wiggling his eyebrows.

Michael waved him off. "Not playing hooky. I'll be working late tonight."

"Or working late on Annalise," Ryan called out as Michael shut the door.

Michael flipped him the bird, and his brothers laughed. There wasn't much that got past them. They knew how over the moon he'd been for Annalise back in high school. Hell, they knew *her*. Everyone knew her—his grandma, his sister, even his father.

His father had thought she was perfect for him.

Michael flashed back to the note in his wallet. The one he kept with him at all times. His father's last written words to him were about Annalise. As he peeled away from the hills and drove back to his home on the Strip, he replayed the thirty-six hours before his father had been killed. The breakfast with his father the day before was a blur; the next morning with Annalise at the airport as he said good-bye was a smudge in his memory, too.

The one starkly clear event had happened after midnight.

A snapshot blazed before his eyes. He swallowed hard, jammed the brakes, and pulled over to the side of the road.

The image was too powerful to drive through.

He'd been in his bed, trying to sleep. He'd bolted upright, remembering he'd left something in the car that day. He'd barely been sleeping anyway. He got out of bed, padded to the front door, and unlocked it. His father's car was in the driveway. He'd been driving the limo that night, taking some teens to the prom, and after returning the limo to work, he drove his own car home.

Michael headed for the car door then nearly tripped.

On his father.

His veins ran cold with fear, then denial, then a soul-ripping agony as he fell to his knees, grabbing, holding, clutching the lifeless body in the driveway. Soaked in blood. Heart no longer beating. Wallet open, ID and photos spilled everywhere along with, he'd learn later, a note his father had likely written to him earlier that day.

The black of night cloaked Michael as he held his father, and he began to know the true meaning of the word *horror*.

Pressing two fingers against the bridge of his nose, he let the memory recede, like a wave rolling out to sea. It would crash into him again, but for now that image sent him back to the investigation. To the role his mother's lover had played in the murder.

The question remained—did Luke want Thomas Paige dead because he was in love with Thomas's wife? Or was there some other motive at stake?

7

"Coffee or tea? Tea, right?"

Becky hadn't answered her. She was hunched over her menu, studying it intently.

"Tea with sugar, right?" Annalise said, speaking louder, trying to get her attention. The waitress had stopped by to ask if they wanted drinks, and Becky hadn't noticed the woman or Annalise's gentle prod.

Becky startled then looked up. They'd met at a hip little breakfast café not far from the Strip, since Annalise was due at today's shoot in an hour for set-up.

Becky's gray-blue eyes looked weary. "Sorry, dear. Tea is fine," she said to the waitress, as her fingers fiddled with the edge of her menu. Becky hadn't seemed like herself this morning. True, Annalise had only spent a quarter of an hour with her so far, and the first few minutes after she'd arrived at the restaurant had consisted of one of the biggest hugs Annalise had ever experienced.

Annalise hadn't expected the intensity of the older woman's reaction. Yes, she liked Becky. Well, she loved her in the way you love an aunt or uncle. Becky and her husband had been her family in America the year she'd lived here, and through them she had gotten to know Michael. Sanders hadn't made it to breakfast today, even though he'd said he would be here. Busy with "some things" Becky had said. "Appointments...you know," she'd added.

Annalise turned to the waitress. "Some sugar for the tea please. And a coffee for me. Black."

The waitress nodded and swiveled on her heels.

"Do you know what you want to eat?" Annalise asked, and Becky shook her head.

"Can't decide." Becky absently ran her finger across her fork.

"Maybe the special, then? I saw it on the chalkboard. Eggs and chives with homemade sourdough bread."

"Sure, fine," Becky said.

After they ordered, Becky continued on like that through breakfast—scattered, distracted, patting her purse, sneaking peeks at her phone as they caught up on the highlights of the last eighteen years. There were highs and lows—awards Annalise had won in journalism, meeting Julien, losing Julien to an early and not unexpected death—all the way through to her work now. Becky shared the latest on her sons and her husband. But every time she mentioned Sanders, something hitched in her voice.

"Is everything okay?" Annalise asked, reaching out a hand and resting it on top of Becky's.

"Yes," she said quickly.

"Are you sure?"

The older woman nodded and then clasped Annalise's hand. She gulped, then fixed on a smile.

"Becky," Annalise said in a soft voice. "Do you want to talk about it?"

Becky's eyes floated closed, as if pained. When she opened them, she wiped her finger under her lashes, erasing the threat of tears. "I'm sorry. I'm not usually like this."

"Is it Sanders?"

Becky's face looked pinched, and the color seemed to slip away. She sighed heavily. "I'm trying to keep it all together. I really am."

"Are you guys okay? Is he sick? Is that the appointment?" But then, if he were ill, surely Becky would be with him.

Her old friend shook her head. "Oh no. He's fit as can be. Well, he has that bad back. But he's all good otherwise. It's just..."

"You're not separating, are you? Divorcing?" Annalise continued, since she'd never been one to tiptoe around a tough situation. Best to be direct. Ask the questions. Most people wanted to talk. Most people were looking for an opening to share their woes. If Becky was, Annalise wanted to be the person to listen.

Becky scoffed and shook her head. "I wouldn't let him out of my grasp. Same for him," she said, her tone chased by a light laugh. "It's just been a tense few months. I haven't really said much to anyone."

"I'm here if you want to talk. Or if you just want me to listen," Annalise offered. Sometimes people shared more with someone they didn't see regularly. Knowing the person across from you was leaving soon could make it easier to say the hard things. If you knew you didn't have to see him or her in the near future, you could open up.

Your secrets would be tucked safely away in their luggage on the return trip home.

Becky's shoulders rose as she inhaled deeply. "Ever since the investigation..." she began, then trailed off. "I shouldn't say anything. I can't say anything."

Annalise squeezed her hand. "I understand."

Clearly, Becky had said all she was able to say. Annalise reached for the sugar, poured some into her coffee, and shifted gears. "So...is the big cruise still happening after Sanders retires?"

"I hope so," Becky said, twisting her index and middle fingers together. "Fingers are crossed it doesn't get put off."

As they talked more about little things, the wheels in Annalise's head started to turn, and she wondered what would defer Sanders's retirement, and why Becky was so tense from the investigation. What on earth would they have to be worried about from an inquiry into an incident that happened eighteen years ago? Sanders was Thomas's best friend back then. They'd worked together.

The wheels picked up speed. Wait a second. Did Sanders know something? Was he talking to the cops?

Her heart squeezed.

Oh.

The appointment.

Was it over the case? Did Sanders have something to hide? Did Becky? As the possibilities took shape, she cycled back eighteen years ago to a night when she'd slipped into the house late, lips bee-stung and bruised, hair a wild tumble, heart racing from being with Michael. Becky had been reading, waiting up for her, and they'd talked briefly in the living room.

"So, the young Michael Paige-Prince. You sure do like him. Is it serious?"

Annalise had nodded with a grin she couldn't contain. "How do you say it? I am crazy for him."

"Yes, that's how we say it here. And I can see why. Smart, kind, and a handsome young man."

"He is," Annalise had echoed, feeling dreamy, the way she always felt when she thought of the boy she was falling in love with.

Becky had smiled dopily. "He gets his good looks from his father."

At age sixteen, she'd barely registered the comment.

Now, years later, she lingered on the remark. *He gets his good looks from his father.* Surely that was nothing, right? There had been no secret affair between Becky and Thomas, no long-simmering desire? It was just a comment, wasn't it? Hell, Annalise herself could tell at that age that Michael was "like father, like son" in the looks department. And she didn't have any weird daddy issues or attraction to her boyfriend's father, but empirically, Becky was right. Michael was handsome, and so was his father. That was all. Case closed.

Annalise quieted her skeptical side, telling herself that Becky's comments from years ago couldn't possibly have anything to do with her odd behavior today.

As Annalise said her good-bye at the end of the meal and slid into the backseat of a Nissan, her Uber ride waiting to whisk her to her shoot, she replayed last night.

The bar, the kiss, Michael's hands. His mouth, teeth, tongue.

His name on her lips.

Her fingers between her legs.

Hot sparks rained down on her, and she shivered. She'd be seeing him this afternoon. The first man she'd ever loved, back when she hardly knew what that butterfly feeling was in her chest—flutters, wings and all.

First love was like that. Enchanting and light, stitched from an endless thread of hopes and dreams. It made you feel invincible and hungry for more all at once. She'd wanted to be with Michael so much when she returned to France. She'd tried so hard to fight the distance through letters. They'd attempted to stay together through the end of high school and on into college.

But just like proximity breeds closeness, distance kills it. Too many days apart, weeks alone, and years gone by. Paper and ink couldn't feed their hungry hearts. Eventually, their love became unsustainable. Stretched too far, it collapsed under the weight.

They drifted apart after the first year of college. Even then, she'd clung to the distant possibility that someday, somehow they'd meet again. Hope powered her even in the years when they no longer talked. She took a job as a waitress at a local café during school, saving all her euros, thinking they'd fund a return trip to the United States. Like a piggybank for rekindled love.

But by the time she'd have been able to use them, she and her high school sweetheart had faded to memories. The fondest ones to be sure, and she'd kept a book of photographs of their days together, a record of her young love.

Besides, the euros had gone to something else.

She'd had to move on. He'd moved on too.

Annalise graduated from university, hunted for jobs across Europe, and eventually landed the gig of her dreams as a photojournalist. There she met Julien, a rival photographer, soon her lover, then her fiancé.

That was what Julien was the time she'd seen

Michael ten years ago. He'd just sent her the most beautiful and heartbreaking love letter, and it had ripped her apart knowing she couldn't respond in kind. Mere days after receiving it, chance had ushered her to the airport in Marseilles on a job, and she'd run into him on a layover. He'd just moved to Europe and was stationed there for his work in army intelligence. It was unexpected and God, the sight of him, a man then, had punched her in the chest. She was in love with Julien, but guilt still gnawed at her when Michael's eyes traveled down her body and landed on her hand. Her engagement ring.

As if she'd broken a promise.

And for the briefest of moments that afternoon, she'd been tempted to break one to Julien. She hadn't. She wouldn't. Straying wasn't in her nature. But had Michael sent that letter before she met Julien, her life might have taken a different course, back to him. As it was, she'd had to march onward, and she did. But with so much that had once been between them, perhaps it was no surprise, really, that the first man she'd ever loved would be the one to rekindle all that was dormant in her body. Last night had ignited something inside her.

Julien had said over and over that he didn't want her to mourn him forever, or at all. "Love, I won't be here always. You'll need to move on. You're young and beautiful and smart and vibrant."

She'd laughed him off, shook her head. "Darling, you aren't going anywhere. I won't let you," she'd said, then mimed digging her claws into her husband's chest as they'd relaxed on a park bench watching the sunset by the Eiffel Tower one evening. But Julien didn't toss back his sandy blond head, or smile his sweet, sexy grin at her.

Instead, he'd tugged her close. "The odds, Annalise. The odds. Five years is much more likely than fifty."

"Stop that," she said. "Let's not talk about this. The sun is falling. The lights are coming on."

The odds were not in their favor. They never had been, and she'd known that before he got down on one knee. He had a lethal arrhythmia, a genetic condition that meant he could die of cardiac arrest at any moment. Well aware she'd likely be widowed young, she'd walked down the aisle anyway. She wasn't blind. She wasn't foolish. But her love for him was powerful. It couldn't be quashed by medicine or odds or statistics.

"Fifty years or five years. I want whatever you have," she'd said to him after he proposed.

She'd gotten eight.

A tear slipped down her cheek as she glanced out the tinted window of the Nissan. The car veered right onto the Strip, and the bright light of the sun pounded down from the sky. Las Vegas in daytime was exposed. Nothing hidden. Every trick, every mirror, every trap was starkly visible in the daylight.

She'd always been so good at spotting sleight of hand, at something out of place, at shining the light in a dark corner. But with Julien, she'd chosen to believe in the illusion—in the glass half-full, in the possibility of fifty years with him. Hope was more powerful than knowledge, love stronger than evidence. She'd loved him fiercely until the day he died in his sleep two years ago.

Knowing the odds had never prepared her for the wreckage of her heart when she found him that morning, unable to be roused. Over the next two years, the only things that got her through each day were routines. Work, walking, shooting photos, taking care of her mother, buying bread. Those simple acts had guided her out of the black hole of grief, as had the change in her career to fashion photography. Her heart had been too heavy for the weight of current affairs.

As the car pulled into the portico at Caesars, she glanced at her watch. A few more hours until Michael arrived.

Her stomach swooped, remembering last night, fast-forwarding to what might happen this afternoon.

Julien had wanted her to move on. Her sister wanted her to move on. She didn't think she'd ever *want* to love again. It was too risky, too dangerous. What if she let herself, then lost again? She shuddered at the thought. Once was hard enough to find the man you love gone from this world.

But a moment, a snapshot of not feeling so goddamn empty and lonely? She'd experienced that last night. She'd held it in the palm of her hands, owned it deep in her chest.

That.

She wanted that. She was so fucking tired of denying herself everything good in the world.

8

Eighteen years ago

"You want to do this?" Thomas scooped some pepper steak from the buffet onto his plate, eyeing his eldest son.

"I do," Michael said with a crisp nod, a fierce certainty in his stare. Thomas's son had his eyes—cool and ice blue. Some people thought that meant he didn't care. Hardly. Thomas cared too much at times. About everything. About his wife and how distant she'd become during the last several months. About his children and how they were growing up so damn fast. About his present job and the one that he wanted to do, the one that would make it possible for him to do more for his kids.

Right now, though—as his sixteen-year-old son spooned lo mein from the silver vat at their favorite cheap Chinese restaurant, the one that boasted all-you-can-eat for $4.29 a person—he cared about Michael. The kid was a chip off the old block. He'd fallen madly in love at such a young age. Hell, Thomas knew what that was like.

He'd been like his son, crazy for the girl in high school. Course, he'd gone and married her a few years later, and they'd had their first kid when they were both only twenty and scraping by at crummy jobs. No college, no nothing. That was why he was heading to night school after this meal, to shore up on his associates degree in accounting. A practical skill, and one that would surely help him get the job he wanted.

If he scored the new gig, that would spell opportunity for his kids. "All right, let's find a way to get you to Paris next year."

"Dad, you think I'm crazy, don't you?" Michael asked when they sat down at an orange booth with cracked vinyl seats.

"For being in love?" Thomas raised an eyebrow.

"For wanting to be with someone who's going to be really far away."

Thomas shrugged happily. "Nah, love is good. Chase it. Embrace it. You're focused and driven in other areas of life, and now you're that way about her."

He'd do everything he could to help Michael follow the girl. He'd help him go to college abroad if he could pull it off. Help him see her more. A love like that, you didn't throw away. Especially with Annalise. She was a special girl; she'd do right by his son. It was a long shot, a Hail Mary pass, but maybe Michael could nab a scholarship at a university in Europe, find some study program for Americans, and learn the French language.

But even if he landed financial aid, they'd need money for airfare and lots of new expenses. Ergo, Thomas needed a new job badly. Being a limo driver only got you so far. Sure, it was a step up from driving cabs, which he'd done for years, but he'd have to reach higher.

"How would we ever be able to pay for it?" his son asked him as he picked up his fork and dug into the steak.

Thomas rubbed the back of his neck. "There's a promotion opening up at work. Think I'm going to apply for it."

"You are?"

"Can you see me being a desk jockey? Instead of a driver?" he said with a wry smile.

"Sure. Why not? You already have to wear a suit and tie."

Thomas wanted that job. Wanted it badly. Wanted the bigger salary to help fund his kids' dreams.

That night at class, he focused on how to apply his newfound math skills to the job application, and when he returned home he told his wife about an upcoming work party.

"We should go. I think it'll help as I try to get a new job. Get to know the people in the other departments," he said as he took off his jacket.

She glanced up from her sewing machine, her green eyes eager for once. He was happy to see that look in them. Lately she'd been so far away.

"Will there be piano again?" she asked, her tone strangely breathless.

He shrugged. "I think so. You mean like at that other party?"

He'd taken her to a holiday party last year, and she'd been transfixed by the Christmas tunes some local musician had tapped out on the piano.

"Yes."

"Pretty sure there will be piano."

"I'll go," she said, and she seemed happy.

That was a relief.

At least she wasn't giving him a hard time about money. She used to do that a lot. Too much. Always nagging him about their finances. She wanted him to make more, wanted to have more. But that had slowed lately, and he was glad of it.

Glad, too, that something so simple would make her smile. They hadn't had the easiest time all these years, but maybe, just maybe, things were changing.

9

A half-dozen beautiful women lounged by the Venus pool at Caesars, closed for a few hours for the shoot. One rested elegantly on a lounge chair, small scraps of bathing-suit fabric covering her long, tanned legs. Another leaned provocatively against the Roman column in the center of the secluded pool, water lapping at her feet, her face tilted toward the sun. A leggy blonde was perched on the edge of the pool, absently splashing the crystal blue waters.

Around them fanned a sea of people. Women in black jeans and tanks stood by with makeup cases, ready to powder a shiny nose at a moment's notice. Attendants carried towels and robes on their fingertips, poised to cover the models the second the camera stopped clicking. A man with a trim beard and skinny plaid pants seemed to preside over the shoot.

The pools at Caesars Palace were lush with palm trees, and rich with stately Roman architecture and statuary. The Venus pool was the most exclusive of all—it was topless, though today all boobs were covered.

Barely.

The whole scene was such a stark contrast to Michael's morning. After his run, he'd met with Curtis, who operated a gentlemen's club that Michael's company handled security for. Curtis wanted to beef up the services, given the increased gang activity across town. That was something Michael had been hearing from many clients these days. Even his brother Colin had recently helped to strengthen security around the community center where he volunteered and his girl-friend worked. Caution was the new watchword, as the Royal Sinners and their crimes made businesses wary. After Michael's meeting with Curtis, he'd finished a walk-through of a bank that had hired more protection in light of some recent robberies.

Funny how he'd gone from armed guards in aviator shades to perfect tens soaking in the rays.

He was liking the way the afternoon was shaping up to be much better.

He'd told the intern—at least, he guessed the young woman with purple hipster glasses, jet-black hair, and a clipboard, who'd done her best impression of a sentry at the pool area door, was an intern—that he was here to see Annalise. The gatekeeper checked the list, found his name, and waved him in. Michael picked a potted palm tree on the terrace, out of the way of the models and the photographic entourage. He could have stared at the blonde, let his eyes travel across the wispy brunette, or roamed his gaze over the chestnut-haired beauty floating on a gold raft.

Nope. His eyes were fixed on the redhead, watching her work. Such a familiar image—Annalise viewing the world through her lens, snap, snap, snapping. Strong arms raised her camera, hands working the shutter, her eye capturing the women in repose. She wore jeans and a black tank top. Her red hair was swept high on her head, some sort of chopstick stabbed through it.

After several minutes she stopped shooting, and the bearded guy in the odd pants clapped and told the models to take a short break. "Get a bottle of water. Have a salad. Be back in twenty minutes. You were all amazing. Perfect. Brilliant. Gorgeous," he said, then blew kisses to the bikini-clad women who scattered from their posts. The man draped an arm around Annalise, and she nodded several times as he talked quietly to her.

The man then joined the models, who were flanked by attendants, while Annalise scanned the pool area. Soon, her eyes landed on Michael and lit up, beaming at him. His heart slammed against his chest at her reaction. She weaved through lounge chairs, around the edge of the pool, and soon stood face-to-face with him, then lips-to-cheek. She whispered, "You're here."

She sounded amazed that he'd made it.

"Did you think I wouldn't show?" he asked, regarding her curiously.

She shrugged as a small smile of admission crept across her lips. "Maybe."

"Hey," he said softly. "Why would you think I wouldn't show?"

She shook her head. "It's not that. It's just..." Her voice trailed off as she raised her chin, meeting his eyes. Her gaze went soft, almost vulnerable. "It's just...you never know."

He nodded his understanding. Yeah, he got that. You never knew if someone would show or if something would derail them, or if a fate would change in the blink of an eye.

She grabbed her camera bag from a nearby table under a big yellow umbrella. He followed her. "Thanks for inviting me," he said, looking at her over the tops of his shades. "Was it a good shoot?"

She raised her face, and little wispy tendrils of red waves moved with her. "It was. These women are terrific. They love the camera and the camera loves them. It makes my job easy, having such talent to work with."

He smiled at her comment. It would be simple for her to say something catty, to toss a quippy one-liner about a too-skinny model. Instead, she'd done the opposite— praised them, not for their beauty, but for their ability.

"I doubt your job is easy," he said. "You've always been good at what you do. Yours is a natural talent as well. You have an eye."

"All I do is point, shoot, click," she said with a wink, then lifted her camera and snapped a candid of him without even looking in the lens.

"Hey now," he teased, covering his face with crossed arms, pretending he was a star avoiding the shutter.

"Too late. I've got you here. For all posterity," she said, tapping the camera. Her gaze drifted to the back of the Nikon. "You look good."

He rolled his eyes.

"I mean it. Come see," she said, gesturing for him to come closer.

He waved her off. "I don't need to see myself."

"Oh, stop being so modest. You are beautiful, Michael Sloan. You were always one of my favorite subjects," she said in her straightforward way, so open and direct. His heart pounded faster, his skin heating up from her

compliments. It grew tougher to keep her in a neat, organized corner when she said things like that.

"Thank you," he said softly, as he moved in near to her,
his arm bumping her shoulder. A slight hitch of breath
escaped her lips as they looked at the image. He resisted
touching her, even though all his instincts told him to.
Instead, he studied himself on the screen of the camera,
and he looked like the guy he'd always been. And yet, as
he saw himself through her eyes, through *her* lens, he
seemed...happier.

Maybe he looked more complete because he'd been
caught staring at her.

"See," she said, nudging him with her elbow. "Your
eyes are so expressive. Your cheekbones are perfection.
And your lips are..."

He picked up where she'd stopped. "My lips
are what?"

She met his eyes. "*Red*," she whispered, saying it in the
same tone he'd uttered the word last night. Her cheeks
flushed pink.

Ah, hell. He was going to have the hardest time not
losing himself in her. She was going to have to stop this
right now. It was past time for him to put an end to all
these sweet nothings, or he'd be utterly ruined. But no
fucking way could he tell her to stop. He liked her compliments too much.

"By the way, I liked watching you work," he said, sidestepping to a safer topic.

"You did?" she asked as she returned to her camera
bag and zipped up a compartment.

"You sort of radiate energy, but it's focused. It's almost
like an athletic event when you take pictures."

Her lips curved up. "Sometimes it feels that way."

"You perform like that. Top of your game. You with your camera, seeing the world in ways other people don't."

She stilled her movements and cocked her head, looking curious. "Is that how it seems?"

"Yeah. It does. Both watching you work and seeing what you saw. I always got a kick out of looking at your photos. Like when you took pictures at the Pearl Jam concert we went to. Eddie Vedder didn't look the same way to my eye as he did to yours. Seeing the pictures afterward was like opening a whole new view of something I'd already experienced," he said, taking off his shades and tucking them on the neck of his shirt. "What's your favorite thing to photograph?"

"Surprises," she answered quickly, as she zipped another compartment.

"What do you mean?"

"Something that's out of place. Something you don't expect to see. A pink sock fluttering on a bush makes you wonder why a pink sock is there. A dog with a goofy expression that makes him appear almost human. The moment before a kiss when the woman is surprised."

"Do you photograph kisses often?"

She shook her head. "Not often enough. I'd like to, though. I'd like to do a photographic book of kisses."

"Would you put yourself in it?"

She shrugged. "Maybe. Depends if I looked like I wanted the kiss desperately."

Oh, that was too easy. He stepped closer, swiped his thumb across her chin, and held her face. A tiny gasp came from her throat, and her lips parted.

"Yeah, like that," he said, his voice rumbling as he held

her gaze. The look in her green eyes was hazy, full of want. "That's the image you want to capture."

"Maybe I don't just want the before," she whispered, her accent thicker, the way it sounded when she was more turned on. She was more French when she was aroused. He brushed the barest of kisses on her lips, a small, gentle kiss that made his skin sizzle. "I want the after, too."

Before. After. In between. He wanted it all with her. One simple kiss and he was on a slingshot into wild longing.

"I want it, too," he said, his voice low and hungry.

She pulled back and blinked as if refocusing. "You keep distracting me from packing up," she said, her voice soft and playful. "And I need to, so I can steal you away from here for a few moments."

He swept his arm out grandly toward her camera bag. "By all means, pack up then."

She tucked the remaining items in pouches and pockets, keeping her eyes on him. "Thank you for what you said about my pictures. About how you see something in a new way from them. That means a lot to me. Sometimes I go back through old photographs and see new details. Some slant of light, or a new angle. Something that wasn't there before."

"Will you look at them all later? Hunting for details?"

She nodded, meeting his eyes. "I will. Including that one of you."

The temperature inside him rose. "What will you search for in that one?" he asked, and when she looked at him like that, her gaze intense and knowing, the breath fled from his lungs, and he felt...disarmed. She was so direct. And yeah, she'd been like that when he knew her before, but it was magnified now, amplified by age and worldliness, as if all her inherent confidence had been strengthened and sculpted over time.

"Maybe I'll remember how it felt to have you in front of me."

His head felt dizzy. His blood rushed hot. "How does it feel?"

"Like a favorite memory is real once more. And real is very, very good."

―――――

She didn't want another ghost. She wanted the solidness of Michael. The warm skin. The beating heart. He was flesh and here with her. That fueled her, made her want to answer this persistent hum in her bones asking for nourishment, asking for all she'd been deprived of.

Contact. Connection. A thread binding her to another human being.

But asking for all that was too much, too soon.

Instead, she gestured to the edge of the pool area as she hiked her bag on her shoulder. "Walk with me?"

"Where are we headed? Are you hungry?"

"Starving." She patted her stomach, flat as could be as they walked. "You know I always have a good appetite."

A smile spread slowly on his face, and he nodded. "Super metabolism," he said, since that was what she'd called it.

"French metabolism," she added.

She was slim and trim, but she didn't deprive herself. She wasn't a pig, but she wasn't a "I'll just have the salad" girl, either. Her secret was simple—she put one foot in front of the other and burned it off.

"Still walk everywhere?"

She nodded and then held up a finger as they reached the doorway leading into the hotel. "Wait. That's not true. I took an Uber today," she said, like it was a confession.

He arched an eyebrow. "Naughty girl."

"I know. I'm the worst. But in my defense, I went several miles away. Breakfast with Becky."

"Yeah? How was that?"

She scrunched her brow. "A little odd, to tell the truth. I'll talk to you about it at lunch. If you want to get lunch?"

He nodded. "Sure. I know some great spots here at Caesars. But do you really only have twenty minutes? Because that would mean taking you to the vending machines on the third floor and springing for pretzels."

A grin tugged at her lips, and she stage-whispered, "That's what they tell the girls. To make sure they're back in an hour. So I actually have about that long." She set her hand on his arm, wrapping it around his bicep. Oh, that was nice. He was so toned, so strong. Julien had been ropy and lanky. Michael was broad, firm, and just...bigger. Stronger. She liked that he felt different from what she'd been used to. "I thought we'd be done by now. That I'd have you arrive at the end of the shoot and then..."

"And then what?"

She shrugged happily. "And then..." She let her voice trail off once more, leaving possibilities lingering in the air. The truth was she'd been hoping for more of last night. For a repeat performance, and then some. She wanted to touch him, to smash into him, to feel him grind against her, and to wrap her legs around him. Call her greedy, call her needy—she'd own up to all of that. But when the director had told her the shoot was lasting well into the afternoon, and maybe the evening, she wasn't so sure she'd get what she wanted. She'd have to settle for lunch. She gestured right at the next corner, indicating the hallway that led to business suites in the hotel.

"Where are we headed, Annalise?"

"I left my purse in our suite—we all use it for the day. It's kind of cool. Like a dressing room, because the models get ready there."

"So it's full of bikinis?"

"Yes. It is"

"Will you model some for me?"

"Would you like me to?" she volleyed back, as the sparks zipped between them. The flirting—the heady, decadent flirting—was fantastic. She wanted to inhale it, let it fill her body like oxygen after too long without air.

"I believe that was established twice—a few minutes ago, as well as on the terrace last night."

"Last night was interesting," she said softly as they reached the door.

He tilted his head. "Yeah? Interesting is kind of vague. What made it interesting for you?"

"Seeing you, of course."

"Was that all?" he asked.

She knew he was fishing. But she wanted him to catch her at the end of his line. She needed him to reel her in.

She leaned in close, her head bending to his neck, her breath traveling across his skin. He smelled so damn good, clean and masculine, his aftershave hinting at the scent of the forest. "Touching you."

His hands shot out, gripping her upper arms. Tightly. "You like touching me?" he asked, his voice low and gravelly.

Like? She fucking loved it. She wanted her hands all over him. Wanted to explore him.

"So much."

He exhaled hard. "One hour, you say?"

Her lips pressed against his neck, then she whispered softly, "Sixty whole minutes. Minus ten now, from the time we spent on the pool deck." She said it like an invitation.

"Let's get out of the hallway then."

She nodded, reached for a key, and opened the door.

10

Bright lights assaulted him. Fluorescents shone starkly from the ceiling, revealing one wall lined with makeup counters, and four mirrors with exposed light bulbs framing each. He reached for the switch to dim the light to a normal illumination so he could be alone with her without retinas frying, when the wispy blonde from the shoot waved a hand.

Ah fuck. That was a buzzkill. So much for the privacy of a room. His shoulders sagged. It was like being in college again, roommates crawling out of every nook and cranny, right when he'd been hoping to have his hands all over Annalise. His fingers itched to touch her.

"Hi, Annalise," the blonde said, stretching her arms over her head, pushing them into a gray sweatshirt. She poked her head through the hole.

Annalise cleared her throat. "Hey, Candy. What are you up to?"

"Just going to do some yoga during our break."

"Great plan. Good use of time. I need to grab my purse." Annalise gestured to a beige couch littered with purses, bags, and jackets. "Then you can do your downward dog to your heart's content."

Candy waved a hand. "I'm meeting my yoga guru. In his room. He travels with me."

"Oh," Annalise said, seeming to rein in a smirk that tugged at the corner of her lips. "That's smart. To have him travel with you."

"Thank you! I better go. I only have a few minutes to clear my mind of dangerous toxins," she said, then seemed to float on her own weightlessness to the door.

She left, and the door clicked shut with a satisfying *thunk*.

"A traveling yoga guru?" Michael asked dryly.

"Don't you have one? I mean, really. How else could you travel?"

He held up his hands. "Can't think of how I'd manage without one," he said, then glanced around the room.

"It's a good thing she had to leave to see him, though, don't you think?" she said.

"It's a fucking great thing. Think anyone else will pop in?"

"It's possible." Annalise gave an indifferent shrug. "But that's what chain locks are for."

She dropped her camera bag to the carpeted floor and slid the lock into place. In a second he was behind her, dragging his nose along her exposed shoulder. "I like touching you, too. So fucking much."

"I like you touching me," she whispered, facing the door, her fingers frozen on the lock.

He dragged his hands along her sides, traveling over the fabric of her tank top, along her waist, up her ribs to her breasts, then back down. With her hair pinned up, her neck was bare and inviting. He dipped his head to the soft, sweet flesh, inhaling her. She trembled, shudders racking her whole body. He kissed a path along her neck, up to her ear, then nipped her earlobe.

"Michael," she said, all low and needy.

"Yes?"

She twisted to face him, looping her arms around his neck. "Last night was...intense."

"Yeah?"

She nodded, then nibbled on her lip.

A part of him knew there was so much to say. Words about time, and distance, and longing. Questions about her heart and her head, and how the fuck she was doing after losing her husband. Practical matters, too, like how long was she in town. Would he see her again today? And did she miss him over all the years with the same kind of intensity he'd missed her?

His brain fought back, reminding him he was being ridiculous. He hadn't missed her. He hadn't thought about her. He hadn't fucking obsessed on her.

This was just fiery lust, and it had been reignited so furiously it blazed white-hot.

"How intense?" he asked, brushing the backs of his fingers along her cheek. "We only kissed last night."

"Kissing can drive you crazy, though, don't you think?"

"I made you crazy last night?" He toyed with her, wanting to hear the admissions from her, the breathless, gasping yeses.

"*Wild*. I was wild," she said, then reached for his hands and led him to the row of mirrors with the lights. She hopped up on a counter, perching on the edge, and beckoned him closer. With his thigh he nudged open her legs and wedged himself between them. Ah, his favorite place to be. The place he wanted to get to know so much better.

Ideally when they were both naked, but clothed was at least a good start.

She roped her arms around his neck and raised her eyes to his. Hers were a confessional. A dirty one. "Last night wasn't just the two of us kissing. When I returned to my room there was more."

"Tell me," he said, threading a hand in her hair, letting the silk flames fall against his fingers. "I want to picture it perfectly."

"Standing up. Against the door. Fast, intense."

He breathed out hard, electric heat sparking through him as his dick throbbed against his pants. Fuck, that was one hot image. "Did I make you come? Like I did all those other times?" he asked, reminding her that he was the first man to bring her to orgasm. His fingertips stroked the denim on her thighs, traveling a path he'd loved when he was younger. She'd loved it, too—falling apart in the back of the car, his hands under her skirt. Her body was such a discovery to him. Learning how she liked to be touched, how she moved, how she felt, so silky hot in his hands. How she sounded when she had her first orgasm. She'd learned all those things, too. They were explorers together, mapping the terrain of her body.

"Yes," she said on a breathy pant. "I moaned your name. The way you liked it."

Desire surged in him, climbing up his spine, spreading over his skin. He'd loved the way she'd said his name when she came.

He cupped her cheeks in his hands, holding her face tight and firm, and sealed his mouth to hers, kissing her hard and rough, the way she liked it now, because she wasn't the same girl he'd made out with after midnight in the backseat. She was a woman, and he was a man. He needed it harder, rougher, hungrier, too. He drew her bottom lip between his, sucking and nibbling as she writhed closer, wrapping her legs around him.

One hand snaked down her tank, brushing the top of a perfect breast, and he moaned deeply into her mouth then resumed the kiss, a commanding kiss that would leave her lips bruised. She arched her back, seeking more closeness.

Traveling from her breasts to her stomach to her jeans, he flicked open the top button. A clock sounded in his head, awareness that time was ticking, that someone could knock at any moment. The lock was in place, but even so, he wasn't going to finally fuck her right now. That would happen when he could spread her out on a bed, worship her beautiful body, and kiss every inch of her skin. It would happen when he could bury his face between her legs and taste her sweetness for the first time, making her come. It would happen, too, when she was ready.

His blood heated as he imagined how intense it would be to have her.

There wasn't time now for all that he wanted, but there were more than enough minutes to make her come. He unzipped her jeans, and she gripped his shoulders, her breath pouring out in a hungry moan. Sliding his hand over the fabric of her panties, his fingertips traced what he suspected was a perfect auburn landing strip waiting for him beneath the lace. He dropped lower, touching the wet panel of her panties.

"And evidently, you're a bit turned on now, too," he said, in the understatement of the year.

"Just a tiny bit," she said, as her lips fell open. Her head rolled back. Legs widened. There was so much want in her eyes. So much need. Wedged between her legs, his cock throbbing and pressed hard against her thigh, he slid his finger inside her panties, brushing wet, swollen lips.

Fuck.

Hot and velvet and so damn wet. For him.

"I can take care of this for you."

"Please." Her voice was feathery, a soft, gasping cry.

He wasn't sure who needed this more—him or her. He desperately wanted to make her lose control, to surrender. Hell, she seemed to crave it like air. Her heady moans, her breathy gasps, told him she was a woman consumed. He could smell her need, could feel it radiating off of her. She was a tuning fork, vibrating at the highest frequency of desire.

He ran his fingers through her slick heat until he was coated in her.

"So good," she whispered, as he traced circles over her clit.

He brought his fingers to his lips and sucked off her taste. Her green eyes widened, watching him. "How do I taste?" she asked, breathlessly.

"Decadent," he answered in a growl.

"Give me some," she demanded.

And that was entirely new. That was not the Annalise he knew before. She'd never demanded to share. He was thrilled at this dirtier side.

"Such a greedy lover," he teased, as he rubbed his finger over her lips. Instantly, she drew him into her mouth, taking his finger all the way in, sucking off her taste as if she were sucking his cock. His dick twitched, hardening to nearly uncomfortable levels in his pants. But he'd take this torture of bliss. He'd fucking live in it for hours, just to witness the sight of her mad desire. She twirled her tongue around him, as if simulating how she'd take him in her mouth. She'd never done that. He'd never felt her lush lips on his shaft, and now he knew what fantasy he'd be jacking off to tonight.

She looked so good like that. So fucking hot and greedy, her cheeks hollowed out as her lips gripped tight. *More.* He wanted to see more of this.

Taking his fingers from her mouth, he dipped them across her slick folds again, then returned them to her lips. He fucked her mouth with his fingers, as he brought his other hand between her legs. As he stroked her, he learned her pace quickly—she liked it fast and hard—and he rubbed her clit like that, in perfect, speedy circles.

She moved her hips against his hand, writhing into him. Then, with her tongue, she pushed his fingers out of her mouth, freeing herself to moan, broken words of bliss in her French accent.

Oh God.

So good.

Yes. More. That. Fuck me.

God, there was so much he wanted to say. So many words that threatened to escape his throat. Words like *dreamed about you, wanted you for so long,* and more, so much more. Words he wouldn't let himself say because those were only the hormones talking, right?

"Did you fuck yourself like this last night? Thinking of me?" he asked, his voice rough as he plunged his fingers inside her slick heat.

"Yes."

"Thinking of how much you want me?"

She nodded as she lifted her chin, asking for a kiss.

He dipped his head, crushing his lips to hers, tasting her as he fucked her pussy with his fingers. With his free hand, he gripped the back of her head, holding her tight against his mouth.

But then, in a flash, everything shifted.

She grabbed his hand between her legs, and gripped his wrist. She circled her hips, jerking her body, rising against him, and holding him in place like his hand was a dildo. Holy shit. He'd become her goddamn vibrator as she rocked into his hand in frantic jerks, desperately racing to come.

"Do it," he growled, urging her on. "Do it till you get there."

She fucked his hand with reckless, untamed need, clenching tight around his fingers until she moaned into his mouth, her lips falling away from his. She cried out, gasping *I'm coming* in French.

That was the girl he'd known. She'd always come in French. On his fingers, in his hand, while dry-humping him in a car, in her locked room, in a movie theater once during a high-octane action sequence. Her words always returned to her native language when she soared off the cliff. Hell, her sexy, breathy moans right now were rich with her accent. It made him even harder, and it made him grin, pride suffusing him.

He lowered his mouth, kissing her neck, dragging his teeth across the tender skin, biting her. He needed to mark this woman who'd haunted him. For years, she'd been the yardstick, the dream, the *what if* fantasy. The trouble was, making her come, watching her lose all control for him, did nothing to abate that pent-up desire for her. The opposite had happened. It stoked the flames. He wanted her more than ever. Wanted to slide his cock inside her, wanted to feel her snug and tight around him, wanted to know what it was like to make love to—*no*. Not that. To *fuck* this woman.

She shuddered, her shoulders shaking. It occurred to him that his fingers were still inside her. Gently, he removed them.

She looked up at him from hooded, sated eyes. "I think I treated your hand like a dildo," she said, a sweet little smirk on her gorgeous face.

"You did. But I'm perfectly okay with you treating my hand, cock, or my mouth as a sex toy anytime you want," he said, and she laughed. He leaned in, moving his lips to her ear. "Because I want you with every part of me. I want to fuck you in every way," he told her. "To have you in any way I can."

She wrapped her hands around his neck. "I want that, too. I want it desperately."

"So what do you want to do about that?"

He waited for her answer, watching her expression change from one of euphoria to something else entirely, something that looked a lot like regret.

His heart cratered.

11

As soon as *I want it desperately* tumbled from her lips, she cast her eyes downward.

A strange sensation washed over her. It felt like...guilt. And it was awful. It wormed through her, eating up the bliss she'd experienced mere moments ago, turning it into something insidious.

She'd just come with another person for the first time in two years. She should feel ecstatic, but instead a seed pushed and shoved against her skin, because it was the first time she'd been with someone new in more than a decade, and that felt traitorous.

It shouldn't.

It really shouldn't.

But as she brushed her messy hair from her face with fingers that had clutched Michael like a lifeline, remorse turned her blood sluggish. She pressed her lips together, holding in this feeling, sucking it down. Maybe she could just ride it out.

When a traitorous tear slipped down her cheek,

Michael tucked his fingers under her chin and raised her face. "Hey. Are you okay?"

His voice was warm, full of concern, and his eyes searched her expression. It was then that she realized why she'd thought he was a safe choice. Because in this moment, he was. They'd always talked; they'd been as open as a couple could be. She brushed the remnant of the tear away, and spoke softly. "I feel guilty, but I don't want to feel guilty."

"I understand why you'd feel that way," he said, taking his time speaking. "And I don't want to push you into anything."

Her eyes widened. "No. God, no. You didn't push me. I wanted all of it. I wanted you."

"Did it bother you, what I said? That I wanted you in every way?"

She shook her head. "No. I loved it, actually."

"You have to know you have nothing to feel guilty about."

"I know. I get it up here," she said, tapping her head, then moved her hand to her heart. "But here, it's hard. That's the first time I've done a thing with anyone since..."

"I just want you to feel good. In every way. Your heart, and your body." He ran his hand down her arm. Her gaze followed the path of his fingertips, and it registered what he'd done. He'd gone from pleasuring her to comforting her. He could do both, just as she could talk freely to him about this pendulum swing of emotions.

She took a long, deep breath, met his gaze, and made a choice. To live in the present.

"Thank you," she said, her voice strong again. She wrapped her arms around his neck. "For that. All of it. Every part."

A smile tugged at his mouth. He looked at his wristwatch. "We need to feed you and get you back to work. I would love to see you again, if you want," he said.

"I want that."

"But I don't even know how long you're in town for."

"Not long. I leave tomorrow for New York."

His smile spread. "Me, too."

The words rang in her ears like a song.

And suddenly, she knew she wanted to live in the present with him for a little bit longer.

———

The Thai restaurant served them lickety-split. With her fork she twirled the noodles and took a bite of her pad Thai. She hummed as she ate. Maybe she was still high from that orgasm, or maybe it was from their plans to spend time together in New York. Quite possibly she might be feeling this way because they'd talked about what was happening, and she'd moved through it, for now.

"The pad Thai...it's that good?"

"Maybe it is," she said, after she finished chewing.

"Or are you grinning about something else?"

She leaned across the table as he worked his way through a shrimp dish. "You," she said with a naughty grin. "Your tongue."

A smile spread slowly across his handsome face, as he licked his lips. "You looking forward to getting to know that part of me?"

She nodded and took another bite, moaning around the food. "Mmm. I bet you're spectacular at that."

"What makes you say that?"

"The way you kiss me."

His eyes darkened. "You have no idea how badly I want to show you other ways to kiss you." He dropped his voice lower. "I want to kiss you until your taste is all over my lips."

She dropped her fork. Her entire body went up in flames. He reached across the table, picked up the utensil, and handed it to her.

"Thank you," she murmured, and she wasn't sure if she was thanking him for the fork, or the orgasm, or the promise of more and in a new variety.

Somehow, she managed to take another bite of her noodles, but she couldn't rein in the grin as she ate.

He laughed, wiped his napkin across his mouth, and took a drink of his water. "I like seeing you...happy. You deserve to be happy."

Happy was one way to put it. *Unlocked* worked, too. That first kiss had turned the key on a closed door in her that had been shut tight since Julien had passed away. She'd shut off the woman who'd loved sex and intimacy and closeness, as if the lack of it were necessary to prove her grief.

But as soon as she'd let herself go there last night, with her own fingers, she'd become a woman unleashed. It was as if that single orgasm against her hotel room door had uncorked her. Like a ravenous, starving woman given filet and chocolate cake and fine wine, she wanted more. Wanted to gobble it all up. A second serving, a third helping, and dessert, please, too.

If she could only keep the guilt at bay. She hoped that brief encounter with it in the dressing room was her last, because she clearly had unfinished business with Michael. He'd been her first taste of love, and the connection they'd shared years ago had been so deep and so strong. Even though loving again was too dangerous, surely she was still allowed to experience passion and erotic joy, right? Especially with someone who'd once been the center of her world.

Perhaps now he could help her move on, help her heal. She had a freedom with him she wouldn't have with another man, a chance to skip the bullshit and come together on a blissful, carnal level with her one-time love. They'd waited for each other when they were younger, but now they'd matured into adults who could have sex without labels. As teens they'd been wildly idealistic; as men and women who'd seen the world, they had the freedom to have unfettered sex. He would be the balm to her wounded body, the warmth to her cold heart. Maybe then she could finally be free to live again, to stop feeling like she was walking around the earth half-alive, with a frozen heart encased in her icicle ribs.

"I am happy. I'm looking forward to New York. It's everything we couldn't do before," she answered him.

"Being young made some things too difficult," he said, his tone both serious and nostalgic.

"Now we can be naughty adults. Do it in taxis, on airplanes, in restaurants," she said, as her dirty dreams spilled forth.

"You want all that? You sure?"

"Yes," she said emphatically, waving her hand behind her as if to gesture to the room where they'd been. "Please don't let my momentary breakdown before scare you off."

He held up his hands. "I assure you, you haven't scared me off."

"And I assure you that I desperately want all of you," she said, choosing total directness right now. She didn't get into the *why*. But the truth was she'd mostly had bedroom sex, and while it had been good, she wanted hot, dirty, thrilling sex. The kind that was spelled with the word *abandon*. The kind he seemed able to give her.

The waitress appeared to refill their water, breaking up the flirty, dirty moment. That was fine, because Annalise needed to return to their prior conversation. "I wanted to tell you about Sanders and Becky," she said.

Michael nodded, a serious look in his cool blue eyes. "Talk to me. What happened?"

"She seemed off. Like something was really bothering her," Annalise began. She hadn't intended to tell Michael at first, and yet it seemed necessary. The more she reflected on the conversation, the more she wanted Michael to know. She'd lingered on the exchange with Becky, and the fact that her old friend had said *ever since the investigation*. She shared the details, adding that Sanders had missed the breakfast because of an appointment. "And Becky seemed nervous, but sad, too."

Michael nodded, his expression now intensely focused, his jaw set. "Sad in what way?"

"She wouldn't elaborate, and I don't want to sound alarms. I have no idea what's going on, but something is on her mind. And I wanted you to know."

"I don't know why she'd be like that. But I'll try to see if it means anything."

She reached across the table for his hand and clasped hers over it. He let out a breath and seemed to relax the slightest bit. She rewound to all the times they'd talked about his loss, to the letters and the phone calls from overseas. He'd shared everything with her—all his hurt, all his pain. She'd heard the man cry once or twice, and she'd comforted him from afar as best she could as he told her the horror of what happened to his family the night after she left town.

The story was shocking to her, especially since she'd seen Thomas Paige less than thirty-six hours before he was killed. She and Michael had had breakfast with him at a little diner, eating eggs and toast as they talked about their plans. He was such a good man, so committed to doing everything he could for his son, and by extension for her. She'd thanked him, hugged him, and even told him she looked forward to the day he became her father-in-law. She'd believed it then—at the time, she was so certain she'd marry Michael.

"How is everything going with the reopened investigation?" she asked, threading her fingers more tightly through his, wanting to be his anchor if he needed her, like she'd been before.

He swallowed, his shoulders rising and falling, then spoke. "They arrested one guy, the getaway driver. And they're looking for the mastermind. T.J. Nelson. He was the guy who brokered Stefano's hits. Apparently, he's wanted for several murders over the years, including this one."

She shuddered, imagining the trail of carnage the man had left behind. "Do they think your father's death was connected to the others? I thought with your mother in prison, and the gunman's confession, that they knew the motive." How much more clear could it be? Dora had her husband killed for the life insurance money so she could run off with her lover.

"Yeah, I don't think that's changed. But the shooter had accomplices, and now it turns out the guy she was involved with is head of the whole fucking Royal Sinners gang."

Her jaw fell open, and her eyes widened. She knew of the gang from all her talks with Michael after the murder. She grabbed her water, taking a drink, processing this newest twist. "She was involved with the head of a street gang?"

"Turns out she was buying and selling drugs from them. That's part of what the cops have uncovered now. She was selling drugs to a whole long list of people, including the two guys they think helped out with the killing. The shooter was her supplier, and the guy she was cheating on my dad with—well, turns out Luke wasn't just some local piano teacher. He's like the 'deep undercover, appears innocent on the outside, but is really head of the street gang' teacher."

Shock coursed through her, spreading from her chest all the way to her fingertips, a cold, liquid sensation under her skin. "Are they arresting him, too?"

Michael rubbed a hand across the back of his neck. "That's the thing. They *know* he's head of the gang, but they have to have specific evidence to link him to a specific crime, so that's what they're looking for. Since all the other players were part of the Royal Sinners, they're trying to figure out if somehow that means my dad's murder was related to the drug trade the gang is part of. The guy who supposedly masterminded the hit, T.J., was involved in a lot of the other gang crimes."

Annalise shook her head, taking it all in. She remembered details that had emerged during the trial—the lover, the affair, the life insurance. Michael had told her everything. Crazy that the crime might have had deeper roots. "Do you think they can find T.J.?"

"I sure hope so. I want nothing as much as I want to see all those fuckers behind bars. Forever," he said, his voice a low seethe, his eyes sharp as knives. "I will never forget."

His hand tightened beneath hers into a stony fist. She rubbed her palm over it, wishing she could comfort him. As she touched him, a memory flickered before her. A party. His mother saying something about a piano.

"Do you think she met her lover at a party? Your mom mentioned something once about a party with a piano."

"You remember those kind of details?"

She nodded. "I have a ridiculously good memory. I remember her making a dress. I asked her what it was for, and she told me."

"A party with a piano?" he asked, raising an eyebrow.

She nodded, then told him bits and pieces from a brief conversation she'd had with his mother in passing one afternoon. "I don't know if that's helpful, though."

His expression seemed grateful. "It's all helpful. Every detail matters."

They finished lunch, and he walked her back to the shoot a few minutes early.

"I can't wait to spend some time together in New York," she said, cupping his cheek. His eyes blazed, and his breathing intensified from that simple touch. For a moment she felt powerful, eliciting that reaction in this strong, stoic man. She stood on tiptoes and pressed a soft kiss to his lips.

"I'm counting down the hours." He'd said he had a dinner with a client that night, so the flight would be the next time she saw him.

Then, because she was feeling frisky, and because things had been one-sided so far, she pressed a hand to his flat belly through his shirt. "Don't think I'm selfish. I'm not," she said, whispering in his ear. "I want to taste you. I want you in my mouth. I want to feel you in my throat."

He swayed closer, a sexy sigh escaping his lips. "You're killing me," he growled.

She wiggled an eyebrow, turned on her heel, and left with a spring in her step, knowing that tomorrow she'd come again.

12

His grandmother kept everything. Which meant it took him nearly an hour to find the box of photos from when he was sixteen. If his hunch was right, his mom had met Luke that year. He grabbed a shoebox from the top shelf in the garage, cluttered with tools, old toys, and clothes headed for donation.

"Found it?"

"I think so," he said, tucking the box under his arm as he climbed down the ladder to join Victoria Paige, the woman who'd raised him and his brothers and sister after his mother went to prison.

"Let's go inside and paw through it," she said, gesturing to the door into the house. Michael had come straight there after lunch with Annalise.

They parked themselves on stools at the kitchen counter, and Michael took the top off the shoebox.

"What exactly do you think you'll find?" his grand-mother asked as she grabbed a thick handful of curled-up photos from nearly two decades ago.

He shook his head. "Honestly not sure, Nana. But I

want to look to see if anything gives me a clue about that guy. Any photo at all. I know he had to have been involved somehow. It can't be a coincidence that she was trying to run away with that man."

She nodded resolutely. If anyone understood the drive to leave no stone unturned, it was Victoria. Michael had lost a father; she had lost her son. That loss tethered them more tightly than a grandmother and a grandson should be. Now they were driven by the same need—the one for justice.

What if it was in their grasp? What if there was a clue in the family photos? Annalise had said photos sometimes held surprises, that when she looked at them again, she'd find things she hadn't noticed the first time. Maybe it was wishful thinking, but hell, if there was a speck of evidence under his nose, Michael wanted to find it. He wanted to know if there were *any* photos that would tell him about his mother's relationship with Luke Carlton, and how it had played a part in his father's death.

He flipped through picture after picture from that fateful year, from posed school photos, to shots of Ryan playing hockey, to pictures of Shannon dancing.

"Let me have that one," Victoria said, grabbing at a photo of his sister on stage, leaping high. "I need to frame that and give it to her."

Michael smiled and draped an arm around his grandmother, squeezing her shoulder. "She'll love it."

His sister didn't dance after she tore her ACL in college. She'd become a world-class choreographer instead.

Michael and his grandmother thumbed through more pictures. Shots of dance recitals, pictures of sunsets, images of family barbecues, including one of his dad flipping burgers with his grandfather, then one with Michael standing at his father's side, laughing together.

A lump rose in his throat, and his fingers lingered on that shot.

"I remember that day," he whispered.

His grandmother's eyes shined with wistfulness. "You do? Tell me more," she said, resting her chin in her hand.

He shook his head, surprised at the clarity of the memory. "It was just an average Sunday in the fall. October, I think. Dad grilling with Grandpa. Nothing special. They were placing bets on whose barbecue sauce was better, and at some point the stakes were so crazy, we all cracked up. We were all there. Hanging out at your house. I think Ryan and Colin were watching college football, and Shannon was playing with the dog you had then."

Victoria smiled widely, her eyes misty. "Rusty. He was a good dog. Your dad liked him. I can see it all now," she said, then tapped the photo. "Why don't I have this one framed, too?"

Michael scoffed and tipped his head to the walls of her home. They were thick with framed family photos. "Can't frame everything."

"But I can try." She snagged that photo, sighing as she regarded that shot of the men grilling. "The barbecue was the day after Thomas went to that party. I remember it now." She traced a shaking finger across the bags under his father's eyes. "He was so tired as they'd been up real late. He and your mother went to a work function."

Michael sat up straighter. That's what Annalise had mentioned. "The party," Michael hissed. "That's what I want to see. Do you think anyone took pictures of the party?"

"Not me. I wasn't there."

"But what if my dad had them? If someone had taken pictures from the work party..." He let his voice trail off, desperate hope coloring his tone.

She gestured to the pile. "Let's hunt."

He wanted to find those photos. He grabbed the next chunk of pictures and methodically studied each one. There was no reason to believe there would be pictures of a party here in his grandma's home, but she saved everything, so there was always a chance. If someone had taken pictures at the event, his dad might have held onto them...

His heart stopped, then started again. He'd found it. A shot of his mother and father in front of a work banner at a company party for West Limos. Flipping to the back, he checked the date. Yep. The year it all went down. He gripped the edge of the photo as dark anger coiled through him. His mother took from him the person he loved most. His insides churned viciously as he studied the two of them. But it was only them posing for the camera, like some kind of company photographer had shot a picture.

He flicked to the next one. A foursome. Sanders and Becky stood next to his parents. Sanders clutched his wife's shoulder tightly, and she smiled for the camera. Michael's eyes roamed to his mother. He saw her looking to the right, just outside the frame.

Determined to follow her gaze somehow, he tore through the other pictures from the party. All in front of the banner, each one a little farther over, like the photographer was moving sideways. There were only a few more. As he lined them up, he could tell where his mother's eyes had drifted just beyond the edge of the banner.

To a man playing a piano.

Luke Carlton.

Was Annalise right? Had his mother met her lover at his father's work party? Why would Luke be at a work party?

"I need to talk to Sanders again. See if he remembers anything from that night. Anything about Luke talking to my dad, maybe. Anything that could make it clear what role he played."

But when he called Sanders a little later from the car, his dad's old friend didn't answer.

13

Michael rapped on the window outside the detective's office. John Winston sat in his chair with his back to him, talking on the phone. He swiveled around, holding up a finger to ask Michael to wait.

As John wrapped up his call, Michael jammed his hands into his pockets, tension curling his muscles tight as the sounds of the police department filtered from behind him—the crackle of the radio, phone calls about cases, the shuffling of papers.

John nodded, then laughed, and at last hung up the phone. He rose, opened the door, and let Michael in.

"How's everything?" John asked, clicking the door shut.

"It's fine." The two of them weren't known for their small talk, so Michael took a seat in the wooden chair offered him.

"What have you got?" John asked. After Sanders didn't pick up, Michael had called John to tell him he had some details to share.

"Are you any closer to getting Luke? Closer to getting T.J?"

John sighed and scrubbed a hand across his jaw. "We're working on it every day. We're doing everything we can."

Frustration slid through Michael's veins at how goddamn easily Luke Carlton had glided through life, avoiding arrest, covering his tracks, operating as a criminal so far undercover. "I don't know if it's a long shot, but I think"—he stopped, pausing before he said his mother's name because it tasted acrid—"Dora Prince met Luke at a work party," he said, then showed the detective the photos.

John nodded several times. "Yeah, I think you're right."

"You think I'm right?" Michael repeated, because he was hoping for something more.

"I've got similar information."

"So this isn't news to you?"

"I've been working leads on this case for a long time. This is one of them."

"Why didn't you tell me that's how they met?"

"Because it's not my job to tell you every detail. This is a police investigation. I'm grateful for all you do—don't get me wrong. But I've got to be able to investigate, and sharing every detail with the family can slow me down on the way to answers." He took a beat and then leveled his gaze at Michael. "The answers we *both* want."

"Fine," Michael said, reminding himself that even though John was the gatekeeper, they had the same end goal. So he tamped down his annoyance. "Let's put our heads together, then. I've got some thoughts."

John nodded. "What's on your mind?"

Michael took his time before he spoke, carefully

weighing each word so that he could extract something from the detective. There was so much on his mind, so much he wanted to know—like why the Royal Sinners were so goddamn powerful, why they were stronger than any average street gang, and why they were smarter, nimbler, and had more firepower. But those were broader questions, and they wouldn't necessarily get him any closer to the answers he needed. Like the depth of the connection between his mother and the head of the gang.

"The question we both want to know is *why*," he said. "We know my mother's lover is the head of the gang. We know the shooter was in the gang. We know the other accomplices are part of it, too. What I'd like to know is *how* my mother got involved with the Sinners, and did it somehow start at my father's work? If she met Luke at a work party, was he a regular there? Luke operates under-cover, and that makes me question everything about where he's been and what he's done. Were the other guys in the gang involved in these work parties? Did they know my dad?" Michael held out his hands. "Maybe I'm reach-ing. But what if there's something to it?"

John met his stare straight on. "That's what I want to know, too. I want to know if work is where they met, and if so, if it sheds new light on the accomplices. Luke played piano at a handful of these parties at your father's company. What does that tell us?" he asked rhetorically. "Not enough on its own, but now that we've learned he's part of the Sinners, we have reason to believe he has knowledge about a number of gang-ordered hits over the years. That's why we want to know if your father's murder had a deeper connection to the gang. Was this just your mother's hit, or a part of something bigger? And did Luke know about it?"

"It seems likely that he knew. Doesn't it?"

———

Yes, it would seem like Luke had to have known about the hit. It would seem, too, that Luke was deeply involved in the planning of the murder. It would sure as hell seem as if Luke fucking Carlton had gotten away with several other murders over the years, based on the information John had obtained from his informants.

But evidence was evidence, and it needed to be hard.

John and his men were getting closer to Luke, but there were things he simply couldn't share with Michael —details he couldn't speculate on with a witness or family member. Things like how the shooter's son, Lee Stefano, had started singing. They'd nabbed him a few months ago on grand theft of iPhones, of all things. The kid was trying to follow in his dad's footsteps, living a life of crime. But several weeks in jail had softened him up, and Lee had started talking. He'd shared more about the two men who'd looked out for him after his daddy went to the big house—Kenny and T.J. Nelson, his father's accomplices in the murder of Thomas Paige.

Turned out, Lee knew some details about T.J.'s whereabouts these days, and John was hoping to piece together enough information to find that slippery bastard and take him into custody, too. John clenched his fists, thinking of the rap sheet on T.J. Nelson, and the long trail of evidence linking him to other crimes over the years. Some of John's colleagues had gathered insight into the gang as a whole, and the way the Royal Sinners had expanded in power, operating a lucrative drug ring throughout the city of Las Vegas and across the state.

Connecting the dots was proving more complicated than he'd expected. Did the hit have anything to do with the gang, or with things Thomas might have learned about the Sinners? Or was this simply what they'd thought all along, a crime designed so a woman could be with the man she loved?

Those questions kept John up at night, but he had witnesses to talk to and leads to chase down, which might bring him answers. As soon as he had the details, he'd get that fucker.

"Listen, I appreciate you doing everything you can," John said, dragging a hand through his dark blond hair, taking his time with each word. "You need to be careful, but I can't tell you not to ask around. What I can tell you is I've heard that T.J. had words with Thomas Paige a few weeks before he died. That conversation took place at your father's work." That was why it mattered to the investigation that Dora had likely met Luke at West Limos. John needed to tie Luke to T.J., and if he could just pull those threads a little tighter together, he'd be able to do it. "I'd like to know why, and what was said."

Michael nodded, an intense look in his eyes. "If you'd like to know, then I'd like to know, too."

14

On the way to the gym that evening, Michael tried to reach his father's friend once again. Becky answered, but when he asked for Sanders, she said, "He's busy for a few days, hon."

"Busy with what?" Michael asked, trying to sound casual rather than suspicious, even though he was starting to feel that way.

"He got called out of town. He has things he needs to get done before he finishes work," she said as he turned on the blinker of his black BMW to exit the highway.

"Hmm. Okay. But I've got to see him soon, Becky. Can you have him call me as soon as he can?"

"Of course, love."

The line went dead.

As Michael hoisted a barbell a little later, he replayed the conversation with John, then the brief chat with Becky, trying to read between their words, to line them up like missing puzzle pieces alongside his conversation with Annalise earlier. As he pushed up the heavy weight in his bench press, he zeroed in on some ideas, but they were fuzzy, hazy around the edges, and he didn't want to jump to conclusions. He lowered the bar, wondering if there was more to Becky's odd behavior, to Sanders's absence, and to the conversation T.J. had with his father.

Now, that—he'd sure as hell like to know more about that.

He'd seen Sanders a few weeks ago, along with his dad's other friend, Donald, at the Golden Nugget. That was where Donald dealt cards, and Michael had joined them for a few rounds, winning handily each time.

"Just like his dad. Thomas always beat us at poker," Sanders had said, shaking his head and laughing, a hint of pride in his voice. Michael had reined in a grin because he loved those comparisons and ate them up like candy.

Anything to connect him to his dad.

They'd all got to talking when Donald's shift ended, and the older men mentioned something about trouble at his dad's company way back when. They didn't have a ton of details, nor did Michael, but he could recall his father mentioning something similar at one of their Chinese restaurant meals. He just wished he knew what *sort* of trouble, and if that trouble was connected to Luke. He had nothing to go on now, since West Limos had come up clean in his research into the company. But the details nagged at Michael as he poked and prodded at his own memories of things his dad had said to him.

He wished he had Annalise's memory—precise and, not surprisingly, photographic. His was blurrier, and he often wondered if it was because of *how* he found out his dad was gone. The image splashed cruelly before his eyes, and he grimaced as he jammed the weights back in the holder. He sat up straight with his hands on his knees, trying to shake off the scene that sometimes replayed unexpectedly.

Taking measured breaths, he focused on the small details around him now. The pounding music in his earbuds. The clang of barbells. The whir of bicycle machines.

They reset him to the present.

But the problem was the present was mired in so much uncertainty. He was on the outside, peeking in, trying to assemble the picture while only having access to the barest bits and pieces. He tried to fill in the blanks as he cycled through all the weights then headed to the rowing machine. Sixty sweaty minutes later, he called Mindy, his sounding board, as he drove home.

"Should we get Morris to look into the company my dad worked at, too?" he asked, mentioning the private eye's name after he'd relayed his conversation with the detective.

"Hmm," Mindy said, seeming to mull over the idea. "I'm not so sure. That's a bit different than having Morris tail Luke Carlton."

"I know," Michael said with a sigh. "That's the issue. Which path to send him down."

"Honestly, I think we need to keep him on Luke, since you know there's likely a connection. And I think you need to talk to the people your dad knew then. Donald, Sanders—those guys. See if they know anything about the conversation with T.J."

"If I can even get Sanders to return a fucking call," Michael said with a huff, as he turned onto his street.

"Go see him, then."

But something about that idea seemed unwise. With Becky acting odd, Michael wasn't so sure how well her husband would take to a surprise visit. He shook his head, even though Mindy couldn't see him. "I've got to work other angles. I'm going to see what I can dig up. I'll let you know what I find."

He said good-bye, then pulled into the parking garage at his building and headed up the elevator to his home. Once inside, he went straight for his computer, logging into some of the databases that he and Ryan relied on for security and background checks at work. He entered the name of the limo company his father had worked for, but nothing new surfaced. He'd been down this road before. When the investigation had been reopened, he'd looked into West Limos. He wasn't suspicious, per se. Just being thorough. It was owned by some guy named West Strassman. For years the same guy had owned it from his home base in Dallas. Now he was retired, living in Canada and keeping busy fishing. But he still owned a bunch of businesses around the country, with managers at each to run the day-to-day operations.

Michael leaned back in his desk chair, sighing heavily. Maybe he was reaching. Maybe the connection was simply that his mother had happened to meet her lover when he'd been playing piano at a work party. Got to know him, started selling drugs for his Royal Sinners to make some cash on the side. Got greedy and wanted more dough to cover her debts. Wanted to run away with her lover.

Killed her husband.

Yeah, that seemed as plausible as anything. The West Limo connection was simply the way in which her world collided with that of Luke Carlton. Luke then became the connection to the gang, the drugs, and the murder for hire. Hell, maybe the conversation T.J. had with his dad was about his mother's affair.

He shut his laptop, padded to the kitchen, poured two fingers of scotch, and let the liquor scorch a path down his throat. He set the glass on the counter and headed for the shower.

Time to put aside the clues that remained cloudy. He had a trip to take to New York, a woman to focus his energy on, and business to attend to.

As the water beat down on him, he bent his head under the spray, letting the heat soothe his sore muscles. He closed his eyes, and soon enough the questions stopped chasing each other. They circled the drain, and he imagined letting go of them until he could talk to the man who might have the answers. As the shower steamed up, his thoughts returned to that afternoon with Annalise.

For the first time all day, he let himself accept that he was going to have some kind of tryst with her. He was going to touch her in all the ways he craved. He could still smell her when he closed his eyes. She didn't smell like rain today. She'd smelled like longing. Like lust. Like the woman she'd become, not the girl he fell in love with.

The woman was like a sexual jack-in-the-box. Wind her up and she exploded beautifully, like diamonds shattering into brilliant pieces. What would she sound like when he tasted her for the first time? How would she move beneath him?

The water pounded his shoulders as he took his dick in his hand. He stroked, slowly at first, and then as desire started to pulse, he tugged faster, imagining sliding his cock into her wet heat.

He'd jacked off to the vision of Annalise more times than he could count, but never in recent years. He'd denied himself that pleasure. Or really, that pain. He'd successfully shoved her out of his mind the day she unintentionally broke his motherfucking heart in Marseilles. The shield had gone up, the walls had risen, and he'd resisted all thoughts of her.

Not now.

Not when he was seeing her again.

Not when he was sure she wanted the same thing he did. She wanted him, and hell if that wasn't the hottest thing ever.

As the water poured down his back, his fist curled tighter.

He breathed out hard, a rough, gritty exhale as his hand worked faster and his mind replayed the dressing room. She'd melted into him, but it was more than that. She *vibrated*—like she was on some other frequency, strung tight, hot, and desperate. The way she'd gripped his hand, rubbing up against him, fucking his fingers, drove him crazy then and consumed him now.

The image stirred up lust all through his body, as carnal pleasure built low in his gut. He groaned as the water pounded mercilessly. His muscles tightened everywhere, his quads tensing as his hand flew up and down his dick. God, he wanted her. Wanted to know how it would feel to strip her to her lacy panties then rip them off. Kiss her, taste her, lick her, fuck her, take her.

His breath raced fast from his lungs, release in reach.

Right now, under the water, in the privacy of his own home, he was free to say her name, to imagine her face, to picture her as he came.

Later, as he lay in bed, he told himself that this

reunion was temporary. It was one day, one moment, one chance. Then he'd move on.

He almost believed it.

15

Eighteen years ago

Something didn't quite add up. Thomas was no expert, but as he finished writing up his log of rides for the day, he grabbed last week's list to make sure he had the correct spelling of the client. But the man's name had been erased, as if the ride Thomas had given him to the airport didn't exist.

He leaned back at the table in the break room and scratched his chin. Why would a ride suddenly go missing? He opened the binder and thumbed through the last few weeks. Here and there, a few others were missing, too.

Flipping to the red tab, he checked out some of the other drivers' records. He remembered his buddy Sanders, who was a mechanic for the same company, had been pulled in to handle a few airport rides. None of those were listed, either.

He shook his head as if he could make sense of the missing info that way. Maybe he'd mention it to Paul, who ran the operations and oversaw all the drivers. Bringing attention to a discrepancy would surely put him in a good light, what with the potential for promotion on the horizon. Paul would have the final say in hiring him anyway. The owner lived and worked in another state and so was never on site.

Thomas finished filling out the details, clocked out, then got into his car to head to his daughter's dance performance. Dora was meeting him there with the boys, except for Michael, who'd been studying at Becky's house with Annalise. As he arrived at the auditorium, he spotted Becky's car and saw his oldest son walking into the event center with his arm draped around his girlfriend. Michael leaned in and planted a kiss on her cheek. As they strolled inside, Thomas pictured them like this a year or two from now, in college, going to a play or a concert, happy together.

But something was missing. Something was off. He rubbed the back of his neck, then an idea slammed into him. Something Michael would need. Something besides money. Not wanting to forget, he grabbed the notebook he kept beside him in the center console and wrote down his thoughts. Tomorrow, he'd make some calls, set things up for Michael. For now, he closed the notebook and headed inside to watch his daughter dance.

————

The next day when he filled out the log, he noticed more rides had pulled a disappearing act. As he packed up, he rapped on Paul's door, figuring now would be a good time to let him know. This would show initiative, that he cared, that he had the company's best interests at heart.

Paul furrowed his black eyebrows when Thomas mentioned the missing rides. "That so?"

"Yes, sir."

Paul nodded and then smiled, a professional sort of grin. "That's good to know. Really appreciate you bringing this to our attention. We'll get it fixed." Then Paul pointed a finger at him, like a gun. "That kind of attention to detail will get you far."

Excellent. That was everything he wanted. To go so much further.

16

Three-fucking-thirty in the morning. Not when he wanted to be awake. Not when he wanted to be dealing with shit. But when the alarm sounded that there was trouble with one of their clients, Michael bolted.

He flew straight out of bed, into his clothes, and to the client's site. He was closer than Ryan, so he called his brother and said he'd handle the incident. White Box, a gentlemen's club, was just a few blocks off the Strip, making it just a few blocks from Michael. He pulled into the lot, parked his car, and ran a hand through his messy hair.

His armed guard was outside, lit up by the glow of the purple and white lights streaming from the art deco sign above the club, a sleek, metal structure that oozed sexy class. The guard stood next to a plainclothes cop, along with Curtis, the VP and biz dev guy at White Box, who'd hired Sloan Protection Resources.

Michael said hello, then gestured to the premises. "So what's the story?"

Curtis cleared his throat and went first. He was a beefy

guy, exactly the type of man physically you'd want fronting a club, if you could choose a manager based on size. His face was like a block of wood and so were his arms. His eyes were brown and warm, though, like a favorite uncle's. "We got word of some gang activity here on premises," Curtis said, disgust in his tone as he recounted details of an attempted robbery and then the arrest of a young man with a *Protect Our Own* Royal Sinners tattoo. Apparently, the guy had tried to steal a watch worth five grand off another patron in the men's room. He'd brandished a knife, turning his crime into an armed robbery attempt. The cops came quickly, and the guy was in custody.

"Your patron, the guy with the watch—is he okay?" Michael asked.

"He's fine. Your man stopped things before it turned ugly," Curtis said, nodding to the armed guard Michael had supplied to the club.

He clapped his guy on the arm. "Good to hear."

Michael breathed easier knowing the incident was routine enough, and frankly the type of thing that happened now and again at these sorts of establishments. When you trafficked in sex and sin, you could sometimes attract the seedier elements.

After another fifteen minutes, all was well enough, and Curtis strolled with Michael back to his car. "Thanks for coming by in the middle of the night to check it out. Charlie and I appreciate the service," Curtis said, referring to the owner of White Box. "He wanted me to extend his gratitude, too."

"It's the least I can do. I'm sorry this happened, but I'm glad no one was hurt," Michael said.

"We're keeping a close watch out for this sort of stuff,

and for gang trouble. It's been heating up lately all over town, so you can't be too safe."

"Couldn't agree more," Michael said, placing his hand on the hood of his car, sensing an opportunity. He raised his chin. "Hey. Question for you."

"Shoot."

"You seen any other gang activity around here?" he asked. This gang was insidious and could sink its claws into businesses like a parasite on an unsuspecting host. Michael didn't want one of his clients to be that host. Selfishly, he couldn't help but wonder if the gang activity here could lead him to Luke or T.J. If the Royal Sinners were encroaching on this patch of land, circling it and threatening the innocent, maybe there was a chance to double down—help his clients, and find the men he was looking for.

Curtis shook his head. "Not too much. This is the first I'm aware of. Let's hope it's the last," he said, his voice determined.

"Let me know if you hear anything else."

Curtis nodded, his face solemn. "We've got high-end patrons here, and we don't want to mess around with that shit, or the Royal Sinners. I'm with you on this."

"There's someone from the Sinners we've got our eyes on. Guy named T.J. Nelson. He's wanted for some crimes over the years. Don't know a ton about him, but he has a gold earring. Scar on his right cheek. Tall, towering frame." Michael gave the scant details he was aware of. He didn't share Luke's name, though. He didn't want to let on he was looking that high up within the gang. Besides, Luke wasn't likely to be seen in public as a gang member.

Curtis nodded. "I'll keep an eye out for him. Let you know if we spot him."

"Good," Michael said as he unlocked the car door.

"Get some sleep," Curtis said with a faint smile.

But sleep was nowhere to be found when he returned home, so Michael settled in to work, plowing through paperwork as dawn spread across the dark sky, casting pale pink morning light over Vegas from twenty stories high. He worked through contract approvals so he was free to get on that plane and focus on the woman. Sure, he had work to do in New York, and meetings to attend that would keep him busy, but he didn't want to squander an ounce of his time with Annalise.

It was best to be ahead of the game, and he was.

That also meant he had enough time to see Donald before he jetted out of town.

———

His dad's oldest friend shook his head, thumbing through a deck of cards at his table at the Golden Nugget—empty for the moment, since it was early in the morning. "He never mentioned anything about someone named T.J. coming by, not that I can recall," Donald said.

"Shit," Michael hissed. "I've got to figure this out. You sure? Not a word?"

Donald held up his hands. "We talked about lots of stuff, but I don't remember him mentioning it. 'Bout the only thing he said was that he was trying to get the new job, and he thought he might have a lead on it when he found something that was missing at the company."

Something that was missing. If so, was that what T.J. had come to talk to him about at work? Michael narrowed his eyes. "And he never said what that something was?"

Donald shook his head. "Sorry, kid. I barely remember

what I had for breakfast some days. I hardly remember the specifics of a conversation that didn't stand out from two decades ago."

"Do you think Sanders knows? Since he worked there?"

Donald shrugged. "S'possible."

"Do you trust Sanders?" Michael asked pointedly, because the question had been gnawing at him.

"With my life." Donald tilted his head, studying the younger man. "But why would you ask? Is there some reason you think you can't trust him?"

Yes. Because he's avoiding me. Because he's avoiding everyone. Because something is up. "No reason. Except I honestly don't know who to trust anymore."

Donald shot him a faint smile and nodded, then stepped around from behind the table and gripped his shoulder. "I hear ya, kid. All I can tell you is this—keep on digging; keep on asking. Your dad was like that, too. He was focused and driven. You got that from him. Stay on it, and you'll find what you're looking for."

Focused and driven. His dad had used those words, too, to describe him—only his father had been talking about Michael's quest to keep Annalise in his life. They were also fitting adjectives for how determined Michael had been to follow his dad's wishes about her. Those words were spelled out in the note he'd found from his dad's wallet, scattered across the driveway with credit cards and photos the night he'd died.

Annalise was his dream, his one-time reality, and his end game.

Then she was gone, reduced to a memory that haunted him. Now, she'd become real again, and he needed to go meet her at the airport.

17

"We will begin boarding Flight Twenty-Three to New York shortly."

Annalise turned in the direction of the gate agent, checking her watch as she talked to her sister in Paris, nine hours ahead of her.

"How is Mom doing today? How was the doctor's appointment?" She paced the boarding area, scanning it for Michael, nerves skating across her skin. It was so weird to be traveling with him. This was what they had dreamed about when they were younger—this sort of freedom, including the freedom to change her flight. She'd been slated for a later one to New York, but had pushed earlier so they could fly together.

She stopped in her tracks, wondering what sort of traveling companion he was, like whether he slept on planes, his head bobbing up and down then crashing on her shoulder? It was an odd image—Michael Sloan dozing on a flight. Did he prefer the window or the aisle? Would he be chatty, or want to watch TV, or work the whole time? Would she want to do the things she normally did on planes—devour magazines like *Discovery*, *National Geographic,* and *Vanity Fair*, which were stashed in the outside pocket of her carry-on—or would they watch some lame straight-to-video release together on the mini-screen? All these details were unknown to her, even though many years ago she'd often imagined traveling with him.

"Her day was all right, but not great, to be honest," Noelle said on the other end of the line, rooting Annalise to the present. Their father had passed on a few years ago, and their mother was alone in a small flat in Paris. That wouldn't be a problem ordinarily, except she'd had a bad fall a year ago, and her hip hadn't been the same since, so she relied on her two daughters. Noelle and Annalise did their best to stay near, check in on her daily, and help with whatever she needed. These efforts were complicated by Annalise's travel for work, but she picked up the slack when she was in town. "Her doctors are switching her to a new medication," Noelle added.

"What kind are they giving her?" Annalise asked, since she'd become far too familiar with drugs and dosages while married to Julien. He took several kinds each day to try to stave off the inevitable, and so when her mother had fallen ill, she'd poured her newly acquired knowledge into researching her mom's meds. As she and her sister discussed side effects and dosage, Annalise wandered through the noisy crowds in the boarding area, weaving through teens slouched on blue upholstered seats, businessmen in rumpled suits hunched over laptops, pecking away at keys, and vacationers playing a final round of airport slots, hunting for that last-chance payout.

Somewhere by the Aladdin one-armed bandit, she spotted him.

Her stone-cold heart thawed again. It shed its jacket like a girl in spring, twirling in the sunshine.

A grin tugged at her lips as Michael walked toward her, dressed in crisp black slacks and a light green shirt with slim white stripes, the top button undone. The man was muscled and sturdy, his chest broad, his arms way beyond toned, his legs strong. Her eyes raked over him, snapshotting every detail, from his trim, tight waist, to his deliciously messy black hair, to the hint of stubble on his face. His jaw was square, his cheekbones strong, his lips so fucking kissable. His ice-blue eyes lit up when their gazes met, a match setting her ablaze with his heat.

As if a tropical sun caressed her, she warmed all over. A slow and sexy smile spread across his handsome face. That was when her focus on the call was officially shot to hell. Butterflies took flight inside her belly, surprising her. She'd expected lust, raging hormones, or the mad desire that Michael had unleashed in her the other night, but this was out of left field, this strange and new stomach flipping. It caught her off-guard, especially when the butterflies soared to the stratosphere as he stopped less than a foot away from her, said nothing at all, and instead just dropped a kiss on her cheek.

Oh God, how she wanted to cup her hand on that cheek, like a young girl capturing a first kiss.

Noelle said something about medicine, but Annalise was simply lost in this moment, her face lingering near his lips, as if all the travelers, all the noise, all the sounds of the world had blurred. These few seconds next to him were bright, crisp, and achingly real, turning everything else mute.

When Michael stepped away from her, she completely lost her train of thought, as well as the words she'd meant to say to Noelle. Her sister rattled off details about milligrams and twice a day. The sound of her voice jarred Annalise back into the reality of the phone call.

She blinked and refocused, but she was still light-headed, just from the brush of his lips and the sight of his face. "Take care of Mom. I'll be back soon to help out. Just a few days in New York for the shoot," she said.

"Fly safely, *mon petite papillon*," her older sister said. "Keep me posted on everything. Love you. Miss you. See you soon."

Annalise ended the call, slipping the phone into her back pocket.

"Hi."

"Hi."

Silly grins and knowing looks passed between them.

"Fancy meeting you here." Her voice was laced with flirtation, and she loved the way it sounded as she talked to him. She thrilled at the way it felt to slide into this kind of woozy chemistry.

"What a surprise. I had no idea you were on this flight," he said, playing along, as if they'd just met.

"Perhaps we can sit together and catch up on the plane," she suggested, as if the two of them hadn't already made those plans.

"I like that idea." He leaned closer, his lips danger-ously close as he said, "Maybe then I can whisper filthy things in your ear as we fly."

She wobbled, his words making her hot. Her hand darted out, and she gripped his shirt, holding on. He looped an arm around her waist, making sure she didn't fall.

"You'd want that, wouldn't you?" he murmured, as he roamed his eyes over her. She wore skinny jeans and heels, and a silky tank top that dared to show a peek of cleavage.

"Yes. So much. Would you?"

His eyes blazed darkly—his *yes*. "I would absolutely love getting you hot and bothered."

She brought her lips closer to his ear. "I'm going to let you in on a little secret. I'm already there."

A few minutes later, the gate agent's voice warbled across the tinny speakers, calling for first-class passengers. Michael swept his arm to the side, letting her lead the way.

As they stepped onto the plane, he asked, "How's your mom?"

The question surprised her, but she answered quickly, "She's okay. Well, she's not great. I was talking to my sister about her," she said and shared some more details. She figured he must have heard the tail end of the conversation, picking up a few French words that she'd taught him once upon a time. Back when they were younger, he'd helped her with her English slang, so it was only fitting that she taught him some of her language. Mostly she'd taught him naughty words.

Which reminded her...

"I need to work on your French again," she teased as they quickly found their seats, comfy gray leather chairs in the second row.

"You think so?"

"Like I did before," she said, jogging his memory. "Have you forgotten it all?"

His eyes twinkled with mischief. "Why don't you try me and find out?"

"Perhaps I will."

The flight attendant strolled by and asked if they needed anything.

"All set," Annalise told her, then carefully tucked her camera gear under the seat in front of her, meticulously taking the time to make sure it was positioned against the leg rests.

Michael tipped his chin toward the bags. "What's the job in New York? More bikinis?"

"We have one more day in some very iconic New York locations for Veronica's. We've actually booked the New York Public Library, and we have some fantastic shots planned of the girls lounging in their PJs on these leather couches, reading old books. It's going to be very cool."

His eyes twinkled. "Can I have your job?"

"You want to lounge in your PJs and read in the library?" she said, nudging him with her elbow.

"Yeah, that's it. Exactly."

"When Veronica's adds boxer briefs, perhaps I'll suggest you model them."

He leaned his head back and laughed, a deep, hearty sound that warmed her soul. She loved his laugh; he'd been so laidback and carefree when she knew him before, quick with a joke or an easy comment. When his chuckles slowed, he lowered his voice to a dirty whisper, "But you don't even know if I wear boxer briefs."

She arched her eyebrow in a challenging stare. "No. But I fully intend to find out the answer to that, and to discover it..." She let her voice trail off, watching him linger on her every word with parted lips before she added, "So very soon."

He drew a sharp breath, and she zipped right back into the conversation. "Then after that, I have a boudoir session with a private client."

"Private client?"

"Just a woman who wanted to have some shots done as a gift for her husband." She'd secured space for the shoot in a studio with a gorgeous, sumptuous bedroom set. The woman was the CEO of a sex-toy company, Joy Delivered, and she'd found Annalise through a mutual contact—her brother worked and lived in Paris with his wife, and Annalise had met them a few times at dinner with friends.

"Do a lot of women do that?"

"Enough to make it a good living for me," Annalise said as passengers shuffled onto the plane, stuffing bags in overhead bins and checking their phones as they searched for their seats.

Michael shook his head in admiration. "Never knew boudoir shots were such a thing."

Annalise nodded enthusiastically. "They've actually grown immensely in popularity in the last several years. More and more women do them. Some just do them for themselves."

He cocked his head, his eyes hooked on hers, then answered in a thoughtful voice, "That sounds very empowering. I suppose you don't have to be Gisele to pose for the camera in a lacy white teddy."

"Yes! That's it exactly. Not everyone gets that, but you do," she said, grateful that he understood something few men truly got. While Michael had certainly indicated his appreciation for the gorgeous women on display yesterday, she adored that he understood that true beauty ran deeper.

He tapped his temple. "I can be a feminist."

"It's hot," she said, raising an eyebrow. "And that's honestly why I love shooting boudoir. Women are realizing that they don't have to be rail-thin to look good in lingerie. You can have curves, you can have extra padding, you can have stretch marks and still put on a black satin bra and sexy panties and feel wanted, feel sensual," she said, moving her shoulders and her hips, demonstrating how a woman might feel sexy. "It's a way of celebrating their femininity. They're capturing sexuality on camera."

"They're capturing their life," he said with a nod and then added, "They're enjoying their life."

"Exactly. I've done photos for women after they've lost weight and want to celebrate their new bodies. And I've done some for others who haven't lost weight but still want to embrace all that they are, and feel comfortable in their skin."

"And you help them do that on the shoot?"

"I try. It's not easy to strip down to your bra and panties and pose sexily for the camera. But my job is to make them feel like they're all the sexiest women in the world."

"How do you do that? What's your secret?"

"I'm...wait for it... *positive*," she said, like it was a punch line.

"Well, that would be a good skill," he said with a quirk of his lips.

"It's also natural to me. Because I do think the female body is beautiful in all shapes and sizes, and I let them know that they look amazing. Thin or heavy, average or above average. Blond, brunette, redhead. Birthmarks or scars. Every woman can be beautiful in her own way."

He nodded. "I like that you feel that way. Ever shoot guys?"

"Shockingly, most men don't do boudoir sessions," she said in a deadpan voice. "But I have photographed a few couples."

He arched an eyebrow, then made a rolling gesture, telling her to elaborate. "Are they getting it on?"

She shook her head. "I'm not a pornographer. But sometimes a newly engaged couple will do a sexy shoot. They want to take photos of their passion for each other. To showcase it."

"They ever invite you to join them?"

She rolled her eyes. "Again, not a pornographer, or a third wheel."

He held up his hands in surrender. "Sorry, I couldn't resist."

"And to answer your question, no, they don't. They're happy together. They don't want a threesome with the photographer."

"I guess it's just me then."

"You'd want a threesome with the photographer?"

"No. I want a one-on-one with her. Only a one-on-one. That's what I want," he said, running his fingers across the ends of her hair, watching it fall from his hand onto her shoulder. "I want to be the one behind the camera, shooting photos of her looking gorgeous in anything and nothing." His blue eyes were fiery, intense. "Then I want to set down the camera and have her invite me to join her on the bed, and all the sensuality she poured into the pose, she gives to me."

Annalise shuddered and swallowed. Her throat was dry. Her skin heated up and then, out of nowhere, a flash of worry touched down. Goddammit. She didn't want to feel an ounce of regret again about her choice to be with him. This time, she made a deliberate decision. She seized hold of that bit of remorse and tossed it in the trash. Instead, she let the heat and the sparks and the sizzle slide through her. "I would do that," she whispered. "I would do that with you. I would give that to you."

The flight attendant began the announcements, and Annalise settled into her seat, her skin on fire, a pulse beating between her legs, desire cloaking her once more. She closed her eyes and breathed, trying to get some sort of hold on these raging hormones, but with him next to her it was futile.

She resigned herself to being wet the whole flight.

It was all his fault. That fucking hot, sexy man.

18

Once they were airborne, Michael returned to the topic of her family. "So you and Noelle help out your mom?"

"Yes. We want to be there as much as we can for her. That's why I try to keep my jobs out of town as short as they can be. Especially since Noelle is so busy."

"How is your sister? Did she ever start the bakery like she wanted to?" he asked, and Annalise loved that he remembered that little detail from their phone conversations years ago.

"Yes, she did. She runs it with her husband now, and she has three kids. So she's been busy." She pictured Noelle and Patrick up before dawn, peddling baguettes and croissants, and loving their little corner shop in Paris. Annalise adored that bakery too. When her sister had struggled to secure a loan to start it up, Annalise had given her the money she'd saved from her café job in college – the money she'd once earmarked to see Michael. But they'd lost touch, and her sister needed the help, so it seemed as if fate had intended something else for her savings. She was glad to have helped her sister start up her business, and that business had provided the foundation for Noelle's family.

"I'd say they've both been busy," he said with a wink, and she returned her focus to him.

"True," she said, laughing. "The kids are great. Nine, eleven, and twelve. She's exhausted all the time."

"I'm exhausted just hearing that. Does that mean you have to take care of your mom more?"

She shrugged. "Sometimes, but that's okay. My mom took care of me. It's only fair," she said, then softened her voice, placing her hand on his arm. "Is it weird to hear other people talk about their mothers?"

His eyes darkened briefly, then he shook his head. "No. It's the way it should be."

"Do you ever see her? I know you did at first, but then you didn't ever want to anymore." They'd talked about his mother, and he'd told her that he'd visited her in prison a few times when he was in high school and college. He'd stopped after that, though.

His jaw was set hard, and he heaved a sigh. "You're right. I used to, a long time ago because I wanted to try—I don't know—maybe to understand what had happened, and why she'd done it. But soon enough it was clear there was no way to make sense of it. I couldn't be near her anymore. I don't think of her as my mother, and I haven't in years."

She ran her hand down his arm. "I understand why."

He turned his head and met her gaze. "Not everyone does," he said in a quiet voice.

"You mean other women?" she asked, and a brief burst of jealousy flared inside her at the prospect of him with other women. Of course, he hadn't been celibate over the years, but the thought of him with someone else was like a hot poker jabbing her flesh.

He ran a hand across his jaw, shaking his head. "Just people in general. My brother Ryan, and even Shan for a while. They wanted me to visit her, but I just couldn't."

"Do you think it's because you were closest to your father, or just because that's simply how you feel?" she asked as the plane began to level out, nearing its cruising altitude.

"Probably both."

"Do you think that will ever change? Your feelings for her?"

"I don't see how it could. Unless she was found to be not guilty," he said with a scoff, as if that were truly impossible.

"Is there a chance of that happening?"

"Not a chance in hell, as far as I can see," he said, then cocked his head, studying Annalise's expression as if he were looking for answers to an unspoken question. "I believe there are other people who are also responsible, but I don't believe she's innocent. So I don't see how I'd ever think of her as a mother again."

"Are you okay with that?" she asked quietly.

"Are *you* okay with that? With me feeling the way I do?"

She nodded resolutely and ran her fingers across the back of his neck. "Of course. It's your life. It's your choice." The tension seemed to lessen in his shoulders as she touched him, and she was struck with a memory as crisp as the images in front of her—a phone call, years ago, a couple months after she'd left Vegas and returned to

France. It was one of the few times she'd heard him shed tears. His mother had just been found guilty of murder for hire, and had said her good-byes to her family before she was taken away in the bus to prison. He was choked up, and it had shredded her to hear him recount the day. But her emotions were nothing compared to what he was feeling at age seventeen with a family pulverized by tragedy. The pain had started to fade from his voice over the next few calls and letters, and he'd told her, "Talking to you is one of the few things that makes me feel okay."

Okay.

Such a small, flat word. But it was all he wanted, and it was enough. To feel okay. Somehow, she'd given that to him. Perhaps she was doing the same now, helping him see that it was indeed okay to *not* want to be his mother's son.

"You sure?" he asked, and his voice was laced with nerves, like he desperately needed her reassurance.

She cupped his cheek and spoke confidently. "Yes. You're a man without a mother. And it's okay to be that way. It's like she died, too, and your mourning for her just took a different shape."

His eyes locked onto hers, and he relaxed further. "Sometimes I wondered if I was too hard on her. Too angry. Too unforgiving. But then she admitted to Ryan that she did it. I don't need to forgive her."

"Some things are unforgivable. Obviously, this is one of those things," she said, letting her hand drift down from his face to rest on his leg. "Do you still miss your dad?"

"Sure. Of course. But you get used to it. It becomes part of your life, doesn't it? The missing," he said, as the flight attendants unbuckled and began to move about the cabin.

She nodded, and though he hadn't said her husband's name, she knew what he was getting at.

"Do you miss Julien?" he asked. Point blank. Direct. The elephant in the room.

She swallowed, her heart rising up to her throat and sticking there. "Sometimes I do," she admitted quietly, looking down at the armrest, the inflight magazine, the screen on the back of the seat in front of her. Then she gazed into Michael's eyes, clear and fixed on her. "But not right now."

The crackle of the speaker interrupted their talk as the attendant announced that they were free to turn on computers and other approved devices. Neither she nor he made a move to do so.

Instead, they talked. They talked as they flew over Colorado, then Kansas, past Illinois and Ohio, through water and club soda, through the afternoon lunch service, and through the movies that others watched. He told her about his family, catching her up on his brothers and sister. She remembered them all from when they were younger, and she savored every detail he shared. His sister's pregnancy was going well, and she was expecting a baby boy; Ryan was engaged to a beautiful philanthropist who made him happier than Michael had ever seen him; and his youngest brother, Colin, had started up a serious relationship with a social worker who had a teenage son. She loved the details, ate them up like fine, dark chocolate, as she pictured the Paige-Princes—now the Sloans—in their new lives, healing from the damage that had ripped them apart years ago.

"What about you?" she asked, meeting his cool blue

gaze. "They all sound so happy. So settled. Are you happy, too?"

The corner of his lips curved up, the barest lopsided grin. "I'm happy now."

Now.

The word echoed. Reminding her that *now* was all anyone ever had. This moment. Make the most of it. Go for more than *okay,* and do it right now. No guilt—only pleasure, only passion, only the present.

She threaded her hand into the back of his hair, feeling those soft, dark strands on her flesh, and he groaned. Low, barely audible. Just for her.

"Come closer and kiss me," she murmured, and he obliged, dipping his head and kissing her like they were the only two people on the plane—flying across the sky, leaving Vegas far behind, and heading to a new adventure.

————

Michael Sloan had always been perfectly content to fly commercial. First class was great, but he'd never longed for a private jet. Not that he'd have minded one, but it was along the lines of a yacht or a mansion—nice to admire in a magazine, but wholly unnecessary for his happiness.

That was no longer the case. A private jet was the *only* thing in the world he wanted right now. No, *want* was too small a word for it. He fucking craved it like air. Because this kiss was different. It was as hot as all their others, but it was something more, too. It was crazed and beautiful. It was hungry and full of regret. For years gone by. For missed connections. For the past and for the present. It was as if everything that could have been between them was bottled up, stored and aged to perfection, all for this one kiss. With her hand on the back of his head, she kissed him deeply, but tenderly, too.

The wildness at the nightclub was gone. The frenzy of the dressing room had slunk away. They would return, but right now this was a kiss that made him a little drunk, like his body was buzzing with some kind of sweet opiate, and that opiate was her. He wanted to pull her on top of him, run his hands over her soft flesh, unzip her jeans, and then slide into her. Wanted to watch her fuck him here on the plane. To enjoy the view of her straddling him, riding him, slow and unhurried, lingering and lovely, as she rose up and down on his cock.

He loved and hated this moment.

This was just a fucking kiss.

But it was so much more.

He'd never kissed like this before. Fierce and greedy. Needy and dreamy.

He wanted to live in this kiss.

At some point, he broke the contact, because he had to. Because another second of her kisses would be too much. He brushed her hair away from her ear. "You keep doing that, and we're going to be putting on a show."

She grinned naughtily. "I think we already did," she said, glancing clandestinely over her shoulder. Some of the other passengers seemed particularly engrossed in their screens and books, as if the sight of the two of them devouring each other had been too much to bear.

"Tell me something," he whispered, "how do you say 'I want you so much'?"

"In French?"

He nodded.

"Je te veux tellement."

He repeated it close to her ear, flicking the tip of his tongue over her earlobe as he said those words to her.

She shivered visibly. "*Mon dieu*. I love the way you say that."

"But see, Annalise," he said, running his index finger across her top lip, "I love the way *you* say it. I want to make you feel that way."

"You do," she whispered, her accent thickening, and he knew she was heading down the same path he was already on.

He slid into another question. "How do you say 'fuck me harder'?"

She shivered and answered, "*Baise-moi plus fort.*"

He didn't repeat it. Instead, he simply raised an eyebrow. "Good. Now I know how it sounds in your regular voice, so I can have a baseline for comparison when you say it later while I'm inside you."

Shuddering, she ran a hand down her front, then whispered, her voice heated, as if she were in the throes of passion, "*Baise-moi plus fort.*"

Lust slammed into him from all corners of the world. He bent his head to her shoulder, dusting the barest kiss on her collarbone. "You'll be saying that later, won't you?"

She nodded, a small, sexy sigh escaping her lips. "I will."

"How wet are you right now?"

"So wet."

"How much do you want to be fucking me on this plane?"

"So incredibly much."

"Is it driving you as crazy as it's making me?"

She opened her eyes. Hers were shining with desire as

she whispered the words to him. "Insane. I'm insane with wanting you."

Soon enough, the plane landed, and twenty minutes after that they were in the town car he'd reserved. He raised the partition, and in seconds her hands were on his pants, unzipping them.

Well, he wasn't going to say no to that.

19

She was a sexy vixen. A fiery lover—a woman who liked to take and who, evidently, liked to give, too, judging from how she rubbed her palm against the outline of his erection.

"Last night," she said, breathy and sexy, her lips near his neck, "I couldn't sleep. I was thinking of you. What you did to me in the dressing room."

"Yeah?"

She lifted her face to meet his eyes. She nodded, her lips now on his jaw as she slipped a soft hand under the waistband of his boxer briefs then wrapped it around his hard cock.

He hitched in a breath, and time fucking stood still as she grasped his hard length, skin against skin at last. It was relief and torture all at once. Her touch was electric. As the town car rolled along the concrete stretch of road away from the airport, she stroked his cock and whispered, her breath ghosting over his skin, "I couldn't stop thinking about you. All the things we didn't do."

He flexed his hips, thrusting up into her soft nimble

hand. He didn't want her to ever stop. "Like what? What did you want most?"

She skimmed her hand lower, down to his balls, cupping them, playing with them. Oh hell, that was fucking fantastic, especially as she dragged her nails across his skin.

"What do you think I wanted?" she countered.

He grabbed the back of her head in his palm and shut his mouth. He wanted her to voice her fantasies. He needed her to want him as desperately as he wanted her. It took every ounce of restraint not to answer her with "Suck me off." Instead, he gritted his teeth and managed in a low rumble: "Tell me what you wanted. *Say it.*"

His chest rose and fell as she played with his dick then moved her hand up his shaft, rubbing a bead of liquid over the head. He groaned, closing his eyes as unholy pleasure swept through him.

With a tight grip, she twisted her hand, rubbing him up and down. He opened his eyes. Hers seemed to twinkle with lust and mischief. She had such a naughty side, and he wanted to explore that aspect of Annalise to the fullest. He had never known this part of her. All he knew when they were younger was that she liked everything he did to her, and that she came easily on his fingers, her moans and cries so sexy when her orgasm washed over her. He was learning that the woman with him now was dirtier, bolder, and so damn passionate.

She bent her head closer, pressing her forehead to his, and whispered, "I want to taste you. Lick you. I want to feel your come in my throat. I want to swallow it all."

He thrust upward into her eager fist as her words scorched a path through his chest, spreading like fire throughout his body. She'd set him ablaze with the match of her lust.

"Did you get yourself off to that?" he asked. "Was that what did it for you—picturing your lips on my cock? Did you spread your legs wide for me, and fuck yourself with your fingers?"

She panted as she pumped him faster. "Yes. I was naked on my bed, knees raised, legs spread, my hand between them, fucking myself as I took you deep in my mouth."

"Fucking Christ." He groaned. His head fell back against the leather seat, hitting the headrest. That was the hottest image he'd ever pictured, and it was scored into his mind now. This naked beauty with her creamy skin, her sheets of red hair, her full tits, and most of all, her abandon.

Her need.

"You tasted so good." She moaned on an upstroke, her lips parted and wet from licking them with the tip of her tongue. He wanted that red-hot mouth on him.

"Take it," he commanded. "Show me how you did it."

In a flash, her red hair spilled across his thighs, and her head was between his legs. Her lips greeted his hard shaft with the warmest fucking hello he'd ever had.

"Fuck me, Annalise," he murmured, dragging a hand roughly through his hair, trying to absorb the enormity of this moment.

His girl.

His first love.

This wild woman.

Doing something he'd craved desperately when he was a teenager. Something he'd jerked off to countless times in those days. A fantasy that had sent him soaring into release on many solo flights.

He'd never had her mouth on him before. Now, as a man he was finally able to experience the gloriousness of those lips, and in a whole new way. Because she'd never have blown him like this in high school.

This was an adult blow job.

Her warm, eager lips wrapped tightly around his cock. Then, in mere seconds, he was all the way in, and she sucked his dick without any teasing. She didn't bother with little kisses, or lollipop licks of the head. She didn't brush her tongue along the underside of his shaft. No, she went full-speed ahead like a hungry, starving creature. The head of his dick hit the back of her throat, and he cursed from the mind-blowing, blackout-worthy pleasure of her mouth.

His entire body vibrated with lust. It spread from his pelvis to every goddamn corner. His nerves were hot, his skin was sizzling, and his brain was lit up from this amazingly sensual woman who loved sucking his dick as much as he loved having her do it. He roped his fingers through her hair, grasping her head tightly. Lifting an arm, she grabbed his other hand, and guided it back to her head.

That was hotter than hell. She wanted it hard and deep. She wanted him to hold her head, control her mouth, shove in far.

"You can handle it like this?" he grunted, needing the confirmation.

She nodded as she sucked him deeper, her lips nice and snug.

"Like your mouth belongs to my cock?"

Another nod.

"What am I going to do with you?" he whispered,

almost to himself, as he gave in to the way they both wanted it, his big hands wrapping around her skull, her gorgeous dark red hair spilling like silk through his fingers. She wanted him to keep her immobile as he fucked up into her mouth. She wanted him to be unforgiving in his desire.

The blow job was both too much, and never enough.

His dick thickened even more in her warm mouth, as white-hot sparks sped through his bloodstream. Flexing his hips, he pumped into her as he held her in his grip in the backseat of a town car speeding into Manhattan. She hummed around his cock. The vibration. Oh, fuck. It made him dizzy. His skin burned. His organs heated. His brain was bathed in pleasure from this most fantastic trip of all—this kind of dirty intimacy with his Annalise. His eyes locked on her swollen lips, racing up and down on his shaft, then she was shifting in her leather seat, her hips rocking the slightest bit, like she needed to be fucked, too.

He'd be taking care of her soon enough.

But first *this*. Her wicked, wonderful mouth. Her eager tongue. Her soft, talented hands that played with his balls as she sucked him without mercy and he fucked her mouth right back.

Unrelenting.

Until he started to lose control. His quads tightened, his spine ignited, and he was helpless to stop the rush. He thrust harder as his vision blurred. "*Coming*," he grunted, barely even managing that one word of warning as his orgasm pulsed through him, fast and hot. He groaned her name, and came in her throat.

He shuddered and cursed. "Holy fuck. That was..."

As the aftershocks subsided, she released his dick

from her mouth. She sat up, sighing happily as she ran a hand through her messy hair. She leaned back in her seat like she was spent.

"Um," he began. "No. Just no."

"No?"

He patted his thighs. "Get on me."

"Are you going to fuck me now?"

"No, but I've got a good feeling I'm going to be making you come in a hot minute."

She climbed on him, straddling his thighs, her hands on his shoulders. "You know I've always wanted your tongue, Michael," she whispered against his lips.

"I know. You'll get it. You'll get it tonight. But for some reason I like making you wait for it, getting you all worked up." He craved her taste fiercely, but he wanted to be able to spread her legs, to feel her bare skin pressed against his cheeks and give her room to wrap those sexy legs around his neck as he licked her sweet pussy.

As he worked open her zipper, he sighed in frustration. "These jeans are so damn tight." He could barely get them off. But he was up to the challenge, and he didn't really need them down far anyway. All he needed was just enough room to glide his fingers beneath the fabric of her light blue panties.

Like that.

Oh, just like that. His fingers slid across her wetness, hot and slippery and fantastic.

"You're soaked."

"I know," she murmured as her fingers curled around his shoulders. "You turn me on. You drive me crazy."

He drew lingering, luxurious circles across her silky, hot clit, coating his fingers in her arousal, but never thrusting inside. She didn't need penetration right now.

She was near the edge already. A few strokes. A couple of circles. Some faster, fevered sweeps of his fingers against her clit, and her hips were arching, swaying, rocking mindlessly against his hand until she cried out and came in less than sixty seconds.

Afterward, he kissed her face, her cheeks, her eyelids, the tip of her nose. Then her lips. That sweet, intoxicating mouth that had driven him wild. She opened her lips for him, her tongue seeking his, kissing like they were drunk on each other. They kissed like they could do it for ages, never wanting to stop.

But eventually they did, and he clasped his hand on her thigh. "Now listen. I have drinks with a client this evening. Then I'm taking you to dinner, and I would really appreciate it if you were wearing a skirt instead of jeans. Can you do that for me?"

She grinned coquettishly. "I can do better. I won't wear panties."

20

Ten years ago

He shouldered his bag and scanned the arrivals and departures board, checking for his flight.

Delayed. For two hours.

He sighed and then shrugged. *What can you do?* He patted his carry-on. It was all he had brought on his short trip, and now he was returning to base. He had a paperback, and music to listen to—a new band that a college buddy had sent him. He'd find his gate, grab a seat, pop in his earbuds, and check out some tunes as he turned the pages.

Heading for security, he reached into his pocket and took out his boarding pass and passport, and ten minutes later, he was on the other side at the small airport in Marseilles. As he strolled past a coffee shop, he focused on the tasks ahead for the week, and the work he had going on in his army intelligence division, doing his best to keep his mind off whether Annalise had responded to his letter yet. Maybe, just maybe, he'd find a reply from her on his return, and perhaps it would be the answer to his greatest wish. Her *yes*. It would be stained with tears of happiness, and it would smell like her.

The sensory memory ran through him of the girl he still loved, now a woman he desperately wanted to see again. He allowed himself that moment, then he blinked, refocused, and turned into the gift shop to grab a bottle of water. Soon enough, he'd have her answer. No need to linger on the unknown until it was certain.

After he paid for the drink and spun around to leave, he spotted the magazine racks. Most of the magazines were French and local, but there were others, including *Vanity Fair*. From behind the column next to the racks, a woman stretched out her arm to grab an issue.

He only saw a sliver of her profile, the shape of her nose, but she was haltingly familiar.

His heart slammed against his ribs. It couldn't be. There was no way. And yet, *what if?* A fragile sort of hope raced in him as he took a tentative step. He swallowed dryly, peering around the rack for a better look at the woman with the long red hair, flipping through a magazine.

And he knew.

The hair on his arms stood on end. Goose bumps scattered over his skin. She was his ghost, his memory, but she was all real now—creamy skin, green eyes, long fingers, and red lips that he'd kissed more times than he could ever count.

Ma petite fraise.

My little strawberry. He'd called her that because of her hair, and because her lips tasted so sweet. He hadn't seen her in eight years, not since he put her on the flight back to Paris and said good-bye, his heart cratering as she flew across the ocean, far away from him.

He hadn't talked to her in five years, not since he was a sophomore in college.

But here she was, and if ever there was a sign, this was it. He'd never believed in them before, but he'd once believed in her. She was his religion. His first love.

His only love.

He took another step and then parted his lips and spoke—a dry crackling sound that became her name. "Annalise?"

She raised her chin, her eyes widening. Her expression changed from curiosity over who was asking her name, to a wistful sort of wonder and surprise. She said his name like a question, too, but it sounded more like amazement that they were both here. "Michael?"

He nodded. "Yeah." His chest warmed, like sunshine was spreading from the inside out. "In the flesh."

As if to test his statement, she dropped a quick kiss on each cheek, then wrapped her arms around him.

It was like falling back in time, landing softly on your favorite moment in the past. All those moments were with her. All his favorite times. She smelled like raindrops and passion, just like he'd remembered, and he inhaled her scent briefly before they separated.

He gestured to her, standing before him in the shop. "How are you?"

It was such an ordinary question, the kind you would ask an acquaintance, but after all the years, it was the only natural way to begin again. Even after he'd sent her a letter a week ago.

"My flight is late. I was annoyed, but now I'm not," she said, her lips curving up in a wide, crazy smile.

Oh shit. He was grinning now, too. Smiling like a fucking fool. She still had that effect on him. His pulse thundered under his skin, hammered in his throat. She had to be saying yes. That must be her answer to his letter.

"Mine, too. Late flight, that is. Also, I'm not annoyed at all now," he said, as hope rose inside him—the hope that they were flying in the same direction.

But when he asked, she was heading to Paris.

"Do you want to get a coffee?" she asked. "Or do you still detest coffee?"

"I would love to...have a tea," he said with a smile, and she laughed, and this was good. So good. Like old times.

They headed to an ordinary airport café, ordered black coffee for her and tea for him, and sat at a small iron table as travelers filtered past them, talking about their trips, their plans, what they needed before their planes took off. It was white noise, the elevator music to this surreal slice of time.

Sitting here with her.

He wanted to cup this moment in the palm of his hands, to carry it and treat it like a precious object, like it could become what he'd once longed for so terribly—a future with her.

He had so much he wanted to say. Things like: *"You're beautiful. I miss you. Why couldn't we find a way to stay together? Why did we have to drift apart? Did you get my letter and will you please, please, please tell me it's the same for you?"*

But when she lifted her hand to reach for her coffee, the breath escaped his chest in a cold rush.

The stone on her left hand was small, but shone brilliantly and horribly, slashing all his hopes.

His throat turned dry and his chest pinched. But he

went for humor, needing it as a shield from the reality. He held up his hand, as if the sun had robbed him of sight. "Whoa. I think your ring blinded me."

Annalise cast her eyes down at it, as if she just realized she was wearing it. She fiddled with it for a second then folded her hands in her lap. Out of sight. "I received your letter. I'm...engaged."

Two short sentences that punctured his lungs. It was something he should have prepared for. Something he knew was always a possibility. But his heart squeezed too tight, and he gasped for breath as nothing but hurt coursed through him. As quickly as it surged, though, he tried to shut it down. To remind himself that he'd been rolling the dice anyway when he sent the letter, and the dice had come up empty.

He inhaled deeply, let the air fill his lungs, then put on his best face. "Congratulations are in order, then. Who's the lucky guy?" he asked, taking the knife and digging it around in his chest a little more, carving out some of that beating organ.

"His name is Julien. We work together. He's...wonderful," she said, her voice faltering, as if she were embarrassed to admit that.

"I'm glad to hear," he said, and he was, in a way, because she deserved someone wonderful. He'd just once believed that someone would be him. He'd believed it a week ago, a day ago, a few minutes ago.

He was a foolish romantic.

But really, what had he expected? That after not talking or writing, he would send a letter, and they'd magically run into each other then start back up again like some romantic movie?

Well, the thought had been front and center of his

mind for the last five minutes, sure. Because when you see the love of your life out of the blue in an airport, it feels like the stars are lining up for you.

Now, it felt like a cruel twist of fate.

He picked up his tea, took a drink, then set it down. They talked and caught up on each other's lives. They discussed their jobs, and their families. She told him about Noelle's life, and he told her that Ryan and he were working for Army Intelligence, that Colin was finishing up college, acing every class, and Shannon was slated to graduate soon, too, and was engaged to be married to her college sweetheart.

The ease with which they had always spoken about everything tugged at his heart, but it reminded him, too, of all that was lost.

Lost with her.

They wouldn't have this again. This was all there was, and he shouldn't feel so let down. He hadn't expected to see her. He didn't think he'd ever see her again in his whole life.

Tell that to his heart, though. It was beating overtime for her, like it had been reawakened and was wishing desperately that this was a new beginning rather than another end.

———

Dear Annalise,

I hope this letter finds its way to you safely, and that you are healthy and happy. It's been so long, too long, since I heard your voice or read your handwriting. I miss both with a deep ache inside me, one that never subsided. In spite of the time that has passed, I haven't stopped thinking of you, not once in all the years since we last spoke. I'm not exaggerating when I say a day hasn't gone by when I don't think of you with fondness, love, and desire, as much, if not more, than I felt before. It seems utterly small to say I hope you are well, but I do wish that for you and your family.

I've finished college now, and am grateful for the scholarship from the army that paid my way through school. Now it is my turn to give back, and I'm doing that, as it happens, in Europe. I'm working in army intelligence and I have just been stationed in Germany, of all places. It's not France, of course, but it isn't an ocean away, either. I am so much closer to you than I ever was before. Perhaps we can see each other again? Perhaps we can do more than see each other? Maybe even start over? I have always longed for you with everything in my heart. Je n'ai jamais cessé de t'aimer, ma petite fraise, my Annalise.

With all of my love,
Michael

———

She wasn't supposed to think he was handsome. She shouldn't be lingering on the memory of how he kissed, how she felt in his arms, or just how damn good they had been together. No, she was in love with her fiancé.

She. Was. In. Love.

But as she sat across from Michael her heart beat furiously, crashing against her skin, fighting valiantly to escape her plans, her future, her pending marriage. She laced her fingers together under the table, and she swore she was on the verge of crushing bones in the effort to keep her hands in her lap, her butt in the seat, her lips to herself.

Some primal part of her was dying to lean across the table, hold his face in her hands, and kiss him like no time had passed.

She resisted with everything she had. She resisted those words he'd written—*Je n'ai jamais cessé de t'aimer. I have never stopped loving you.*

Receiving that letter last week had been hard enough. Knowing how to respond was even tougher. Seeing him now was the most difficult part of all. Because as they talked, she slipped back into what they'd had in high school and that first year of college, and all that they'd been for each other.

All and everything.

She'd needed him to feel at home in America when she'd been alone, and he'd done more than that. He'd given her so much happiness. He'd needed her to survive the tragedy in his life, and she'd been there for him, even across the miles. She had thought she would marry him. She thought she'd be with him forever. And she hated that it had been too hard to stay together when they were young and so dependent on their families.

Now they were older and could find a way, and that was what he'd been trying to do when he sent that letter.

Except.... She toyed with the ring on her finger.

Her heart climbed into her throat, lodging itself there. She wanted to cry, and she wanted *him*, and she wanted to not want him.

She was happy, and she would always be happy with Julien. She just wished seeing Michael wasn't so damn tempting.

And easy.

And good.

Soon enough, the clock ticked closer to boarding time.

He walked her to her gate, and each step was a door closing, each second the final turn of the pages in a book. At her gate, they stopped, and unsaid words clung to the air like fog.

There was so much to say, and yet nothing that could be spoken. This was the last good-bye.

She swallowed her tears and choked back her emotions. "It was so good seeing you," she said, and wished her words didn't feel so inadequate.

He nodded. "And you."

I'll miss you. I'll think of you. I can't think of you. I won't miss you. You have to understand how hard this is.

He moved first, raising his arms, and she practically fell into his embrace then lingered for a few more seconds, breathing in his scent one last time before she pulled away.

Remaining faithful. Staying true. Vowing to march forward and love her husband-to-be with everything she had.

Damn the past. The past was not her future. She wouldn't look back.

21

The jeans were gone. Mercifully.

In their place she wore a short green dress that hugged her fantastic body, showing off her breasts, her small waist, and those long, endless legs.

At the table in the far corner of a restaurant that Brent's brother had recommended, Michael couldn't take his eyes off the woman. Ask him a month ago if he'd be having sushi dinner in the Village, listening to Annalise tell stories about her sister, and he'd have said no fucking way. She was nothing but a mirage, a sepia-tinted photograph of days gone by. Now, she was eating a salmon roll, and he was having the best time. They weren't staying at the same hotel, so he'd picked her up at hers, the breath knocked clear out of his lungs when she'd answered the door.

In that dress.

And heels.

And, very likely, no panties.

But as much as he wanted her right then and there, he

craved the anticipation, too. He was a patient man, and he wanted to take her out to dinner. To savor every moment from picking her up to walking to the restaurant to enjoying the meal. It was so simple, but this was what he'd dreamed of having with her. A freedom that wasn't possible when they were kids, and now it was all theirs. No curfews, no rules, no regulations. A real date with this woman, and as the evening unfurled, a new sensation spread through him, a freedom from care he hadn't felt in years. An ease.

"One time when I was helping out at Noelle's bakery, an American woman came to the counter, and she tried so hard to speak in French," Annalise said with a smile, continuing her tale of working with her sister from time to time.

"I bet you hate when they do that."

She clasped her hand to her chest. "Me? No. Why would you say that?"

"Doesn't it make the French people crazy when we try to speak French?"

"No," she said, shaking her head. Then a guilty little grin appeared on her face. "Only if it's very bad French."

He laughed as he picked up a yellowtail slice and swirled it in soy sauce. "Was her French very bad? Tell the truth."

She held up her thumb and index finger. "Only a little. It wasn't good, but she tried, so she got credit for that. She said she wanted *un yaourt abricot*, but she pronounced *yaourt* like *tarte*."

"In her defense, yogurt is one of the hardest French words to say."

She gave him a curious look. "You know *yaourt* is yogurt?"

"You taught me some French words," he said, then popped the sushi in his mouth.

"Did I teach you *yaourt*?"

He nodded as he finished chewing. "Isn't yogurt an important word to know?"

She set down her chopsticks, crossed her arms, and fixed him with a stare. "I taught you words like *kiss*, and *come*, and *fuck*. I did not teach you yogurt."

"Must have picked it up on my own then when I was in France. I spent a few weekends there."

Something dark passed through her eyes. "I remember," she said, sadness coloring her tone. She reached for his hand. "I remember seeing you at the airport."

He straightened. "You do?"

"Of course. How would I ever forget?"

He shrugged, wincing. The memory still hurt. He hadn't forgotten a single detail.

"I remember everything about it," she said softly but confidently. Her bright green eyes held his captive, never looking away. "I remember the way your hair was shorter, how you looked at me in the gift shop, then the hurt in your eyes when you saw my ring. You have to know I never wanted to hurt you."

"I know," he choked out, and the memory of that day slid in front of him, in all its hope and heartbreak.

"I hated feeling like I broke your heart, but I had no idea you were going to send me that letter," she said, and her voice sounded like she was shattering now, too.

"Of course you didn't know."

"I opened it with nervous fingers. Part of me hoped it would say all that it *did* say, but I also hated myself for wanting that. Michael, I loved my husband." She inhaled deeply, as if she needed the air to fuel her. "I loved Julien with all my heart. And though I had loved you that desperately too, you were the past. The most beautiful, wonderful part of it, but still the past. Then you sent me that note, and I was already with him, and I felt torn to pieces," she said, pressing a fist to her heart.

"I didn't want to make you feel that way." A fresh wave of guilt crashed into him. He should have tried to research her relationship status, but that was hard to do a decade ago. He'd simply sent the letter to the last address he'd had for her.

"You didn't make me feel that way. My damn heart did. I thought about you every day in college. I missed you every day. Getting over you was near impossible, but I was finally doing it. Living my life. We tried so hard to be together, but the fates were against us. We were too young. We only moved on because we had no other choice. And then you blasted back into my life with this letter that was a thing of beauty, and I was unprepared for how much your words would stir up my feelings of all that we'd had."

He shook his head, his throat hitching. He hadn't thought about how his words might have wounded her. "I didn't mean to mess with your head."

She reached for his hand and ran her fingers across his palm. Her touch was comforting and maddening. Because it felt right, and like the only touch he'd ever want.

"You didn't," she said, stroking his hand. "Not at all. I just want you to know it wasn't easy to get over you the first time, and it was gut-wrenching to let you walk away in Marseilles. But I had a fiancé and what kind of wife would I be if I even let myself linger or wonder about what could have been with my first love?"

He swallowed thickly, unsure how to answer, or if it

was even necessary. His whole life since then had been spent lingering on his first love. He remained silent.

"If I was like that, if I had entertained anything more than a passing notion of you, I would have been the worst wife. When I boarded my flight that day, I had to shut my heart and mind to you and give it thoroughly to Julien." Her eyes welled with the threat of tears. A waiter walked by, balancing rectangular plates of sushi.

"And you did," he said, and he understood deeply why she'd had to do that.

"I did," she said, then took a drink of her water. "And I regret nothing."

"Regret is a terrible feeling. But I've got to know," he said, clasping her hand tighter now, needing her answer, "why are you telling me this?"

"Because I want you to know that I was faithful. Always. That I am a faithful person. And I told you that you're the first man I've been with since he died, but you're also the only man I've even thought about. I let go of you years ago because I had to, and then when I was finally able to think about this again," she said, gesturing from him to her, "you were the only one who even came to mind. The only one I could even imagine sharing anything with."

The only one.

A rush of heat flooded him at those three words. He wanted to be the only one for her, even if he was only able to have her for a small moment in time. He would take what he could get, and he would savor it. She was here right now, with him and no one else.

"You have no idea how glad I am that I'm the one you thought of, Annalise," he whispered.

A smile tugged at her lips.

Then, he went for it. Just fucking let it all out. A hope, a wish, a *what if* question. "Do you ever wonder what would have happened that day if you weren't engaged? If you'd never have met him?"

She shook her head. "No. I don't think about it. I don't have to wonder," she said, her tone steady and certain as she looked straight at him, the rest of the restaurant fading into a blur. "Because I know what would have happened."

His hands shook and his heart stuttered as he rasped out, "What would have happened?"

She leaned in closer, placing a hand on his cheek. "I'd have stolen you. Taken you away from the army. Brought you home with me to Paris. Kept you all for myself for all the years and made up for lost time," she said, and his heart beat furiously, slamming against his chest, loving those words.

"Stop saying those things," he whispered, shaking his head.

"What things?"

"Things that make this harder for me."

"Why is it hard for you?"

He drew a breath. "Because you say things like that and it makes me want to steal you away. Maybe this is my only chance."

"What if it is?"

That was the question, wasn't it? What if this night, this trip, these hours were all they'd have? He didn't know if he could risk putting any more of his heart on the line for her. One thing was certain—his original notion that one touch and she'd be out of his system was well and truly gone. "Then we make the most of it."

She nodded. "We are making the most of it. Right now."

Before he tumbled into the land of no return with her, before he gave her every part of his heart and soul, he cleared his throat, returning to simpler matters. "Are you ever going to tell me about the yogurt?"

She laughed, her head leaning back, her long elegant neck exposed. "She couldn't pronounce *yaourt,* so it came out like *tarte*, and we gave her an apricot tarte. She seemed quite happy about that." She picked up her chopsticks and grabbed a piece of sushi as the patrons at a nearby table raised their sake glasses in a toast to a new deal. So odd that a business dinner was transpiring at the same time that they were discussing love, fidelity, and possibilities.

And yogurt.

He laughed softly. "A tarte sounds better than yogurt."

"My sister's bakery makes the best apricot tartes. Come to Paris sometime and find out."

He arched an eyebrow. "Come to Paris for a tarte?"

She jutted up a shoulder. "Or more."

"Like what? What else should I have with the tarte?"

She set down her chopsticks, the sushi untouched, then tilted her head and murmured, "*Me.* You should have me."

His blood heated, and his head swam with dirty thoughts. This meal seemed wholly unnecessary. He had no more interest in fish and rice. He could subsist on her, on this talking, these confessions, and these touches that promised what was to come.

He was ready to call for the check, but the waitress was nowhere to be seen. He glanced around, then tossed his napkin, stood up, and reached for her hand.

She rose, not even asking a single question. He led her past a table, around the corner, down the hallway. He knocked on the door of one of the restrooms. No one answered, so he turned the knob, pulled her inside, and locked the door.

"*Michael*," she said, all sexy and low.

"Yes?"

"What are you going to do?"

He lifted her up and set her on the sink cabinet. "Have my dessert first. I want you so much. I've wanted you for so damn long, and now you're here with me, and everything that comes out of your mouth makes me crave you even more." His voice was rough and hungry as he ran his fingertip across her bottom lip.

Her breath rushed over him. "It does?"

"So much. So unbelievably much." He dragged his finger down her neck. In its wake, goose bumps rose on her skin as he traveled along her throat, down her chest, between her breasts. He reached her waist, and squeezed her hip. Touching her was such a privilege, such a complete and utter gift. "Lift your dress. Let me see you."

Trembling, she reached for the hem and lifted it, and all the air rushed from his lungs as he stared, just fucking stared like a starving man at her beautiful, pink, wet pussy.

"So fucking pretty." He ran a finger through that slippery wetness. "I've wanted to taste you forever. I've wanted to have your sweetness on my mouth. Will you give it to me?"

"Please take it," she said on a pant, arching her back, raising her hips.

He kneeled, pressed his hands on her thighs, and took

his first taste. He groaned the second he touched her. She was heaven on his tongue.

She gasped and clutched his head, her fingers threading through his hair. He was intoxicated—utterly fucking buzzed on her. His mind turned hazy with pleasure and possibility, with the sheer magnitude of this sensual dream becoming his visceral reality at last. She was better than all his fantasies. She was real, and wet, and hot, and she wanted him as much as he wanted her.

His bones hummed, and his mind ignited as he flicked his tongue against the soft rise of her clit. She moaned, a long, delicious sound that seemed to vibrate through her whole body. He kissed her pussy deeply and then drew her swollen clit into his mouth, sucking it between his lips. She bucked against him, seeking more, and he gave it to her.

He gave her everything, and he was sure he'd never want this from anyone but her.

Ever.

———

His lips. His tongue. His hands gripping her thighs, holding her tight.

At once it was all too much and not enough. She felt like she was ready to fly to the moon, to launch into orbit, and she still wanted to ride higher, go farther. Everything was silvery as her body dissolved into his touch. He caressed her with his masterful tongue then sucked hard on her clit. In some kind of delicious harmony, she moved with him, rocking into him, hips shifting, keeping a sensual pace with him as he ate her out on the edge of the sink in the restroom.

The lights were low, a soft, blue glimmer against the black tiles on the wall, and somehow the glow fit. This was a decadently lit space for a deliciously dirty deed—sex in a restaurant bathroom. She didn't care where they were. She hadn't thought she would survive a minute longer without some kind of contact, and bless this man, he *knew*. He knew precisely how to meet her needs, and exactly how to lick, kiss, suck, and drive her wild. She felt untamed with him, on the edge of control, ready to let it all go. Her hands curled tighter around his head, her fingers laced through his hair. She looked down, and the sight of his face between her legs, devouring her, made her wetter, hotter.

She moaned his name, loved the way it felt on her tongue, the shape it took on her lips. Loved how he licked faster and hungrier each time she said it. They were like a feedback loop. His name fell from her mouth, and he consumed her. Like he was drinking her up. Like she was the only one he'd ever wanted.

Oh God, she felt that way right now. Nothing could even compare.

Pleasure climbed through her legs like vines, spreading across her whole body, filling her with a desire so deep and so far, she felt like it would never end. This feeling—this mad, crazy bliss—was everything. Gripping his head, she moved with him, moaning and sighing with every stroke of his tongue, every kiss of his soft, fuckable lips, and soon she melted into him, boneless and mindless with pleasure. She was losing touch with the world around her as her pulse beat rapidly across every inch of her skin, as heat flared in her chest, and her face flushed as she chased her climax. There it was, rising up, swelling, and her nerves blazed. Her hold on reality shattered as she thrust into his face, coming, and coming, and coming.

She squeezed her eyes and sealed her lips, trying desperately to quiet the little noises that escaped. And she shook. Her body just fucking shook from the orgasm that thundered through her, blowing her mind, blasting her once-cold world into nothing but scorching heat and lust.

All she wanted was more of him. All of him. She wanted to feel everything with him. Everything she'd denied herself, and everything good in the world.

As her release ebbed, Michael rose, cupped her cheeks, and whispered, "You taste divine. *Ma petite fraise.*"

"Take me back to your room," she whispered, revealing the depth of her desire for him. "Spend the night making love to me. I need you so much."

22

The door fell closed with a loud creak. In seconds, his hands were on her face, her breasts, her waist. Everywhere.

He pressed her to the wall of the foyer, trapping her with his body, touching her all over, as if he could memorize the feel of her curves with his palms. She writhed against him, and he groaned, low and deep in his throat.

As he lifted her arms over her head, pinning her wrists with his hands, he couldn't help but wonder if this was an all too vivid dream. Everything with her felt so insanely good it bordered on unreal.

How many times had he fantasized about this? How many nights had he taken her to bed in his mind, his own fist a pale substitute for this woman? She was a jewel, as brilliant and beautiful, her eyes sparkling. Her body was lush and warm, and her hungry lips hunted for his mouth. Her breath, her pants, her noises played in his ears like a sultry song.

His lips were fused to hers, her body was sealed tight to him, and he didn't intend to let her go.

He kissed her like the world was ending, but it was only the beginning of something entirely new between them. He couldn't get close enough to her, and he could barely accept that she—his *what if* girl, though she was all woman—was moaning softly in his mouth, pressing her breasts to his chest.

With his hand caging hers above her head, he pushed against her, craving this frenzied foreplay of clothed bodies, of clawing at each other to get close. God, he wanted her with a desire that couldn't even be measured. It felt like the kind of want that could scale mountains, invade countries, and send men and women to the moon. He broke the kiss, breathless, and held her face in his hand, getting lost in her emerald eyes.

"I've dreamed about this so much for so long. I can't believe it's real," he said, fighting so hard to hold in all the other feelings. If she knew how much and how deeply the need to be with her had defined him, had driven him to learn new ways of living, he might scare her away.

His muscles tensed from the restraint inside him as he reined in all the words he wanted to say. It was too soon, too much to share.

"But I'm real, Michael," she said, breaking free of his grip to place her hands on his face. "Feel me. Touch me. I'm here."

He closed his eyes, and his skin turned electric from the tender possession in her touch. No one had ever made him feel this way. All the other women were right. They had been completely right in their assessment when they'd said to him: *You're in love with someone else.*

He was.

Irrevocably.

This was his fate in life, to fall in love with the same woman over and over.

A rush of air escaped his lungs with the sharp, clear realization. He was in love with Annalise once more. He'd been madly in love with her before, and now it was happening all over again as he fell for the woman she had become—for her fragile but strong heart, her open mind, her willingness to try, her compassion, and her understanding of him.

He was dying to tell her, to imprint on her flesh: *I'm in love with you.*

Instead, when he opened his eyes, he chose his words carefully. "All I want is to touch you. To feel how real you are." He tugged off her dress, drinking in the sight of her in a black bra and nothing else.

A groan rumbled up his chest, then he dropped his face to her collarbone and slid his hand between her legs, the temperature in him soaring as he touched her silky heat. Lightly he stroked, teasing her, drawing out gasps and moans, sexy little sighs and sweet, heady murmurs. He pushed the cup of her bra over one breast, freeing a nipple and sucking it deep, then nipping her.

With each bite across her flesh, he imagined tattooing her with words. The words he wouldn't give voice to, he left as marks. A kiss on her throat. A long suck on the swell of her breast. A pinch of his teeth on her neck. Each one said, *I'm so in love with you.*

"Michael?"

His name was a question. He looked up, dazed from touching her. She spread her hands across his chest, her fingers toying with the buttons on his shirt. "I don't want to use a condom. I want to feel you completely. I'm on the pill, and I'm safe," she said, meeting his eyes. Hers shone with desire.

His mind and body latched onto the image of sliding into her, no barriers. His dick grew impossibly harder, straining against the zipper, fighting its way to get to the Promised Land.

That land just got even sexier.

He swallowed thickly, nodding. "I'm safe. I haven't been with anyone in a year."

Her eyes went wide. "You haven't?"

"That surprises you?"

As she worked open the buttons on his shirt, she said, "You're so handsome, I can't imagine you would be alone."

"I'm not a player, Annalise," he said roughly, as her long fingers undressed him.

"No, you're not a player. You've never been one. You always had your eyes on the woman you were with, and only her." She said it generally, as if the statement applied to his approach to relationships, and it did. But God, if she only knew it fit her precisely.

"Look at you," she murmured as she opened his shirt. Dipping her face to his chest, she planted kisses on his pecs, biting a nipple. He hissed in a breath. "You are so strong," she said, dragging her fingernails across his muscles as she pushed off his shirt.

"You're going to ruin me with all your compliments."

"Your body," she continued, as her eyes roamed over his chest and arms. "I love it. I love looking at you. I love touching you."

And he loved being touched by her. More than anything in the world. Especially when her hands went *there,* to his belt, unbuckling it then unzipping his jeans.

He helped push them down then off his feet, along with his shoes.

He glanced at her, then back at himself. "Feels like we've been here before. I'm kind of thinking we want to get to the next level of naked."

She laughed. "You mean the completely naked level?"

"Yes, that one," he said, and led her to the bed. He sat on the edge of the mattress, and looped his hands behind her back, unhooking her bra, letting it fall to the floor. His hands shot out and cupped her breasts, pinching the nipples as she arched into him. He raised his face and stared up at her, still in awe that she wasn't a mirage.

"You're here," he said in disbelief.

"I'm here," she echoed.

Naked before him, totally revealed, and the most beautiful thing he'd ever seen. He wanted to kiss every inch of her body, to catalogue each feature, from the tiny little appendix scar on her belly, to the small spray of freckles on her chest, to the strength in her legs.

"Michael, this isn't fair. Please take your clothes off."

He stood and shoved down his boxers. Her eyes blazed darkly as she stared at his cock, licking her lips. *Fuck*. He wanted to live in this moment, to return to it again and again—her unabashed lust. Her deep desire. Her stare made him hotter, made him burn. He reached down and stroked his cock, letting her watch and loving her reaction.

"Are you thinking of me?" she said naughtily. "When you do that?"

"Now. And always."

She trembled and then joined him, wrapping her hand over his, stroking along with him. "I think of you so much now. I'm so worked up being near you. So wound up. You drive me crazy with want."

He gripped her shoulders, guided her to the bed, and regarded her naked frame.

"Fuck." He groaned as she lay back on the sheets, resting on her elbows. "So beautiful. All I want is to make you feel so fucking good."

"You already do," she said, then raised her knees and let them fall open.

He was helpless to resist. He bent down and buried his face between her thighs once more, kissing and licking her sweetness, rubbing his stubble all over her slick, wet heat. She moaned and rocked her hips into him, faster, harder, then just wilder. Her hips shot up as he thrust his fingers inside her and sucked her sweet clit between his lips until she came, flooding his tongue, her pleasure all over his face.

Seconds later he crawled up her, wedged himself between her legs, and dragged the head of his cock through her heat.

She gasped, her head falling back against the pillow, her lips parted.

"So greedy," he said as he toyed with her, loving the feel of her wet pussy against his hard dick. This was what he'd craved for so long. The chance to be with her. The thrill of fucking the woman he'd never stopped loving.

"Please don't tease me. I need you. I need you now," she said, so desperate, so sexy, so beautiful.

"*Je te veux tellement,*" he said, repeating the phrase she'd shared on the plane.

She trembled, whispering desperately, "Say it again."

"*Je te veux tellement,*" he said roughly.

"You're even sexier when you speak my language."

"I'm only speaking the truth. I want you so much. So fucking much."

"Have me. Take me."

He eased inside her in one hot, tight thrust.

Then the earth stopped spinning. The stars melted away from the sky. Gravity had no hold on him because he was falling, falling, falling into her.

After all these years. After all this time. It was exquisite and so unbelievably fucking good. She gasped, her breath spilling out as she made the first move, her hips rising up, her legs wrapping around him.

"Closer. Come closer," she whispered, and he lowered himself, their chests nearly touching as he braced on his elbows, flexing forward in slow, steady thrusts, taking his time, savoring the feel of her bare, sweet pussy.

Their heated bodies moved together. He was lit up everywhere, his entire being electrified as he pushed in and out, then deeper, hitting her right where she went wild, her back bowing off the bed, her mouth falling open, and a beautiful groan that became his name.

"Say it." He growled. "Say it now."

"Baise-moi plus fort."

God, it was music from her. It was heady and thrilling to hear her say those words.

"I knew you'd sound crazy for me when you said it like this," he groaned, then buried his face in her neck, kissing, biting, marking.

"I am. I'm crazy for you," she said, and then it was her turn to nip. She went for his collarbone, and he nearly exploded. He loved her roughness, and she knew it because seconds later her hands were on his shoulders, then she dragged her nails down his back, digging into his flesh.

"Let me feel you all over me," he said as he fucked her faster, harder.

She ran her nails down to his ass, curling her hands around him. He pushed deeper, the start of his orgasm barreling through his body. She arched up, grabbing his head, crushing his mouth in a crazed, fierce kiss, full of teeth and tongue and madness. Then she let go, his name tumbling from her lips in a raptured cry as she shattered beneath him, arms and legs grabbing, twisting, tugging him even closer, like she'd never get enough.

Her need for him set him off, igniting a mind-blowing orgasm that blurred his vision and torched his veins as he followed her there, in perfect fucking bliss.

Like heaven on earth.

He collapsed on her, a sweaty, tangled mess of limbs, and lips, and desire, sated at last.

She ran her hands through his hair and sighed softly against him. It was unequivocally the best night of his life, but he also winced inside with the awareness of how much harder it would be to say good-bye now that he'd experienced all of her.

Until she said the next words.

23

Wow.

Just wow.

That was out of this world.

She lay on the bed in a sea of rumpled sheets, Michael's strong arms wrapped around her sweat-slicked frame, her heart beating like a hummingbird, and she blinked open her eyes.

All her senses were heightened, and she felt new, like she was experiencing having a body again after a deep, dreamless sleep.

Breathe in, breathe out.

Each inhalation sent air rushing through her blood, waking her up, nudging her, reminding her that this was life, this was sex, and this was good.

It had been so much more than good.

She'd seen stars, tasted heaven, breathed rare air. Her skin tingled all over, and her blood pulsed hot and fast from her climax. She'd never come like that before. She felt it humming in her bones. Skimming across her skin.

And hammering in her heart, insisting on being

heard. She wanted more of him. So much that the thought of not having him again already hurt—like a phantom pain, a promise of how it would feel if she let him go. The prospect of flying home in two days and leaving this bliss behind made her chest ache, like it had been carved out once more.

She was tired of hollowness. Tired of hurting. She wanted more of the good. She turned in his arms, facing him. "Michael..." Her voice sounded hoarse to her own ears; all that moaning his name had taken a toll. "I'm going to need so much more of that from you."

Her gaze locked on his, watching the slow spread of his smile, the way it stretched across his whole face, how his blue eyes seemed to flicker with happiness.

He kissed her cheek, whispering soft and sexy. "With me, you can have everything."

The sentiment made her shudder, and yet she wasn't talking about more sex, per se. Or even more sex in the next few days. She pressed a hand to his naked chest, needing to make sure he understood *exactly*. "What I mean is..." She stopped to let a breath fill her lungs, fueling her admission. "I want to see you again. I don't want this—whatever it is—to end when we leave New York."

His features froze. His lips were parted, his jaw was set, and his eyes were vulnerable. He didn't move, as if he were slowly absorbing her request. Soon enough, though, he found words, his voice gravelly. His question came out as a scratch. "You do?"

She nodded vigorously. "I do. Maybe that is crazy. Do you think it's crazy?"

He shook his head. "*No!*" flew off his tongue.

The speed of his response emboldened her. That,

combined with the endorphins still rushing through her system, drove her on. "I just," she began, running her fingers through the fine hairs on his chest. "I just would be so sad to leave New York and not see you again. And I don't have a plan, or an agenda, or anything beyond the here and now. All I know is I want to see more of you. Which probably sounds..." Her voice trailed away, lost in the noises of late-night New York floating through the window.

"Sounds what?" he asked, prompting her.

"You probably think it sounds too hard, since I'm in Paris and you're in Las Vegas, and that's how it was before," she said, worried that they were facing the same obstacles, those very ones that had splintered them years before.

That sexy smile returned, tugging at his lips as he shook his head. "No. It's not crazy at all. We're not the same as we were before. The distance—it's not as daunting. We have the means to deal with it."

She nodded. "Yes, we do. And all I know is that I don't want this to end."

He pulled her closer, held her tighter. "That's enough for me to fly across an ocean for you."

He dusted her lips with his—a soft, sweet kiss that was both gentle and thrilling at once. On his lips, she swore she could taste his happiness, and she kissed more, taking some of it for herself.

They chatted in bed, talking about friends and family, work and music, photographs and security. Every now and then a small shard of latent guilt stabbed at her, but she pushed past her nagging worries. She wanted to savor these moments with Michael. This time with him was the sweetest thing she'd experienced in a while, and she'd rather revel in it, especially after so long of having felt the opposite.

Soon enough, their lips found each other again, and they kissed, slow and lazy, the kind of kiss that made her wetter and him harder, that led to fingers slipped between legs and dirty words like, *Get on your hands and knees. I want to take you that way.*

She didn't need to be asked twice. She wanted to be fucked that way by him, with her palms flat against the navy blue comforter, her knees sinking down, and her ass in the air. Michael ran a hand down her back, inch by torturously slow inch, each touch making her wriggle and writhe.

"Mmm," he murmured, his big palm tracing her flesh, pushing her spine low, forcing her to raise her ass higher. "Look at you. Look at my Annalise. So fucking wet. So fucking hot. So needy for me."

Like a sparkler igniting, those dirty words set off a fresh wave of desire. Heat pooled between her legs as she lowered herself to her elbows, her breath coming fast. "I do need you. I need you in me, Michael."

He dragged his fingers through her sex, and she moaned, closing her eyes, giving in to the fevered rush in her body, surrendering to her desire to be fucked.

Sheets rustled behind her as he moved, straightened up on his knees, and positioned himself. When he rubbed the head of his cock against her pussy, a wild cry ripped from her throat. *Mon dieu*, who was this woman in her body? Inhabiting her, taking over her mind, using her mouth to speak such dirty things? "*Fuck me. Hard. Take me. I'm yours.*"

He took, fucking her as she'd never experienced before—rough and beautifully cruel, fingers digging into flesh, hands gripping her breasts and pinching her nipples, teeth on her shoulders. Deeply buried inside her, he fucked her savagely. She moved with him, moaned with him, slammed her pelvis back on his cock, letting him know that the more he filled her, the hungrier she was. Sliding a hand up her backbone, he grabbed her hair, wrapping it around his fist. She gasped and her noise turned into a long, animalistic cry as he yanked.

"Rougher. Harder," she bit out.

She wanted to be bruised, to feel used, to be fucked so hard she felt him for days. Michael Sloan was more than willing to give her all of himself, to plunder her body with his cock, to take her mercilessly until her hands grappled at the sheets, clutching and twisting as pleasure spiked then slammed into her.

A shattering.

No warning.

Just a rapturous crash as her climax rattled her body, jarring her bones. It shocked her, the power of this kind of orgasm. It had a magnitude measurement as it thundered through her. With a final thrust, growling her name in her ear, he came. She'd never felt anyone go so deep inside her. Never felt so in tune with her body.

But it was more than that. She'd never felt this kind of physical connection. Raw and hungry.

And boundless, too.

That may have been what surprised her the most— this endlessness of the pleasure. She supposed that was how any sort of new passion felt. Infatuation was the most powerful magician in any land, and it could trick you into thinking something was true and real. But there, in the dark of the night, in the middle of a city of millions, tucked away in a hotel room, she believed in its promise.

She believed in fate, too.

In second chances.

As he spooned her, brushing soft kisses against the back of her neck, tonight seemed precisely why she'd landed a job in Vegas, exactly why she'd said yes to the New York gig. As if the cruel mistress of circumstances who had toyed with them and yanked them apart when they were younger was working in their favor now.

Bringing them back together in a whole new way.

After that rough, punishing sex that bruised her hips, and made her sore everywhere, she was sure she'd fall asleep sated. She did. For a bit.

But sometime in the middle of the night, she woke. Not with a start, but with a slow, unhurried shift of her hips. His erection grazed her backside, and she wiggled her rear against him.

"Mmm. That's a nice way to wake up," he said, all rough from sleep.

"It's not even time to get out of bed yet," she whispered, rocking into him.

"You mean it's time for more of this," he said, sliding his hand along the back of her thigh and shifting her knee to make room.

"Yes. Please. You've made me insatiable."

"Good, I like you that way. Hungry for me," he said against her neck as he eased inside her. He made it a lazy and luxurious coming together, as if they were two lovers who'd spent countless nights entwined. For a moment, she wondered if either of them could come like this, with this unhurried kind of love-making, but the question turned to dust as the warm pleasure in her hummed, tension coiling, and she climbed to the edge once again. She cried out his name, and then out of nowhere, a sob escaped her lips, mingling with her noises, obscuring the evidence of her pain.

A tear slid down her cheek.

She swallowed it quickly. Judging from the way he grunted and shoved deep in her, he didn't notice. A storm of emotions swelled, gripping her chest, squeezing her heart like an invisible hand trying to choke up the mess brewing inside—guilt, joy, sadness, elation.

She inhaled sharply, willing the air to spread through her lungs, to free her from this specter of remorse. She didn't want to feel it. There was nothing wrong with having sex. Nothing at all.

Yet her heart was fracturing at the same time as it was stitched back together. Sex with Michael was both wondrous and bittersweet.

And she understood precisely why she felt so fucking good, and so fucking awful at the same time.

"It's so good with you, Annalise," he said a minute later.

"I know. It is. It's so good."

It was unlike anything she'd ever felt. It was better. It was the best.

That was the problem.

24

The beautiful blonde stretched on her belly on the white duvet—heels kicking in the air, lips red and pouty, as seductive as she was real. Even when she was posing, there was nothing forced about her client's beauty.

Casey Sullivan had one of the best smiles Annalise had ever photographed. Fresh-faced and all-American, she possessed a gorgeous grin. The woman also knew how to give "come fuck me" eyes to the camera.

She was thinking of her husband, Casey had said, so it was easy to gaze at the lens that way—like she loved him and wanted him at the same damn time. Now they were in the last series of shots at the boudoir studio space. Casey wore an emerald-green satin push-up bra and matching lace panties. "Nate always likes me in this shade of green," she said.

"I suspect your husband likes you in anything, everything, and nothing," Annalise said as she finished shooting.

Casey laughed. "Yes, that does describe him perfectly."

"Then he is going to be one very happy man when he

sees these photos. He won't know what to do with himself. His jaw will drop. Guaranteed," Annalise said, as she showed her some of the pictures on the back of the camera.

Casey shrugged into a robe and peered at the images, and she squealed with delight as they flipped through the frames. "These are amazing," she said, then ran her hand over the outline of her belly. "You can't even really tell I had a baby six months ago."

Annalise shook her head. "You look radiant, happy, and beautiful."

Casey blushed and waved a hand in the air. "Stop, you flatter me."

"No. I don't have to. The camera loves you because you're so happy and so in love."

Casey met her eyes. "You can really tell from how I look at the camera?"

"Of course. It's in your eyes. Everything is."

Casey narrowed hers, and studied Annalise. "Hmm. What's in yours, then?" she asked playfully.

A red flush crept across her cheeks.

Sex, hot sex, more sex. Dinners, days, sleepless nights. Idle chats, deep conversations, sweet nothings, and so much coming together. The last three days and nights in Manhattan had passed in a blissful blur. She'd cancelled her hotel room and stayed with Michael. During the days she'd finished her shoot for Veronica's while Michael had worked with clients, and in the evenings they'd gone to dinner, or to a club, and sometimes they hadn't left the room at all.

New York with Michael was a great escape from the past and the present.

The only trouble was she couldn't rid that nagging

guilt that gnawed at her for having such an immeasurably lovely time. As if she shouldn't be allowed to enjoy herself —at least, not this deeply, this quickly, this intensely. Most of the time she turned the volume down on that voice, but still it spoke up, worming its way around her heart like an insidious creature.

"You're happy, too." The declaration came from Casey. Annalise's heart skittered. The woman was so straightforward and so direct.

"Of course I'm happy," she said, in her best cheery tone, keeping things businesslike. "I love what I do."

"But something is holding you back?" Casey pressed on, undeterred.

Annalise knit her brow together. "Hmm?"

"From truly being happy," Casey elaborated. "I can see a sadness in your eyes, too. Barely there, but it comes into focus now and then."

Annalise swallowed and fiddled with her camera. The woman was too astute, too observant. She didn't answer.

"If something holds you back from your happiness, you should try to move through it," Casey said softly.

Annalise looked up, her client's gentle words threading into her. "Spoken from experience?"

"Sort of. I had to get through my fear that my husband and I would lose our friendship if we became long-term lovers."

"And you didn't, clearly."

"We didn't but we had to walk through that fear. Live in it. Roll around in it for a while."

"And you think I need to roll around in something?"

"I think whatever is making you sad, you should face it."

On the cab ride back to the hotel, Annalise lingered

on her client's advice. Rubbing her thumb against the outline of the lens in her camera bag, she wondered if Casey was right. She had to face this thing, this voice, this knot in her stomach that stood in the way.

That night she dressed in jeans, heels, and a soft black sweater, and perched on the edge of the bed before they headed out for dinner. She waited for Michael to emerge from the shower, and when he did, her heart thundered. His hair was damp, and a white towel hung on his hips, revealing his flat, toned stomach and the trail of hair that led to her favorite place. God, she wanted him so badly, in ways that went beyond the physical.

"I feel guilty for enjoying this," she blurted out, ripping off the Band-Aid.

He sat next to her on the bed, gesturing from him to her. "Us?"

She nodded and inhaled deeply. This was the hard part. The deep and dark truth. "Because it's so good with you."

His lips twitched and he looked down, then back up at her, schooling his expression. "The sex, you mean?"

She nodded. "That. Yes. It's amazing. It's better than anything I've ever had."

He nodded, as if she'd said something as simple as "This salmon is delicious." She hadn't expected him to beat his chest at the compliment, or grin with masculine pride, but she was doubly glad for his tact. "That doesn't mean you didn't love him," Michael said, as a droplet of water from his shower slid down his chest. "It just means we have good chemistry."

She shook her head vigorously, strands of her hair slapping her cheek. "It's not just chemistry, Michael. You know that. We have so much more than simple chemistry. We have history, and now we have the present too."

"I know," he whispered.

"That's part of what scares me. The sex is amazing in and of itself, but it's also incredible..." She slowed her words to run her fingers along the back of his neck and into the soft strands of his damp hair. "For other reasons."

A small smile slipped across his lips. "I feel those reasons, too."

"I don't want to be sad about this," she said, keeping her voice strong, as if announcing her intentions to move on would rid her of this hard stone inside her chest.

"There's no shortcut. You just have to let yourself feel," he said, leaning his head back against her hand and closing his eyes, almost as if he were demonstrating how to feel again.

How had he gotten to be so wise? Where was the carefree, easy guy she fell for decades ago? But of course, she knew the answer. He'd had to let go of who he was. He'd had to walk through all his own grief, too.

As her fingers toyed with his hair, she asked, "Is that what you did? For your father?"

"Yes. Most of all, once I stopped feeling so awful every day, I chose not to beat myself up for enjoying being alive. It gets to a point where you *can't* miss a person every second. Or even every day. And you stop getting mad at yourself if you dare to laugh, or joke, or even just do something mundane, like have fun watching an episode of *CSI*."

She latched onto that last one. "Are you saying we should watch TV?"

He laughed and opened his eyes, shaking his head. "Hell no. But I learned to just have a good time hanging out with family. Enjoy work. A good hard run. That's the only way through everything. Keep on living—keep on feeling."

"I want to be there. I want to feel." But as soon as she spoke, she wondered if she was further along than she thought. Hadn't she done all that? Let herself feel everything? She hadn't shied away from grief. She'd faced it head on, experiencing every tear, every ounce of heartbreak, every moment of missing him. She'd gone all in when it came to remembering, and longing. Maybe it was time to do the same for moving on.

Go all in.

So when she went to dinner with him that night, she chose to relish every ounce of the happiness, to lose herself in the joy of being with this man she cared for so deeply. When they returned to his room for their last night together, she knew there was one more thing to do. One more way to give her whole heart to moving on.

"Take my picture," she said. He scrunched up his brow as she handed him her camera. "I'm always the one behind the camera. I'm always the one with something in front of my eyes. I want to be the subject, and I want you to photograph me getting naked for you. That's what I want to feel tonight. What it's like to give myself to you."

His eyes blazed darkly, shining with desire, and something else—something she'd wanted desperately when she was younger. Something that scared the hell out of her now. But maybe if she was on the other side of the camera, she could handle everything she saw in him, and let him see the parts of her no one else was privy to.

25

He wasn't a photographer, but he didn't need to be to know she was a breathtaking subject. Gorgeous, real, and heartbreaking. Written in her eyes was a mix of emotions —trepidation, courage, excitement, determination.... He tried to capture them all as she tugged her black sweater over her head, then unbuttoned her jeans.

She didn't pose or mug for the camera. She simply *did*, and he simply shot.

She reached for the zipper of her jeans and worked it open.

"Mmm. It's getting harder to concentrate," he murmured as he snapped a shot of her undressing.

She laughed, and he caught that on film, too. "*Harder*. Ha ha," she said with a flirty smile. That was captured for posterity, also—her playful side shining through. He caught every moment of her getting ready for him.

Her eyes met the lens, as if she were able to peer behind it to see him. Even though he was the one with the camera, somehow he felt studied at the same damn time. She was so fucking *knowing*, observant through her bones, down to her marrow, even when being photographed. Those green irises held him captive as she gazed at him, taking her time undressing, pushing the denim of her jeans down one hip, then the other, giving him a strip show.

She wiggled her eyebrows. Licked her lips.

His chest rumbled as his dick hardened. "That's what I was talking about earlier. You enjoying yourself."

"I am."

"I want you to enjoy yourself with me."

"I do." She let her jeans fall to the floor. She stood in her black bra and panties, and he snapped an image of that, too, as his skin grew hotter and desire flashed inside him.

"You like it when I take your picture?"

She nodded.

"Then lie back on the bed. Hair on the pillow. That's one of my favorite looks of yours. All those crazy red strands spilling across the white pillowcase."

"Tell me why you like that," she said, scooting back on the bed, assuming the pose.

"Because you're vulnerable and raw. Because you look real, and sexy, and you look like you want me."

She swallowed, and he snapped quickly, cataloguing her reactions. "I do want you."

"Let yourself want me," he said quietly, capturing more as she reached to unhook her bra, then more as her breasts spilled free.

"Fuck," he muttered, his erection straining against his jeans. "So fucking turned on. Can't concentrate on the picture."

"Don't concentrate. Just shoot," she said, as she tucked her thumbs into her underwear, and he hit the button again, his length thickening as a heavy need thrummed in him. The need to have her. To take her.

She pushed down her panties, revealing the soft auburn landing strip. His mouth watered. He wanted to rub his face against it, to feel her slickness on his jaw. To taste her heat on his tongue. He groaned but somehow managed to click again and again, as she skimmed off her panties and lay naked on a hotel bed.

"Open your legs," he instructed.

She raised her knees, and let them fall open.

Gripping the camera harder, he swallowed thickly. Her pussy was so fucking pretty, so goddamn ready for him. "Don't let anyone else ever take your picture like this," he said, as possessiveness stormed through him. He hated the thought of anyone ever seeing these photos, let alone seeing her naked. Thank God the pictures were on *her* camera, which meant they'd be safe where they belonged.

"Never," she said in a heated whisper. "No one ever has," she added. "This is only for you."

He inhaled sharply, her meaning registering. She was giving him something her husband had never had. Something that was a first.

Now.

Fucking now.

He couldn't take it anymore.

In a flash, he set the camera on the bureau, and unbuttoned his shirt.

With her index finger, she beckoned him. He recorded that image in his mind—her calling him to her side. Him heeding her wish. He'd play those few seconds over and over again. The story of his heart, given long ago, only to her. "Come to me," she said. "Join me. Fuck me like you wanted to when you were taking the pictures."

He shoved off his jeans. "On your stomach then," he said, and didn't take his eyes off her as she flipped to her belly. With her cheek pressed to the pillow, she watched him. Watched him as he stripped off his boxers and as he reached to stroke his cock, hissing in a breath because it felt so fucking good to touch himself as she stared, her eyes flaming with lust. But something else, too. Longing, desire, and also a new kind of freedom, it seemed. Like she was finally letting herself feel everything.

She lifted her rear, inviting him home.

"*You*," he gritted out as he climbed on the bed and brought his dick to her ass, rubbing it against the soft flesh of her rear. She moaned, rising up into him as his hard length slid between her cheeks, like a filthy tease of what he wanted to do to her someday. She pushed back, and he filed that reaction away in the dirty vault to bring out again when they were both ready. For now, he moved lower, gliding the head of his dick against her heat. Fuck, she was slick and wet, and so damn ready for him. Her soft velvet folds were like a beacon, and his dick pointed its way home.

"I want you so much. I love wanting you. It feels so good," she said, her eyes on his, and he fell even harder for her as she let herself open up to him, and to pleasure, and to this chance to feel again, to live again, and hell, he hoped maybe, just maybe, to love again. He covered her with his body, and she let out the sexiest purr, then the most intoxicating moan as he pushed the head of his dick into her slippery sweet entrance. He sank inside in one slow, deep, decadent move. So snug—so fucking perfect for him. They moaned in unison. She fit him deliciously, and he couldn't imagine not having her like this.

"Did you like it when I took your picture?" he asked once he was fully nestled in her.

"God, yes," she panted.

He pushed deeper. "Why? Why did you like it so much?"

She moaned. "Because I love being naked with you. I love being with you. You make me feel so good."

"Just let me make you feel this way. *Let me.*"

"I will. I am. Oh God, please."

As he fucked her like that, slow and unhurried, she moved with him, shifting her hips, aligning her body, sliding against him. He cupped her tits, squeezing, then pinched the nipples.

She gasped as he tugged at them, and that drove him. Burying himself deeper in her, he gripped her hair in his hand.

"Yes," she said, urging him on, and he knew she meant both the fucking and the tugging. He wrapped those gorgeous red strands around his fist. "Hard. Pull hard."

Yanking her hair, he pulled her head back, raising it off the pillow.

"Oh God, yes, like that, like that."

"You like it rough?"

"With you, I do. So rough."

He gave it to her the way she wanted. Driving in deep. Gripping her hard. Fucking her relentlessly.

With each thrust, she cried in pleasure. With each pinch, she groaned his name. With every nip of his teeth, she gushed.

And he was consumed. Utterly consumed.

Sex with her was a revelation. It was as if he'd discovered life on another planet, to know that it was possible to have this kind of sex. Savage yet tender. Cruel but gentle.

To know she wanted it the same way. Her sounds told him she wanted to feel it everywhere. In her body. On her skin. In her heart. Oh God, he fucking hoped she wanted him in her heart. So deep in her heart that he could never be removed. *Always*. Like he was the end of the line for her. Just like she was for him.

Love me, he wanted to say. *Just fucking love me*.

But he couldn't say that. Not now. Not yet. Instead, with her hair tight in his hand, and her throat exposed, he gripped her shoulder, digging his thumb into her collarbone.

"Like that, just like that," she cried out, this time in French, in that heated way she spoke when she was close to the edge. Her pussy clenched around his shaft, so tight, so fucking perfect.

"And this?" he asked, biting down on her shoulder. *Love me.*

"Oh God."

He thrust harder. Brought his lips to the shell of her ear. Spoke harshly. "Do you want me to leave marks? Ones that say you're mine? You're fucking mine. I want to fuck you till you're mine."

"Yes. Yes. Yes," she urged, and he let himself believe she was answering his greatest wish. *I'm yours.*

He pressed his lips hard to her neck, his teeth biting down, digging in as she went crazy beneath him, rocking and thrusting and losing all control as she cried out and came undone in a fevered frenzy.

Then his balls tightened, and his vision blurred. The rarest pleasure, the kind that came from total carnal bliss, surged in his bones, igniting him until he came long and deep inside the woman he loved.

He just fucking loved her.

And it was so goddamn hard not to tell her, in her language or his. He tried to swallow the words, to choke them down, but the moment got the better of him. "I'm so mad about you. So completely crazy for you. All the time. I can't stop this feeling," he whispered, barely scratching the surface of how he felt.

She tensed all over. Then she scooted out from under him, her hands on his chest, her eyes meeting his. "You speak French. You speak perfect French."

Fuck.

He hadn't meant to say it in French. He hadn't meant to let on he'd understood everything he'd heard her say in her native tongue.

26

Sixteen years ago

As he rounded the corner of the long hallway in the languages building, he opened the note yet again. The one he'd found scattered in his driveway, wreckage from his father's wallet. Like a treasure hunter, Michael had salvaged it, clutched it in his hand, gripped it tight that night, like a precious thing. And it was. He'd held onto it ever since. He probably always would.

He folded the note and tucked it back into his wallet when he reached room 403.

Freshman year French.

He wrapped his hand around the knob, opened the door, and roamed his eyes across the sea of desks. Nerves whipped through him. He wasn't a natural at languages. He was good at business, at strategy. Those were his skills. But he'd taken a night class during his senior year of high school, and he was committed to seeing this through. He wasn't so romantic that he believed his father had left a dying wish. His dad had no notion that he was going to be killed and surely if he had, he wouldn't have left such a practical note.

Michael was wise enough to understand what the note was—one of the many reminders his father had left for himself. *Get milk. Pick up Shannon at 6:15. Remind Michael to study for math.*

But even so, this reminder was bigger. More important than a day-to-day item on the to-do list. This note was part of the plan—the plan he'd discussed and hatched with his dad. The plan to apply to school in France, to be with Annalise, to make a life with her.

He hadn't been able to get into college in France, and she'd had no luck in the United States.

But he could keep trying. Because...there was always a someday.

"Reminder: Tell Michael he's signed up for French classes in the evening. A gift to him. He needs to learn the language for when he goes to school there. He needs to learn French for Annalise. So he can find his way back to her."

That was it. That was all. But that was enough. His father's wish for him. Dead or alive, it didn't matter. Michael would fulfill it.

He stepped into the classroom, daunted but ready, and started working his ass off to learn another language.

Six years later, at age twenty-four, he was fluent. During those six years, he and Annalise had lost touch, but by the time he was done with school, on his own, serving his country, he was ready to find his way back to her.

He tracked her down and sent her the letter. *Je n'ai jamais cessé de t'aimer.*

He didn't have to turn to Google to translate his heart.

27

She sat up in bed, staring at him like he'd skydived in from another planet and landed kaput on her bed.

"Michael?" She raised an eyebrow.

He rubbed his hand over his jaw. "Yeah?"

"Did you just have a conversation with me in French?"

His shoulders tightened, and he silently cursed himself. There was no denying it. He'd done nothing wrong, but he couldn't pretend he hadn't said those things. Not just the whole *I'm crazy for you* declaration, but after she'd said, "*Yes, like that, just like that*," every single word that tumbled from his lips had been in French.

"Not a whole conversation. Just a few words," he said, desperately trying to sidestep.

"How did you know what to say?"

His heart slammed against his chest. He didn't want to tell her. Not yet. He didn't want to expose himself like this. He didn't want to reveal the full extent of what he'd done for her. That his desire to find her again, to be with her again, had driven him to learn a whole new language. "Just a few words. That's all," he said, then glanced at the clock on the nightstand. "You have an early flight. Let's get some sleep."

"Okay," she said in a strained voice.

He turned out the light. "Come here. Come closer," he murmured, and wrapped his arms around her.

"I'm already close."

She snuggled into him, giving in on this count.

"Closer still," he said.

"Michael," she said, her tone pleading as she pressed her warm body to his, skin to skin.

He kissed her hair. "Not now."

"I want to know."

"Just let me hold you."

She sighed, relenting as she wriggled closer, giving in. "Thank you."

"For?"

"For taking my picture."

He smiled into her neck and kissed her there, inhaling her scent. Tonight she was rain and sex and him. "I want you to be happy. Tell me you won't regret this. Or me."

She shook her head. "I don't regret you. I could never regret you. But I want to know—"

He whispered into her hair. "Shhh..."

He just couldn't go there tonight. He would break.

———

His breathing evened out, and soon he was asleep. She stared at the bright green letters on the hotel clock. After midnight. She had a five a.m. wake-up call, and the world's earliest flight to Paris.

Back home.

Her chest ached. She missed him already.

She hadn't realized when she sought him out how much she needed *this*. Contact. Emotion. Passion. She'd been so shut down, but one flip of the switch from him, and the electricity was powered on, bright and shining, lighting up a whole city.

Perhaps that was why she'd searched for him when she went to Vegas. Yes, she had neatly tucked him away when she'd married Julien. She hadn't thought about Michael at all while she was another man's wife. But with that bond severed, she was free to roam, to return to wondering *what if*. To her first love.

Such a big love.

Maybe she'd always been destined to find her way to him again. She'd told herself he was safe, but she wasn't looking for safety, as she'd quickly learned in a few short days with him. She was on the hunt for connection, for that sliver of a thread between two people. She may not have realized it that afternoon at the Bellagio, but she knew it now, and she had unearthed the mother lode with him.

But tonight she had something new to noodle on. A twist. A surprise.

Something she hadn't expected.

His sudden fluency.

It perplexed her that he'd talked to her in French, then tried to deny it. There was nothing wrong with him knowing her language, but she was so damn curious for details. How he'd learned it. Why he'd hidden it. Admittedly, it was odd that he hadn't told her. They'd had so many conversations—especially the one about yogurt—when it would have been natural to say something. Especially since he'd told her years ago that he started taking classes in college. Never had she imagined he'd gone all the way.

But the clock told her it was too late to press.

―――――

The next morning, she showered, stuffed her toiletries into her suitcase, and checked that her car service was on the way. But she couldn't seem to let go of Michael's newfound language proficiency.

Perhaps it was the former journalist in her, the part of her that chased answers, that hunted for truths.

Even as he kissed her hard against the wall of the hotel room, whispering hotly in her ear, "I want to make love to you once more, and to fuck you at the same time. So you won't forget me while we're apart."

She liked that he used both *fuck* and *make love*, because she'd learned that was exactly what she wanted from him. Both. Especially right now. "You have to know it's that way for me too. And I would *never* forget you," she said.

"Let's just be sure of that," he said, low and dirty, as he pulled down her panties, hooked her leg around his hip, and slid inside her.

He was tender, touching her with a sort of adoration that she longed for. But he was also willing and ready to manhandle her in a way she'd hadn't experienced before. It seemed to awaken her, to remind her that her body was designed to feel good, and sometimes good meant sore and bruised and used. She let go for one last time with him as he took her against the wall, and they came together.

They straightened up, adjusting hair and clothes. She checked her watch. Ten more minutes. She couldn't wait.

She blurted out, "Why did you hide from me that you know French? It's driving me crazy. I want to know."

He scoffed and looked away as he grabbed the handle of her suitcase. "I hardly know it."

"But you spoke French to me last night." He was quiet as he rolled her bag to the door. She followed him, shouldering her purse. "You always told me you wanted to learn it. You told me you wanted to be able to speak to me in French."

"I don't really know it well."

But he looked away from her as he reached for the door handle, his cool blue eyes glancing anywhere but her face.

That was her answer, but she wanted the confirmation. She stopped him from opening the door. She placed her hand on his arm, then ran her fingers up to his hair. She turned him to face her. Pressed her forehead to his. And spoke to him in French, rapid-fire. "You're amazing, and I adore you. I want to see you over and over. I want you to do everything to me, and with me, and on me. You make me feel happy again, and when you come to Paris I will show you everything, and you can have me in alleys and staircases, and we can fuck in museums and in restaurant bathrooms, and then you can make love to me in bed. You can talk dirty to me and tell me how much you want me, and I will tell you the same because I do. So much I ache for you now."

He trembled and bit his lip like he was holding in all the things he wanted to say.

Determination spurred her on. "And you make me feel again. I feel things for you I haven't felt in years. Or for anyone. Do you know how terrifying that is for me?" she said, laying her heart bare. She was heading to the airport in ten minutes, jetting away from him once again. What did she have to lose? She'd already lost once, so rolling the dice on this truth of her heart was a chance she should take.

His eyes squeezed shut, his expression pained. Then he opened them and met her gaze.

"Yes," he admitted. "I know. And I want all that, too."

She inhaled deeply and cupped his cheeks. "Why didn't you just tell me?"

She was dying to know the answer.

28

Because it revealed everything, that was why. Because it showed all his cards. It told her his full and true heart, as pathetic as it was.

Slumping against the door, he dragged a hand through his hair.

And stopped.

Stopped keeping it all inside.

Stopped biting his tongue.

"Why didn't I tell you I learned French for you?" He tossed out the question like an attorney cross-examining. "Why didn't I admit I spent six years studying a language because I was in love with you?"

He'd wanted to hide it, to keep it from her. It wasn't hard to pretend you didn't understand. But those words, those things she said...he was only human. How could he hide his reaction?

She pressed her hand to her chest. "You learned French for me? Even though I know English?"

"You make it sound foolish."

She shook her head. "No. I'm just processing. It's big. That's a big thing. How did you do it?"

"I started freshman year of college. It was my father's idea. He even wrote me a note about it," he said, softly, so his voice wouldn't break. "He knew me better than anyone. He knew you were all I wanted. He wanted me to be with you. I still have the note," he said, reaching into his back pocket, opening his wallet and taking out the worn, threadbare sheet of lined paper with the last words.

Annalise covered her mouth. Her bright eyes glistened with the threat of tears. "Your father wanted you to learn a language?"

He nodded and swallowed thickly. "He was practical, and he was romantic. He knew I wanted to be with you. He wanted me to have the means to, including the ability to speak the language and get a job. So I could live and work and be in France with you." He rubbed his hand across the back of his neck. "I took classes in college. I used to think I was doing it for him. And maybe in some ways, that was how it started. A way to feel connected to the man who was gone. But I didn't let myself believe that for too long."

"It wasn't for him?" she asked softly.

He shook his head. "No. His note might have been the reason I started, but you were the reason I never stopped. I wanted to be with you."

"I wanted it just as much. You have to know that," she said, her bright green eyes wide open and honest, not shying away.

He glanced at his watch, trying to avoid this deeper dive. "Your car is here in five minutes."

"I know, but this is important."

"So is not missing your flight." He grabbed her suitcase, let the door fall closed behind them, and headed with her to the elevator banks. He pushed the button and then met her curious gaze. God, this was hard. Putting himself out there. He waited for her to go next.

"I knew you were taking classes, but I had no idea you'd become fluent. After we lost touch, why did you keep learning?" she asked as they stepped inside the car.

Ah hell. What did he stand to lose now? She was getting on a plane, leaving again. She might as well know. The elevator doors slid closed, and he fixed her with a serious stare. "Because I never got over you. I never stopped loving you. Even when we fell apart, I wanted to find my way back to you."

There it was.

His heart. Served up. Given to her once again.

Her lips parted. She stepped closer. "I wanted that, too," she said, placing a hand on his chest as the car chugged downward. "Don't you know that?"

But that was the thing. He didn't know. "No. How would I have known? We didn't talk."

"I thought about you all the time. I saved up every cent I earned from my job at a café. My airfare money, I called it. I was setting it all aside to see you again. I had enough for a few trips."

"You did that?" he asked, surprised.

She nodded. "Yes. The year we tried to stay together and then through the rest of university. I wanted the same thing, Michael. I wanted to find a way back to you."

His heart beat faster. Knowing she'd wanted the same thing even then thrilled him. "What happened then?"

"We'd drifted apart, and my sister needed money for her bakery, and I gave it to her. To help her. We weren't together then, and if I wasn't going to use it to see you, I wanted it to go to something that mattered," she said, then returned to her questions, tugging at his shirt collar. "But I want to know more about your secret language skills."

The car cranked its way to the lobby. Closer to good-bye. He'd kept such a tight lid on his emotions since Marseilles, squeezing them in, stuffing them into an airtight box, denying he felt a thing for her. He was tired of it. He was in love with her. He wanted her to know the full scope of his love, how far and deep it went. How it consumed him. Drove him. Carried him through the days and nights. The last time he saw her, he lost her. He might not have had a chance with her then, but he had a chance with her now. He wanted her to know.

The doors opened, and he walked through the lobby and out to the crowded avenue, thick with morning traffic and the din of horns and screech of tires. He peered down the street. Her car wasn't here yet. He turned to her. My God, she was beautiful, and she was here, and he wanted her to know who she was to him.

Everything.

"Please tell me," she implored, her tone both gentle and full of need. It did him in. It unleashed his hidden truths.

"Annalise, I wanted to find my way back to you. I learned French so I could be with you. If I had to be with you in France, I needed to know the language. I wanted to be able to be with you wherever you were."

She nodded, listening. Waiting for him to say more.

He gripped her shoulder. "I know how to say *I love you* and *I've always loved you*, and *I want you*, and *you're the only woman I've ever loved*, and *I don't know how to stop loving you*. I know how to say a million other things like"—he switched to French—"you came back into my life now, and it's the same you, the same girl I fell in love with eighteen years ago, but better. You're strong, and yet more fragile. You're tough, but terribly vulnerable. And I want to take care of you and love you. Because," he said, placing a hand on her cheek, with her red hair blowing in the breeze, framed by the concrete strip of Park Avenue and the morning traffic lurching and cruising behind them.

Her tongue darted out, and she licked her lips, anticipation evident in the set of her jaw, the look in her eyes.

He swallowed, saying the last of his piece. "Because I've been in love with you forever. I've been in love with you for eighteen years. And nearly half of those years, you were married to someone else."

She pressed her teeth into her bottom lip, her shoulders rising and falling.

"And it's driving me insane," he said. "I hold the words inside. But every time I'm with you I want to mark you with the truth of how I feel for you. That I love you, I'm in love with you, and I've never ever stopped."

His admission echoed down the avenue, ringing across the entire city. His confession. His whole entire heart.

Trying desperately to read her reaction, to find out if this was a one-way path again, he searched her face. In her worried eyes, he saw fear and uncertainty. He wanted to kick himself. Perhaps he should have waited. Held back until they were on solid ground, far enough along that he knew she loved him, too.

"Michael," she whispered, and her voice sounded feathery, like it came from another part of her.

Her car pulled up. The driver cut the engine.

"You need to go," he said, tipping his chin toward the black vehicle.

She wrapped a hand around his bicep. It felt too good. He couldn't be tricked by the feel of her. "I want to reciprocate. I want to say the same things back to you. But I can't say that yet. I can't tell you I've been in love with you all through the years and ever since we were young. I can only tell you I feel so much for you now."

His head understood. But his heart wanted all of her, all the time. Even though he knew that was hardly fair.

"Look, I didn't say this for you to reciprocate. I said it to be honest. Because it was eating me up. And I want you to know—I love you, and that's just a fact of my existence." He waved at the car and shot her a rueful look. "And you need to go. And that's a fact of yours."

She placed her fingers on his cheeks and held his face in her hands and kissed him. "I will miss you so much."

That was all for now, and it had to be enough.

Seconds later, he lifted her suitcase into the trunk and walked in the other direction, not looking back.

29

Four months ago

When he heard the siren, Sanders cursed and banged a fist against the steering wheel. With a frustrated motion, he flicked on his blinker and pulled to the shoulder of the highway.

A yawn erupted from his mouth. He was so tired from the drive. So damn exhausted, so many hours spent trying to finish up these last few runs to make the money he needed. Fucking college loans. Goddamn bills. Too many doctor's appointments for his bad back. They all added up to the need for more greenbacks, so he'd taken on more runs like this one. He'd barely slept on this quick trip to California, and he'd just wanted to get home to Vegas sooner after visiting his sister in the Golden State. As he cut the engine, he peered in his rearview mirror to see the cop open the door of his state trooper sedan and walk toward him.

He should have relied on the tried and true tricks for a long drive.

Gum. Coffee. Loud music.

Any or all of those stay-awake aids. Maybe even tried one of those damn apps his sons were always telling him to use to avoid the speed traps. But smartphones were agony, and he'd always followed the speed limit.

Until now.

Because he wanted to get home to sleep in his own bed next to his wife. So he'd gunned the engine.

He lowered the window. Boots crunched over the gravel on the side of the road.

"Afternoon," the officer said, his voice cool, his eyes obscured behind aviator shades. "License and registration, please."

"Hey, there. Sorry about that, sir. I was going a little too fast," Sanders said, opting for patent honesty, hoping it might do the trick.

"Yeah, I'd say," the officer remarked, humorless. The young man studied him from behind his sunglasses, then whipped them off. Sanders felt naked and exposed, and he blinked several times, unsure of why he was under such scrutiny. The trooper scrubbed a hand over his chin as Sanders reached for his wallet in the center console. It slipped from his fingers, and he gripped it more steadily, shaking his head. Damn, he needed to get some sleep.

He fished in his wallet, and handed the cop his ID.

The cop raised his chin. His mouth curved up, and his eyes narrowed as he glanced from the ID to Sanders, then back again.

"Funny thing, Mr. Foxton," the cop began in a drawl. He clucked his tongue and tapped his finger to the ID. "Your eyes don't look so bloodshot in this photo."

He sat bolt upright. "Come again?"

The cop cocked his head. "You been drinking? Smoking, maybe? You look like you might be enjoying some substances."

Sanders's jaw tightened, and he shook his head, fear prickling along his skin. "No, sir." He'd never done that, never would. But when the cop's eyes roamed the car, spotting his bag on the backseat, the man arched an eyebrow. "What have you got in there?"

"Just my stuff."

"What were you up to? Where have you been?"

"Visiting my sister. In California."

"Mind if I have a look?"

"What are you looking for, may I ask?" His voice was etched with worry.

"Whatever you're on," the cop said smugly.

Sanders held up his hands. "I'm not on anything. I swear."

Doubtful eyes stared back at him. "You were swerving in the lanes like you're drunk or high. Your eyes are bloodshot."

"I'm just tired. Been driving a lot. Trying to get home and sleep in my own bed."

"If you're just tired, you won't mind if I have a look around."

Oh shit. His stomach plummeted. "Go ahead," he said, trying to sound like he wasn't terrified.

Five minutes later, the cop gave him a sharp, knowing stare. "You want to start talking about what you're transporting across state lines?"

For more than eighteen years, Sanders had been making these runs. He'd been fucking flawless. He hadn't asked questions. He hadn't wanted to know. He'd simply taken the packages and brought them to the addresses he'd been given.

He'd never been pulled over, never gotten questioned. And now, four months from retirement, he was nabbed.

This was just his luck.

For the first time, he felt the cold grip of fear that the authorities would find out all he'd done.

30

The grocery store. The piano shop. His house.

That was what the private detective had said Luke Carlton's daily life consisted of. The day Michael returned from New York, he shoved aside all thoughts of Annalise.

Narrowing his focus on the investigation, he conducted some recon of his own.

He pulled into the parking lot at Luke's regular grocery store on his usual evening to shop. Maybe it was an act of desperation. But hell, this guy was slippery. And Michael didn't like slippery. He wanted the man to be caught. Put behind bars. Locked the fuck up.

Maybe he could find a clue. The detail that would tip the cards in the favor of justice. He sat in his car and waited, like he was the private eye.

And hell, if this job didn't suck.

But Luke was clockwork, and at six p.m., he walked through the front doors of the store. Michael got out of his car and kept a decent pace behind him, clenching his fists.

How could that man—that Royal Sinner—have such an ordinary, average life?

Luke pushed a cart through the aisles, buying bananas, a whole chicken, some cereal, toilet paper, potato chips, orange juice, and a can of white beans.

Each aisle Luke wandered down, Michael was tempted to confront the fucker. To grab him by the collar of his short-sleeve button-down shirt, slam him against the canned peas, and ask him what the fuck he had done eighteen years ago. How he'd gotten away with it. How he was still getting away with everything, including buying bananas.

Michael hated bananas.

But somewhere between the bathroom supplies and the salty snacks, he slowed his pursuit and tamped down the treacherous ball of anger inside him. Talking to Luke, confronting Luke, spitting on the man's face—none of that would help solve the crime. Those would only serve to mess with the investigation. To tip him off.

Michael turned around, marched to his car, and yanked open the door. Once inside, he dropped his head to the steering wheel and cursed up a blue streak.

When he looked up, Luke was depositing grocery bags in the trunk of his car a few rows over. Shrugging, Michael decided to follow him when he left. Keeping a reasonable distance, he drove behind him for a few miles on a long stretch of road, stopping at traffic lights, never going above the speed limit. Luke turned into a strip mall, and Michael followed, too, watching as the man parked and headed into a piano shop.

The bastard probably needed more "London Bridge is Falling Down" sheet music.

Michael loathed him for that, too.

For his boring fucking life.

Work consumed him. The next few days roared by in a sea of trouble, triage, and shit storms. He'd been called to one of the financial firms that employed them for private security to deal with some threats against the building. Then he and Ryan tackled an issue with one of their banks involving an attempted robbery of an armed vehicle. Bad mojo was going around daily, and Michael was tense, poised for the next shoe to drop. It was like one of those weeks of celebrity deaths, where bad things happen in threes.

The next one would come any second...

And it happened on a Thursday night.

Michael and Ryan were working late at the office when the call came, Michael at his desk, Ryan poring over paperwork on the couch.

Michael answered the office line on speaker. "Michael Sloan here."

"Hey, Mr. Sloan. We had more gang trouble at White Box." It was their on-the-ground guy at the club.

He groaned as Ryan looked up from the contracts.

"What happened?"

"Actually, it all worked out," the man said, and Michael breathed more easily as his guy recounted what went down. "Some dude from the Royal Sinners tried to solicit one of the dancers."

"But that happens all the time at a club," Michael pointed out, as Ryan nodded silently, following along.

"True. But he wasn't just trying to get her to go home with him. He wanted her to be part of a prostitution ring."

"Jesus," Michael said, seething.

"But don't worry. We handled it. Threw the guy out."

"Good," Ryan chimed in.

"Thanks for the heads up. Glad it was all taken care of," Michael said, and when he hung up, he met Ryan's eyes.

They were thinking the same thing.

"We should go there and touch base. Check in," Ryan said.

Michael nodded. White Box was far too important a client.

Fifteen minutes later, they walked into the main doors and quickly found Curtis and Charlie at the sleek, silver bar. Women in next to nothing danced on stage, and scantily clad waitresses delivered highballs and scotches, as low techno music thumped through the club. Patrons lounged on red velvet couches, mostly businessmen, judging by the sheer number of suits and ties. In the far corner, a group of men puffed on expensive cigars in the smoking lounge.

"Everything work out okay?" Ryan asked after saying hello to Curtis and clapping Charlie on the back.

They both nodded, and Charlie stroked his chin. "If I wanted to run an escort service, I'd do that myself," he huffed indignantly. "Obviously, that's not the business I'm in. I can't stand those street thugs trying to recruit the women here." He counted off on his fingers. "My dancers are salaried. They have health insurance. I even have a retirement plan for them. This isn't how I run this place. They aren't ladies of the night."

"Sorry that happened," Michael said.

Charlie waved him off. "No apologies needed. It comes with the territory. But I will be breathing easier at night when the authorities finally break up the gangs. They are making business difficult for many here in town. They draw an element we do not want."

"Trust me, we all want to see the street crime problem lessen," Ryan said sympathetically.

"But your men handled the problem beautifully, with none of my regulars the wiser, and I am grateful for that."

Charlie liked to run a high-class business, and while it *was* a strip club for all intents and purposes, White Box was geared to the more discerning crowd.

"Glad it was handled discreetly and well."

"It was perfect. Exactly what we hired you for," he said and flashed a brief smile before lacing his fingers together. "What do you think we can do as private business owners to combat the gang problem?"

Michael eyed Ryan, and a look passed between them. These guys were speaking their language. They loved having a client who cared so much, who wanted the same things.

They spent the next thirty minutes strategizing, brainstorming, and discussing best practices for private citizens and companies to handle the problem.

When they were through, Curtis glanced at his boss, and Charlie nodded, giving him permission to say what was on his mind.

"This is why we want to do more work with you," Curtis said. "We want you to handle security for our clubs in Phoenix, Dallas, and Miami."

More business sounded good, so Michael took his brother out for a celebratory round of poker and beer. That was a welcome end to a shitty work week.

With so much trouble still on the streets, Michael and his brother decided it made sense for them to start carrying again. They both had concealed weapons permits and knew how to be safe. With crime on the uptick, it was a necessary precaution.

Michael said good-bye to his brother. As Ryan headed home to his bride-to-be, a pang of sadness hit Michael. He was happy for Ryan, and he also couldn't help but want some of that for himself.

With one woman in particular.

As he shut the door to his home with a *thunk*, his phone buzzed. It was Friday morning in France, and there was a note from Annalise lighting up his screen.

31

Annalise ran her finger over the computer screen, tracing the contour of her own body. She'd turned the image of herself on a hotel bed into an arty black-and-white photograph. In this one, Michael had captured a full nude shot, but from the side. Nothing too porny. Sure, he'd taken some of *those* pictures, and she had no interest in gazing at her parts. But this picture? She rather liked it. In it, she looked at the photographer out of the corner of one eye, one knee raised, and her hair spilling down her back.

From her desk by the floor-to-ceiling window in her home, she adjusted the contrast a bit more, then she leaned back in her chair, crossed her arms, and studied the screen.

She gazed at it as if she could find the answers to her heartbreak in a photo. To some it might seem narcissistic, but Annalise comprehended the world from behind a lens.

Her world.

Her heart.

In all its brokenness.

But here in this photo, she felt...whole again. For the first time. So odd that a nude photo, a shot of her turned on beyond any and all reason, would make her feel that way. But it did. Because her body had been a part of the heartbreak, too.

Her body was healing.

Perhaps it was no surprise too that this photo on her screen was next to the shot of him at Caesars. The candid of him by the pool. She hadn't yet decided how she wanted to frame it or crop it. If she would edit it, or leave it untouched.

Keep it raw. Maybe because she felt that way with Michael.

She pushed away from her chair and roamed around her flat. Sex with Julien had been good. They'd had an active sex life, tried many positions, and never went more than a few nights without making love. She'd always been a physical woman, had always longed for that kind of triple connection between heart, mind, and body. She stopped at a bookcase and picked up a photo of Julien taken in one of the covered walkways in Paris. He'd emerged from a store full of maps, a gleeful look in his eyes, like he'd found treasure. She picked up an image of him sipping espresso, coolly staring in the distance, contemplative. Then another of him thumbing through postcards at a sidewalk dealer along the Seine, sweetly complimenting her work in comparison.

He was her handsome, thoughtful, kind, inquisitive love.

Her throat hitched as she considered the picture.

But the lump disappeared as quickly as it came.

No tears threatened her. No pain rattled around in her chest. No ache descended on her body.

Did that mean something? Anything?

An idea seized her, and in minutes her purse was slung on her shoulder, flats were on her feet, and the metro was rattling its way to this very spot from the first photo—one of the passages of Paris.

Soon she walked past the map shop, stopping outside the window to stare at the vast collection of maps of the world. Julien had loved history and geography. That was one of the reasons he'd become a photojournalist. He'd always been drawn to the big world beyond this city. And she'd been lucky to spend time traveling with her explorer man. She ran her finger over a map in the window, tracing a line over Italy, to Turkey, over to Singapore...all the places they'd been...recalling the times they'd had.

She looked at her watch. She was due at her mother's in two hours to help her with dinner and to fix her broken sink. That gave Annalise time to walk past some of the haunts she'd shared with Julien. At the café they loved, she tapped their regular table for good luck. She wandered across their favorite bridge on the Seine, marveling at the gray ribbon of water that snaked through Paris, then along the antique shops and art dealers near the Musee d'Orsay, one of her most beloved spots in the city, and past the sidewalk dealers by the river, peddling postcards.

He'd once joked that she'd set up shop someday, selling her photos there. She smiled faintly at the memory.

Then, when she was done with her tour, she turned her face to the sky, looked heavenward, and said her final good-bye.

"Love, I won't be here always. You need to move on. You're young, and beautiful, and smart, and vibrant."

It was okay to feel again, to want again, to live, and maybe even to love.

And it was okay to let him go.

When she arrived at her mother's, she knocked then let herself in, and walked over to her mother, who was reading a book on her couch, a news station playing softly on her radio. Her mother set down the book and greeted her with a hug and a warm hello. "How was your day, *mon petite papillon*?"

"It was completely necessary," she answered, and her mother raised an eyebrow at her response.

Annalise explained what she meant as she made dinner, then fixed the sink, chatting about the news of the day. Her mother was a newshound, and Annalise had always loved world affairs. Later, Annalise fell asleep on the couch. When she woke up the next morning, she stretched, brushed her teeth, and said good-bye.

Outside, as the sun rose in the Paris sky, she snapped a photo of a coffee éclair in a bakery window. She captioned it: "*Are coffee éclairs on your hell-no list, too? Wait. Don't tell me. I want to discover all the things about you I do not know. Will you let me?*"

———

"And then you will hand me the ring for Ryan," Sophie said to Michael, as she gestured grandly to the waterfalls raining behind them. They were at Mandalay Bay's outdoor terrace, framed by gentle waterfalls that would form the backdrop to Ryan and Sophie's ceremony next month. The walk-through was early, but Sophie had said she wanted to be prepared.

Michael was the best man. Well, one of them. Ryan

had decided to have two best men. Both Colin and Michael would stand with him. John would be the one to give his sister away, but he wasn't here today. Sophie said he'd been called away on police business, and Michael could only hope that was code for "close to cracking the murder investigation." Of course, Michael was well aware that John was a busy detective and had many cases he was working. His father's was one of them, though Michael felt, selfishly, like it was the only one that mattered.

It had been a quiet several days on that front since he'd returned from New York, but his private investigator, Morris, had messaged him the other day to say that he had some leads and hoped to get some solid intel soon.

Soon couldn't come fast enough, especially after Michael's pointless pursuit of Luke several nights ago.

As they finished the quick walk-through of the ceremony, his cell phone buzzed, and Michael's new Pavlovian response kicked in, a dart of lust flaring in him.

His phone had been glued to his side since he'd left New York, but even more so after Annalise's note the other morning. *That note.* It was a window opening and sunshine pouring in, and of course he'd said yes. She hadn't said *I love you*, but in the last few days she'd given him so much of her time and herself, even from an ocean away. She sent him sweet little messages throughout the day, and often included photos, too. She took pictures of her lunch, her coffee, her life in Paris. A flower planter in a second story window of a flat she walked past in the Fifth Arrondissement. A couple lounging on a blanket on the grass by the Eiffel Tower. A shop window with impossibly tall silver mannequins on display. The rain on a cobblestoned street corner. She captioned them all.

In French.

He answered them. In French.

That wasn't all, though. She also gave really good naked Skype strip shows. The best, actually.

Last night, for instance, she'd shown him precisely how a cheektini looked on her succulent ass. She'd modeled no less than a dozen, sliding them on, gliding them off. Yeah, he was okay with how things were. Because at least they had something. He didn't try to define it, or to pressure her for a declaration. Maybe just voicing his own feelings on the street had been enough. He was no longer carrying that hard knot of tension inside him, that secret knowledge that he was a man wildly in love with a woman. His feelings were out in the open, and somehow that made things better, especially after she threw the line back to him with her note. *I want to discover you.*

But as he pulled the phone from his pocket, his thoughts of her vanished. Morris's name flashed across his screen.

"Michael," the man said in a gruff, gravelly tone befitting a PI. "I got something for you."

He straightened and glanced over at Ryan and Sophie, who were wrapped up in each other, laughing, whispering. They probably wouldn't care that he was busy on the phone. He walked away from them and down the aisle that would be covered in peach tulip petals for the wedding.

"Tell me what you've got."

"Meet me in person in thirty minutes. There's a diner off the highway. It's busy enough, but far enough away, too."

Morris gave him the address, and Michael repeated it. When he hung up, he headed to the happy couple and dropped a hand on Sophie's shoulder. "Hey, I need to take off, but I'm all set on the ring and what I need to do."

"What's going on? Client stuff?" Ryan asked. "On a Saturday? Wait. Don't tell me there's more trouble at White—"

Michael cut him off. "Nothing work-related. Just something I need to do."

He didn't want to say anything in front of Sophie. Not that he was worried it would get back to John, but the fewer people that knew about his own investigation, the better chance he had of gaining information. He'd learned that over the years in business.

"Fine, fine. Just take off," Sophie said with a pout, shooing him away. "We were going to invite you to get a bite to eat or coffee, but now we won't."

Ryan laughed and tugged Sophie closer. "He hates coffee."

"Well, he could have had soda," she said. "But now he can't. So toodle-oo."

Michael smiled and pressed his palms together as if in prayer. "Rain check?"

She waved a hand as if wiping away his transgression. "You are forgiven. Oh, wait. Are you going to bring Annalise to the wedding?"

Michael stared at her like she was an oddity. That hadn't even occurred to him. "I don't know. I hadn't thought about it."

"Think about it. It would be so nice."

Michael shifted his attention to Ryan. "I don't believe I've said much about Annalise, and now you're telling Sophie to invite her to the wedding?"

Ryan shrugged. "You don't have to say much. Your constant texting, emailing, and Skyping says it for you.

Oh, that and the fact that you were madly in love with her in high school."

Sophie's eyes lit up. "Tell me everything. I adore romantic tales of love rekindled."

He shook his head. "I seriously need to go."

"Bring her," Sophie called out as Michael turned on his heel.

"It's more than a month away," he shouted back.

"Gives her time to plan."

Michael laughed once more, pretending he had no interest in asking Annalise. But as he headed to the parking garage, he found himself considering it further. If they were really doing this long-distance thing, and it seemed they were, why not bring her to his brother's wedding? They'd already been tossing out options for his first trip to see her in a week or so. Maybe they could plan the next one, too.

For now, though, he shifted gears, calling Mindy and picking her up along the way.

"My fingers are crossed for big news," Michael said as he held open the car door for his friend.

She wrapped her index and middle fingers together. "Me, too."

At the diner, Morris was working his way through a mug of coffee when Michael slid across from him, shaking his hand in greeting. Mindy said hello, too, and sat next to Michael. Fifties music played on the sound system, and waitresses took orders decked out in pink diner uniforms.

"This place has great fries. You should get some," Morris said, sliding a well-worn menu to the two of them before scrubbing a hand across his jaw, complete with day-old stubble.

"Far be it from me to refuse great fries. Want to split a plate, Mindy?"

The blonde nodded. "That I do."

After they ordered, Michael raised his chin. "So, what have we got?"

Morris took a deep breath, dipped a hand into his messenger bag, and pulled out a manila folder. It was so old school, and Michael kind of loved the Phillip Marlowe vibe. The guy just needed a fedora to finish the look.

Taking his time, he flipped open the folder and stabbed his finger against a photograph. It was upside-down, but Michael could tell what it was. He glanced at Mindy then at Morris, then leaned closer to study the picture, his muscles coiled, tension threaded tightly inside him. "The piano shop? The place where he buys sheet music?" he asked in a hushed tone.

Morris nodded.

"Okay. What of it?" Mindy asked.

Morris raised both eyebrows. "I've been casing it. And our target. All day long. All night long. Stuff cops don't have the man hours or resources to do."

"And?"

"There's a lot more that goes on in the back of the store than sheet music."

Michael swallowed. "Like what?" he asked, so fucking eager for information.

"It's where the Royal Sinners fence all their stolen goods. It's their goddamn fucking headquarters. Everything runs through there. Electronics, iPhones, all sorts of stolen shit. As well as guns. They've got themselves a huge illegal gun sales operation they run from this joint." He lowered his voice even more, licked his lips, then made his pronouncement. "Bust the guns, you've got your man."

Time froze...then sped up. Michael's fingertips tingled, and the possibility of justice tore through him. A smile spread across his face, morphing into a thrilled grin. He looked at Mindy, and she beamed, too. They raised their hands, smacked palms, and treated Morris to a cheese-burger and the best fries in Vegas as he shared the rest of the details.

Later, Mindy and Michael went to meet John at a Starbucks.

"This is good stuff," the detective said, his eyes glinting with excitement.

"Is this enough?"

"I can't make any promises, but if I can't at least get him in custody with this, then someone should take away my badge."

Mindy laughed, and John turned his attention to her, as if he were seeing her for the first time. Maybe even checking her out. Well, that was certainly an interesting development, too.

32

Eighteen years ago

Any day now, Thomas would learn if he'd landed the promotion. The increase in salary made him even hungrier for the job, and he was sure he'd nailed the interview with his boss. Paul had seemed impressed, and had asked him a ton of questions about how he'd uncovered the discrepancy, and what they could do to prevent those sort of accounting errors in the future.

"We should have an answer in a few days," Paul said at the end of the interview, then extended a hand and flashed a toothy grin before walking Thomas to the door.

The next day, he entered his last ride in the logbook in the break room. After a hearty swig of his coffee, he set the mug down, closed the binder, and stood up to leave. He was joined by a young guy. He didn't know the fellow's name, but he'd seen him around, operating as sort of a jack-of-all-trades. He had a short Mohawk, a gold earring in his right ear, and he helped out Paul from time to time.

"Hey," Thomas said, with a nod of his chin.

"Hey," the guy replied. He wore a black T-shirt and had arms like iron and height like a basketball player. "Got a minute?"

Thomas stopped in his tracks. "Sure. What do you need?"

The guy scratched his chin and then waved broadly to the break room. "Listen. I get that sometimes things might seem odd around here." He tilted his head to one side. "Was this written down?" Then the other side. "Was this *not* written down? It can be confusing remembering if everything was there, if it wasn't there."

Thomas frowned. "You work closely with Paul?"

The guy nodded, then flashed a smile. "That I do, and listen," he said, clamping his hand on Thomas's arm, "let me give you some advice. Things here are more complicated than they seem. I had to learn it the hard way, but I learned it. You're just better off if you don't let all those details worry you."

"I'm not worried," Thomas said, straightening and shrugging the guy off his arm.

The man clapped him on the back. "Good. Because there is nothing to worry about whatsoever."

"Okay, then. So we're good."

"We are so good. Just remember," the man said, tapping his broad chest, "you have any questions, you ask me. I'm here to help." He lowered his voice. "The key to lasting a long time here, to getting the good gigs, is to know what's important and what's not important. I want to help you get there. Let me help you."

Thomas nodded and said, "Sure," even though he was pretty damn certain he wouldn't be turning to this guy for help. "What did you say your name was?"

"T.J." He repeated it. "T.J."

Thomas rubbed his hand across the back of his neck and said thanks, then headed off to meet Sanders and Donald for their Saturday afternoon poker game at Sanders's house. Once he arrived, he settled in at the table, grabbed a beer, and caught up with his buddies as Donald dealt, focused on the cards.

"How was the interview? Think you'll get it?" Sanders asked.

Thomas shrugged hopefully. "Hope so. I think he was impressed with some of the things I brought up for improvement, as well as how I can apply what I've been learning about in night school." Sanders sat up straighter and raised an eyebrow as Thomas elaborated. "There were some extra trips and missing trips in the logbook. Seemed a problem area to me. But then after the interview some guy made a big deal about how there was nothing to worry about. Whatever that means," he said, doubtful about the whole incident.

"Was he talking about the missing trips?" Sanders asked as he perused his cards.

"He didn't really say, but it sure seemed that way."

"Huh." Sanders scrubbed a hand across his jaw.

Conversation halted as Annalise popped into the kitchen. "Oh hello!" She gave a quick wave to each of her host family's guests—to Donald and to Thomas. "I'm going to get a snack," she said and reached for an apple in the fruit bowl on the counter.

"Hey, Annalise," Thomas said, tipping an imaginary hat. She was leaving in a month or so, heading back to Paris, and he and Michael were concocting a way for them to stay together. "Good seeing you. Michael said you have plans with him later today, right?"

She nodded. "Yes. We're going to the movies."

"Want a ride over when we're done here?"

"I would love that. Thank you."

As she left, Sanders shook his head and smirked.

"What are you laughing at?"

"Those two. So young and in love."

"It's nice to see," Thomas said, then winked. "Does it remind you of Dora and me?"

Donald snorted. "Ha. Not exactly."

It was no secret among his friends that his marriage had run into some trouble.

"I know, right?" Thomas said, shaking his head, half amused, half irritated. "She's been all over me about money. But we're getting by, and I feel good about this promotion. Besides, I told her if she wants money, she should just smother me and collect the life insurance."

Sanders cracked up, and Donald raised his beer. "Let's hope she doesn't take you up on it," he joked.

Thomas laughed. "Yeah, she thought it was funny, too. Besides, everything is fine. I've got plans in place for all the kids, and college, and life. It's all good. She doesn't need to worry. I'll get the promotion, I'll show them what I can bring to the table, and it will all work out fine."

———

Sanders took a long gulp of his beer to cover up the nerves flaring inside him.

He knew about the rides. He knew why they didn't exist in the books. But unlike his buddy, he didn't fucking ask questions at work. He took the cash and did the job. The company had been good to him, plain and simple. No reason to sniff around and ask about things. The less you asked, the better off you did. Head down, nose to the grindstone, mind your own business.

The company offered ample opportunity for making money. Sanders wished he could tell Thomas how to do it. But the man was too good. He wasn't one for bending the rules.

Ever.

As Becky wandered past the kitchen on her way to the garden in the backyard, he caught a glimpse of his wife.

A man had to do what a man had to do. Every man had to take care of his family in his own way.

He met Thomas's eyes and nodded. "Yup. It will all be fine."

———

"How was your day, Mr. Paige?" Annalise asked, as she slid into the front seat next to him an hour later.

"Not too bad. You?" He turned on the engine. She was such a sweet girl, and he was so damn happy that Michael had found her.

"It was good. I'm *good to go* for the history test," she said with a wide smile, using one of the more Americanized phrases she'd learned during her stay. "And did you have a good morning at work? You work hard on a Saturday."

He tapped the dash as he pulled out of the driveway and rolled down the street. "Doing my best. And yes, work was good."

"But there is something you worry about?" she asked, tilting her head. "I was not eavesdropping, but I heard some of your conversation as I walked into the kitchen. I hope you don't mind me asking."

Thomas smiled and shook his head. "Nope. Don't mind at all. I admire your curiosity. You'd make a good journalist someday."

She smiled widely. "Thank you. That's what I hope to do. With my photos."

"You'll do great. And to answer your question," he said as he flipped on the blinker and turned right, "there's just something odd I noticed at work, so I mentioned it."

He shared a few details with her, since she was such a good listener.

"Maybe there is a reason for it all? There has to be. Things don't just disappear," she said. "You are probably onto something. Some connection."

He nodded. "That's what I think, too."

He slowed at a red light near the strip mall. He glanced over and narrowed his eyes briefly, catching the silhouette of a man walking into the nearby piano store. Holy crap. The guy looked like T.J. Big and broad, and toweringly tall. Annalise's eyes followed his. The man turned around before heading inside. Yup, that was T.J.

"Some guy who works with me just went into the piano shop. He gave me a hard time earlier today. I'd never have pegged him as a musician."

She flashed a smile. "People surprise you. They do things we don't expect."

———

As her husband stripped off his button-down shirt, she fiddled with a necklace on her bureau, averting her eyes. Dora could hardly look at him anymore. She didn't want him. She'd had no interest in him since she'd fallen in love with another man.

She hadn't planned to. But Luke had given her so much. He'd given her hope. He'd helped her find a way to make more money, to earn well beyond her meager seamstress wages and Thomas's paychecks. The cash she'd amassed from her side business had helped her make ends meet and then some. Luke understood that. He knew she'd needed more, and he'd helped her find a way to get it. Something Thomas wouldn't do. Ever since that night she'd met Luke at the work party—not Narcotics Anonymous like she'd told her sweet Ryan—he'd understood her deepest needs. To provide for her children. To give them the opportunities she'd never had. So what if she had to bend some rules to make it happen? Break some laws, even?

Luke was wonderful, and sweet, and paid attention to all her needs. She longed to be with him. Ached to have a life with him. She was sure he was her future, especially now. She ran a hand over her stomach, still flat, but not for long.

Could she go through with it? She'd lined up all the players. Luke had helped her find the right men, connecting her with a broker who was flawless in arranging hits.

She knew T.J., had sold to him and his cousin. She knew Stefano well, too, since he was her supplier.

Her stomach churned at the thought, but she pushed those feelings aside, denying them. She was tired, so fucking tired of scraping by for everything. Every last penny. Every goddamn dime. Besides, she wanted to raise her family with Luke. Was that so wrong? How could it be, now that God had put this baby in her belly?

Still, her chest heaved as she placed her necklace in the bottom drawer of her jewelry chest.

"Everything okay?" Thomas asked

She pressed her lips together and nodded. "Just fine."

She ran a hand over her stomach, a fresh wave of nausea kicking in. She gritted her teeth, not wanting to let on. She'd had morning sickness that lasted all day long with her other pregnancies. No surprise she'd have it again with this one. She hadn't slept with her husband in months, so she'd never had any doubt who this baby's daddy was.

This baby was her reason.

She'd gotten in too deep with the drugs, and the gang, and the selling. But now, she had a way out. If she could pull this off—and Luke had assured her that Jerry Stefano was the best—then they had a chance.

Luke had promised he'd leave town with her. They'd escape with the money and go to Arizona, Florida, Texas... anywhere. Start a new life with the man she adored. Be with him, her baby, and all her kids. All five of them under one roof with the man she loved madly.

It was her only choice. It would be worth it, the end result, the freedom.

Thomas walked behind her and placed a hand on her back. "Come to bed. You're so tired these days. Get some rest."

He kissed her hair and she shuddered, wondering again if she could go through with this.

33

"The piano store?"

To say Annalise was surprised was an understatement. More like shocked, but also excited. The latter because Thomas has driven past the piano store with her once, and made a passing comment about a guy from work being an unlikely musician. But she'd never have thought it was the epicenter of the local gang that had ripped Michael's family to pieces.

She gripped the edge of the iron latticework table in her fifth-floor flat and stared at him through the computer screen with wide eyes. "I drove past there. With your father. We drove past it one day."

"Holy shit. What happened? Why?" he asked from the other side of the world. He was in his home, the steel counters of his kitchen framing the video screen.

"You and I went to the movies one Saturday afternoon, but before then your father had come over to play poker with Sanders and Donald. He drove me to your house. Do you remember?"

It was all so clear in her mind. It wasn't as if she had

been lingering on that particular memory for any reason, but now that he mentioned the piano shop, that day splashed to the surface of her thoughts with a particular kind of clarity.

"That's where the Royal Sinners run the operation from," he said in a breathless whisper.

"A piano store. That's so clandestine," she said, as the flutter of the French news station from a television a floor below drifted up through the late fall air. The weather was cool and crisp, and her terrace doors were open. The Eiffel Tower stood proudly a few blocks from here, and if she leaned far enough out the window, she could catch a glimpse of the flickering lights that lit it up at night.

He nodded. "My private detective found out last night. Apparently they run everything from there. Did you learn anything when you drove past it? Did my dad say anything unusual?"

She shook her head. "No. Not all. He simply noticed someone from work heading there. He didn't give a name, but I remember he was big and broad, and incredibly tall."

Michael's eyes narrowed, and he hissed the name. "T.J. Must have been T.J."

She clasped her hand over her mouth, shock coursing through her. She collected herself and said, "That was T.J.? Your father was surprised that he'd gone into the piano store. That was literally all he said about the place. It was a very fast conversation at the traffic light. But before then, we were chatting about work."

Michael gestured for her to tell him more. "About the promotion he was looking for? He always told me he was hoping to impress the guy who ran the company. But nothing came of it. Obviously."

"I overheard him and the others talking about 'extra work trips' at the game. I believe he said someone at work told him to stop asking so many questions. Then when we drove past the store, he said the guy heading into the shop had been giving him a hard time at work, but that was all."

Michael's jaw dropped. "That's got to be the missing link. That must be how it's all connected. If T.J. worked there, too, the Royal Sinners must have been operating somehow at the limo company." He scrubbed a hand over his jaw. "We looked into his employer when the case reopened, and the cops did, too, but nothing came up as a cause for concern. Even the guy who ran the place—he was squeaky clean, and now he's long gone. Retired in Canada. Not a single blip or issue, but hell," he said, stopping to blow out a long stream of air. "That's how they operate. Under the radar."

"Yes. If they run out of a piano store and have been avoiding capture for years, they're smart. But you've figured it out," she said with a smile, because she was so damn proud of him. His work had gotten the investigation that much closer.

Michael paced in front of the screen. "Everything must have been flowing through my dad's company, I bet. Maybe the owner didn't even know, and it was all right under his nose. And that's how my mother met Luke in the first place. At a work party. I found pictures. So Luke must've been running everything—all these illegal operations through the back of the piano shop, but it was actually being funneled through West Limos. The drugs and the guns. And my mother was a part of it, since she was involved in selling drugs. That must be why the investigation was reopened. My mother was behind it all, but there were other people who had no problem offing my dad.

Jesus fucking Christ," he said, dragging a hand through his hair.

Annalise nodded sadly. "He said something about finding some discrepancies at work. Rides or items that were missing. Maybe they were missing because the Sinners were transporting guns or drugs, through the company and perhaps to the piano store."

He snapped his fingers and pointed at her, his eyes lighting up with that *aha* moment. "You know, you're beautiful and brilliant?"

"So are you."

"I need to tell John."

She waved him off. "Go, go. This is important. I'll see you soon," she said, and she was ready. Ready to have him come see her here in Paris, to have him in her home, to share some of her life here with him. She wanted to show him the local bakery, wander through the alleys, through the shops, take him to some of her favorite places in Paris. To make new memories with Michael.

"Nothing could stop me from seeing you."

———

No one was home. Detective John Winston knocked on the door of Luke Carlton's house at a quarter past ten. But the sound of his fist rapping on the wood echoed without an answer.

He turned around, scanning for Luke's car on the street. He hadn't seen it when he'd pulled up, but even so, he looked once more.

Course, the man not being home didn't mean much. He might be at the piano shop. He might be at the grocery store again. It was hard to say.

John leaned to the right, trying to catch a glimpse through the window into the home. It looked just the same as it had when John was here over the summer. He'd interviewed Luke when the case was re-opened. The man claimed to know nothing. He played up the whole fear factor, sticking to his story of being terrified the Royal Sinners would come after him. In truth, they were in his back pocket, and the man probably figured he was still getting away with it. That his long and time-honored practice of hiding behind his fake life and pushing others to take the blame would keep working. Hell, even the handful of gang arrests made recently were for other crimes; none were related to the murder.

And so Luke kept going about his business.

If the man stuck to his schedule, and he sure seemed like the type, that meant John might need to track him down at the piano shop this evening. But as he returned to his car, heading out of the neighborhood, he considered whether arresting the man at that place was the smartest approach.

That would be like walking into...well, into target practice. The shop was the center of their gun trade, and if John wanted to keep this arrest as quiet as he possibly could until he had T.J., too, he needed a different way in.

Food was the path.

———

When evening rolled around, John's partner headed inside the grocery store, strolled around the aisles, and reported back via text.

John nodded to himself with a small sense of satisfaction. Luke Carlton was indeed a man of routine. That routine was his camouflage. It had shielded him for years. His clockwork schedule had made him appear one way to the world, and that masquerade made it possible for him to live a life of crime undetected.

John waited by the automatic doors of the super-market—ready.

Tension coiled in him, but a kind of excitement, too. This was why he did what he did. The chance to clean up the streets. Put the bad guys behind bars.

After his best friend had been paralyzed by a drive-by gang shooting when he was fourteen, John had vowed to always do his part to keep this town safe. Sure, Luke Carlton had done so much more than sell guns. But all John needed was probable cause to take the man in. Thanks to Michael's tip, coupled with the weeks of investigation, John and his men had been able to amass the necessary evidence.

He could taste the possibility of justice in the air.

The doors slid open, and his partner crossed from the tiled floor of the grocery store onto the sidewalk.

Briefly, a small knot of guilt wormed its way through John as he thought of Marcus, the courageous boy who'd helped them start down this path. Marcus and the rest of his family would be safer, though, he reminded himself. The sooner John could dismantle the Royal Sinners, the better off everybody in this town would be.

Sixty seconds later, Luke Carlton neared the exit of the grocery store. It was a little after six on a Tuesday evening. He carried two bags of groceries. He wore jeans and a short-sleeved shirt. His gray hair was freshly combed, as if he'd taken a shower before he ran his errands.

Luke didn't notice the two men in slacks and button-downs loitering outside the local market. He kept walking, his keys in one hand, whistling under his breath. Sounded like Beethoven, something he'd probably taught to a young student recently.

John burned with frustration over the freedom this man had enjoyed for so many years. But it was also Luke's Achilles' heel. He thought he could keep it up indefinitely, living like an average guy.

John stepped away from the brick wall he'd been leaning against and stopped in the path of the head of a dangerous street gang. An average, ordinary guy.

"Pardon me," he said, shifting to the right to avoid John, as if he'd truly just bumped into him. Funny how Luke didn't even look up. If he had, he might have recognized the detective he'd lied to a few months ago.

Fucking mild-mannered piano teacher, my ass. But the guy had pulled it off, living a double life for years. That was about to be blown wide open.

"Good to see you again, Luke Carlton. You're under arrest," John said.

The second the words left John's mouth, Luke dropped his grocery bags and bolted. It was an instant reaction—he took off along the sidewalk of the cavernous store, running like hell.

John went after him, sidestepping the bunch of bananas, the trail of cans, and the chicken that had spilled from the bags. Luke had more speed than John would ever have expected. He ran past a line of shopping carts, grabbing the handle of one and yanking it out onto the sidewalk.

John dodged the cart, and his partner was right behind him as Luke rounded the corner into the back lot to the side of the store. Luke seemed hell-bent on escape, and John completely understood his drive. The man had lived a scot-free life for two decades. That could drive a man to run like hell. But so could the pursuit of justice, so could dogged determination, and so could years of running every morning before the sun even rose.

John had all that in his favor.

Even though the bastard was fast, he wasn't fast enough. No fucking way was John letting Luke Carlton get away from him in the back parking lot of a grocery store.

With his heart pumping, his feet pounding, and his breath coming in fast, powerful spurts, John neared him. Ten feet, five feet away now. John closed the distance across the asphalt, stretched out his arm, grabbed the back of his shirt, and tackled him.

Luke twisted in his arms. "Let me go. You've got the wrong man."

He was like an eel, flinging and swishing and desperately coiling his body. But John wasn't letting go, and as his partner reached them, the cuffs were ready.

John yanked Luke up, pinned both wrists, pushed him against a dumpster, and slapped on the handcuffs.

He breathed out hard. "As I was saying. Good to see you again, Luke Carlton. You're under arrest for illegal gun trafficking." Then he rattled off a litany of violations that this man had committed over the years, from selling guns without background checks, to peddling weapons to convicted felons, to giving firearms to fugitives.

And at last, they took him in.

———

The next morning, John paid a visit to Lee Stefano, to see if he could get that punk to serve up some details on T.J.'s whereabouts. Weeks in jail had worn him down. He wasn't so keen on "protecting their own" anymore, so he named a few spots that T.J. had been known to frequent. An interesting list, to be sure. John had a hunch where they might be able to nab the guy. Bringing in T.J. would require some stealth. The man was already wanted, so John would need the element of surprise on his side, and he knew how to pull it off.

He called Michael Sloan to ask for his help. Michael said yes, then John cleared his throat, shifted gears, and asked him for the number of the cute blonde. He'd had Mindy on his mind since the night he met her.

34

"You want us to set a trap?"

"Yeah. I would really like that," John said, his tone somehow casual but also intensely serious.

Michael's eyes swept from John to the two men he was making this request of. Leaning against the back of a royal blue lounge chair, Curtis scratched his square jaw with his thumb, glancing at Charlie before answering. "So we've got to bring those fuckers back into our business?" he asked, arching an eyebrow skeptically as he waved a hand around the club, quiet now during the day. Jazz music hummed from the same speakers that played dance music after midnight.

John nodded. His arms were crossed. "I know it's not what you want, but if we bring him in, and I've got the warrant for his arrest, we can take the gang apart. He's the last linchpin left, now that we've got their head guy. One of my witnesses has named the places he's been seen."

Curtis shook his head. "This isn't one of them."

"No. But by using the guy who started trouble here a few weeks ago with the knife in the bathroom, we think we can lure him. That guy is willing to invite T.J. here. Make it look like just a regular night out. Once he's here, you make the call and we'll take him in."

Charlie blew out a long stream of air. "I don't like bringing them in here. We've been trying to keep guys like that out. I don't want any guns in my club."

"I hear you loud and clear," John said. "But we're close, so close to blasting them apart. We'll have plainclothes cops here. They will be the only ones with weapons, besides my men and myself. We'll do thorough checks at the door to make sure. And Michael's team will ramp up security. We will keep your business safe."

Charlie hummed and raised his chin at John. "I heard you talk at the benefit a few months ago."

Michael's ears pricked. He hadn't attended that event, but both Ryan and Colin had. It was a fundraiser for the local community center where Colin volunteered. His girl-friend Elle ran it. Colin's company was one of the main donors, and so was White Box. These guys were committed to cleaning up the city, and Michael hoped they'd take this chance, even if it put them at risk.

"You had a friend who was injured when you were younger," Charlie said, meeting John's eyes.

The detective nodded.

"I know what that's like," he said through tight lips. "I lost one of my brothers when I was younger. To street crime, too. That loss changed me. Led me to make some choices I wasn't so proud of. Now, I'm trying to live a better life, in his name. He would have wanted this."

Curtis nodded and patted Charlie's shoulder. "He would have. He really would have."

Charlie turned back to them. "We will help you."

———

The waiting was miserable. Minutes ticked by as if they were hours. The days were elongated, like melting Dali clocks. Michael walked through town as if in a surreal dream. He was glued to his phone, and his phone was stuck to him. Just in case there was news. In case Morris, or Mindy, or John, or Ryan, or Annalise, or his White Box guys called.

Waiting sucked. Waiting was torture. But he understood this was the safest way to bring in T.J. The fucking mastermind of multiple hits had gotten away with so much, but with Luke now behind bars and facing a possible trial, and T.J.'s cousin arrested, and many of his guys on the streets locked up, too, the power structure of the Royal Sinners was cratering. They were caving in on themselves. T.J. was the last man standing, and once he was down, Michael would breathe again.

He was slated to fly to Paris in a few days, and he had half a mind to cancel the trip. But that was silly. He wasn't the guy who'd make the arrest. He was simply the man waiting for justice. Justice would happen, one way or another, he was sure.

He went to the gym late one night, hoping a workout would burn off some of his tension. At the end of his weights session, his phone rang.

———

John was playing pinball when the call came. He'd just sent a silver ball screaming up the board and into the waiting maw of Jabba the Hut at his favorite game in the arcade hall not far from White Box. The phone trilled.

Mindy eyed his back pocket. It was their second date, and the first had gone exceedingly well. "Want me to grab it? So you don't miss a ball?"

He nodded, his eyes focused on the game. Turned out she was a tenacious competitor. Turned out she kissed like she'd never wanted anyone so much before. He felt the same for her, and he sure as hell liked her hand in his back pocket, grabbing his phone.

"You might need to take this," she said, her tone serious.

Immediately, he let go of the buttons, saw his colleague's name flashing across the screen, and answered the call from his guy on site at the club. "He's here."

John wanted to punch the sky. "I'm on my way."

"You want us to arrest him?"

"If I can't get there in time, yes. But I'm five minutes away. Don't let him out of your sight."

Soon he walked through the door of the club, the neon lights bright and beckoning. Once inside, he nodded to Curtis, who watched the joint like a sentry. Curtis tipped his forehead to the cigar lounge.

John sent a silent thanks with his eyes, found his colleagues, and made his way to the lounge, two men behind him. He peered in through the glass window into the small room. A cloud of smoke engulfed three guys, and one of them laughed.

The man was bigger, brawnier, and tougher than the rest of them, and even though John had never laid eyes on him before, he knew T.J. Nelson in seconds. The gold earring. The arms the size of barrels. The missing tooth now capped with a gleaming white one. And the tattoo on his right bicep.

Protect our own.

The last puzzle piece. The last man standing. A sense of calm descended on John, mixed with the thrill of victory. This was why he'd dug into this case. He'd known he could solve it. Known he could find the accomplices. Months ago, as soon as the shooter's ex-girlfriend had come to tip him off that two more men were involved, he'd been determined to hunt them down and put them behind bars. Three, it had turned out, since those two accomplices the night of the murder had operated under the tutelage of Luke Carlton.

Inhaling deeply, John reached for the door handle, turned it, and entered the dark, smoky room. There was no way out. Three pairs of eyes met his, and T.J.'s were the hardest—dark brown, cold, and full of hate.

He didn't say a word, just raised his chin, waiting for John to go first.

"T.J. Nelson?"

"Maybe. Depends who you are," the man said, his voice deep and menacing.

"I'm the man you've been avoiding for eighteen years. But your lucky streak ends tonight," John said, moving quickly, drawing his gun from his holster and aiming it. T.J.'s hands darted behind his jacket, but John was faster, and since the other men had helped to lure him in, he was sure T.J. didn't stand a chance—even when the broker brandished a long, gleaming knife.

His eyes turned to slits, and he raised the weapon. For a second, John's blood went cold. The club had a metal detector for guns, but somehow T.J. had managed to slip this knife through. This was precisely why John had needed to trap the guy, capture him in a corner, some-place his suspect could let down his guard.

This was as far down as John suspected it went—T.J. with a knife instead of one of his precious guns.

"You don't know who you're messing with," T.J. hissed as he lifted the weapon higher.

"But I do. I absolutely do," John said coolly, keeping the gun trained on the man he wanted behind bars.

T.J. tried to stand up from the leather couch, but in a flash, John's partners moved in, quickly overpowering him, each man pinning an arm. One grabbed the knife, and the other cuffed him.

Then, as John tucked his gun away, he said the words he'd wanted to utter for so long. "I have a warrant for your arrest for the murder of Thomas Paige. You have the right to remain silent. Anything you say can and will be used against you in a court of law. You have the right to have an attorney. If you cannot afford an attorney, one will be appointed for you."

T.J.'s eyes widened. The expression on his face was white-cold fear.

Good.

As it should be.

As it absolutely should be.

———

Many glasses of champagne were raised. In the kitchen of his grandparents' house, the very home that Michael and the other Sloan siblings had bought for them a few years ago as their way of saying thanks, Michael lifted a glass. Cleared his throat. Said words he'd longed to utter.

"To justice. At long last," he said.

"Hear. Hear." It was a chorus sounded by everyone.

His grandmother nodded as a tear slipped from an

eye. They clinked glasses, Michael with Brent, Ryan, Sophie, Elle, his grandparents, even Mindy. He tapped his glass to the flute of Diet Coke Colin held, and to the water glass in his pregnant sister's hand. He suspected John would be in attendance at the next event, by Mindy's side, but for now he was still busy, still working, and Michael was glad of that. He hoped that Marcus would come back soon enough to join them. Maybe for Christmas.

"At last," Victoria echoed, and they all drank.

There was something incredibly odd about celebrating an arrest. And yet, it wasn't the least bit bizarre.

Since his world had been wrenched upside-down and shattered eighteen years ago, he'd grown accustomed to the unexpected moments. In a family that had seen a father killed by a mother, that same mother in prison, and a half-brother born behind bars, life became unexpected.

Celebrations could take on the strangest forms, moving well beyond the usual festive occasions of birthdays, anniversaries, and weddings.

Michael knocked back a hearty gulp of champagne and wrapped an arm around his grandmother. She looked up at him and flashed a smile rich with relief.

That was what this feeling was.

The long, overdue exhalation.

It was blissful relief, hard-earned justice, and delicious victory. Nothing would ever change the course their lives had taken that fateful night, but at last, at long fucking last, there was the promise of peace once again. It tasted so good.

Shannon beamed, and Brent rubbed his hand on her belly. Sophie began slicing the cherry pie she'd made for the occasion, as Ryan once again thanked her for the key part she'd played in helping decode the names of the accomplices. Colin wrapped his arms around Elle and kissed her cheek, then whispered something in her ear. She shot him the sweetest smile, and for a moment Michael found himself wondering if Colin would be down on one knee, too, popping the question to the woman he loved.

Love.

There was so much of it here in this house. It was a surplus. They had an embarrassment of riches when it came to love. His brothers and sister. Their husbands, girl-friends, and fiancées. His grandparents. Even the dog had joined in, rubbing his side against Michael's grandmother's leg.

After he'd taken a bite of pie, his phone buzzed. Grabbing it from his back pocket, he felt his heart warm as he found a new photo from his girl.

A shot of her legs. She looked to be sitting at a sidewalk café, and he pictured her perfectly—watching the world go by, observing it all, drinking it in, and thinking of him.

The caption read: *Waiting for you. Not much longer.*

He'd be seeing her in mere days. The past was behind him. The present was free of its weight. The future was in his grasp, on the other side of an ocean, waiting for him. He could have it, taste it, touch it, love it.

Love her, if she'd let him. He hoped, and he hoped, and he hoped that she was ready.

She was the love of his life, and he'd been given a second chance with her.

Perhaps that was part of this newfound peace.

35

A blue and white teapot called out to her. Ceramic, with a line of blue ivy snaking along the top, it was pretty and artsy at the same time. Her hand darted out, carefully avoiding the mass of kitchen items crowding it on a table at a sidewalk vendor. Grabbing the teapot, she held it in front of her, brandishing it for Michael's opinion.

"I need this, don't I?"

They were at the *marché aux puces* at Porte de Vanves, a massive weekend flea market, spread across many blocks.

He gave her an inquisitive stare. "Didn't you buy a teapot yesterday at a fancy shop in the Marais?"

Busted.

"I know," she said with a pout. They'd wandered all over Paris the last few days, seeing museums, stopping at bakeries, popping into shops, strolling along the Seine, and flipping through vintage postcards at the street-side dealers. She stroked the porcelain. "But it is so pretty."

He shook his head, laughing, and squeezed her shoulder. "I would never have pegged you as such a hoarder."

"I just like cute little objects. If you came to my flat,

you'd see. I have all sorts of little trinkets," she said, nudging his side, trying to convince him.

"Someday," he said softly, looking away.

She chose not to press. He hadn't been to her home yet. His trip only lasted four days. He'd booked a hotel room, and she'd spent her nights there and the days traveling across the city with him. She understood why he didn't want to stay at her house. He had been upfront about it.

"I want to make new memories with you," he'd said. "I hope you understand I just can't step foot in the place where you lived with your husband. Not yet."

Her home was rich with history, with the story of her time with another man. She couldn't fault Michael for not being ready to open the green door to her two-bedroom apartment and walk inside. She didn't want him to feel like a second choice, because he never felt that way to her, so they'd stayed away, enjoying a little vacation in a hotel room.

She set down the teapot and took his hand, threading her fingers through his. He glanced down at their joined hands and dropped a kiss to her cheek. She shuddered at the sparks that raced through her, even from a little kiss like that. He was so affectionate, and he loved touching her. Holding her hand. Wrapping an arm around her. Planting kisses on her face. Anywhere and everywhere. She loved walking through Paris with him touching her so possessively, as if he was telling all the world that she belonged to him.

"My father and mother used to take me here when I was younger. To this flea market," she reminisced as they wove through the crowds of shoppers along this stretch of vendors. "They loved to bargain shop. My father would come here to buy tools and skeleton keys and dusty old books. Funny thing is, he never actually used them. We had to donate them all when he passed on."

"Why did he want them?"

"Honestly, I think he loved to haggle."

Michael nodded. "Now that makes sense. I'm quite good at haggling. You should see me do it. It's amazing that Ryan thinks he's the negotiator for our firm, but it's really me. I make sure we get the best deals."

She squeezed his fingers. "Will you haggle for me then? For the teapot?"

He arched an eyebrow, and they stopped, other bargain hunters pushing past them, bumping and nudging in hot pursuit of a deal on corduroy jackets, old costume jewelry, baroque mirrors, and more.

He lowered his mouth to her ear. "Will it turn you on so much that it makes you want to fuck me again?"

She shivered in response. "That's a silly question. I pretty much always want to with you."

"But will you want to even more?" he asked, his voice gritty, dirty. He ran his fingers down her arm. Since it was November, she wore a jacket, but goose bumps still rose on her flesh.

She stood on tiptoe and leaned in close to him. "I'm already turned on from the question."

"Let's get your teapot," he said, turning around.

Suddenly, the flea market had become foreplay.

They returned to her teapot seller. *"Combien ça coûte?" How much?*

"Cinquante euros," the man barked back. A cigarette dangled between his yellowed teeth. *Fifty euros.*

Michael shook his head, offering twenty. *"Vingt."*

The man scoffed. Waved his arm dismissively. Flubbed his lips. *"Quarante. Pas moins!"* Forty. No less.

Michael huffed. *"Ça ne les vaut pas." That's not worth it.*

The vendor sneered, growled, crossed his arms. Michael rounded on his heel, and Annalise's eyes widened. He was walking away.

"Revenez," the man called out. *Come back.*

Michael turned and waited. The man wrapped up the teapot, and handed it over in a flimsy white plastic bag. His annoyance was part of the game. Michael handed him the bills. *"Merci."*

As they strolled away, he whispered to her, "Did it work?"

"Hot and bothered."

"Let's see how much."

She tipped her head to a café across the street, the words *Bouledogue* painted across the front in red letters, alongside an illustration of a canine of the same breed. Once inside, they took the staircase to the basement where restaurant bathrooms were usually located. Michael rapped on the door. Empty.

He tugged her inside, locked the door, and hung the plastic bag with the teapot from a hook.

He thumbed the hem of her skirt. "I love that you wear skirts with me now."

"I've learned my lesson."

Wrapping an arm around her, he tilted up her chin so she looked at him. His eyes searched hers, full of so much passion that she heated up all over, her skin tingling. He pushed a strand of hair away from her face and kissed a path along her jawline. Her legs turned to jelly. Her knees went weak, and heat pooled between her legs, dampening her panties. One kiss, one touch, and she was ready.

He ran a hand along the inside of her thigh, and she quivered, melting into him. He gripped her waist and backed her up so she was pressed to the door. Cupping her jaw in his hand, he gazed into her eyes. Her mouth fell open, and the entirety of the universe narrowed to the way he stared at her, drawing out the anticipation. To his beautiful face. To his words as he said, "Now, let me fuck you, my love."

Her eyes floated closed, and she lingered in the rapturous bliss of his way with her. His need for her was so intense it nearly scared her. Except it didn't, because she knew precisely how he felt. The same need drove her. Made her want to smash into him, grind her body against his, bring him close and then closer still. Want thrummed between them, radioactive in its intensity. Her hands worked open his jeans, unzipping them, freeing his cock. The aching desire to be filled by him spread to every bone, every nerve, every cell. She ran her hand along his hard length, thrilling at the feel—the skin so damn soft, while he was so incredibly hard.

Then his hands grabbed her ass, and she let go of him. In seconds he'd lifted her, wrapped her legs around his waist, and tugged her panties to the side.

"Michael, do I have to be quiet?"

He shook his head as he rubbed his cock against her wetness, sending an electrical charge through her. "I don't care who knows that you're in heaven when I fuck you." He eased inside her, and that current surged, igniting her, crackling through her being. Her head fell back and she moaned. Loudly.

Heaven.

That was precisely what this was. Sex with Michael was a faraway land of ecstasy, of endless fiery pleasure.

"It's so good, there's no way I can be quiet," she murmured.

"Then moan. Cry. Scream. It doesn't matter to me. Fucking you is something only I get to do, and I don't care who knows how completely consumed you are."

"I am. I am consumed."

His fingers dug into her ass as he thrust. Deeper. Harder. Farther.

He pumped, swiveling his hips, pushing, his cock moving in sharp jabs that sent ripples of desire everywhere. Each one was more powerful than the last. He dipped his face to her neck, whispering her name as he fucked her. Whispering kisses across her skin that made her shiver. That made her burn. "You knew it would be like this with us, right?"

She nodded on a breathless pant as he stroked inside her. "Yes, God yes. I knew."

"You knew I would need to take you like this." He growled as his shaft rubbed against her clit, hitting her just right.

"Anywhere. Everywhere," she said.

His breath came fast, ragged against her skin. "I can't hold back from wanting you like this. From fucking you against doors. From making you come."

His hips moved in relentless thrusts; her back slammed against the wood. Her body sought more of him, chasing the release. "Michael," she groaned. "I need to come so badly."

"Come on me, my love. All over me," he said, and she knew from his pace, from the low timbre of his voice that his climax was imminent, too. She knew also from this deep, exquisite ache in her body, and most of all from the mad fury in her heart, that he was fucking her into falling.

That his words and his deeds and his care and his love made it impossible not to fall for him again.

With his dirty voice in her ear, alternating between sweet nothings like *you're so fucking beautiful,* and harsh growls of *get there, fucking come for me*, she broke. Her orgasm crashed over her, swept through her, stole her senses.

She cried out.

He grunted, with a deep, powerful thrust. His orgasm followed hers, their bodies shuddering, their hearts beating fast. A minute later he lowered her, holding her waist, letting her find her land legs again.

When she did, she cupped his cheeks and looked deeply in his eyes. "I'm falling."

He sighed happily, as if she'd taken the weight of the world off his shoulders. His eyes shimmered with something that looked like joy. "Then I'll catch you."

She pressed her face to his jawline, rubbing her cheek against his stubble, terrified and elated at the same damn time.

Terrified that now that she loved again, she could lose again, and that her heart couldn't be put back together a second time.

―――――

They crossed the Seine on the walk to his hotel, stopping to gaze at the slate-gray river and the city unfolding on each side. Fog drifted over the water, curling like smoke as night fell on Paris. Streetlamps cast their halo glow on the sidewalks. He'd only been to Paris once before, for a brief stay during his overseas service. That was a functional trip.

This was a dream come true.

Especially when Annalise tilted her face to look at him, a sweet smile on her red lips. "How are we going to do this, Michael?"

He brushed a thumb across her cheek. Not touching her was impossible. "Like we've been doing," he said, since he wasn't going to let time zones be an issue.

"Does the distance scare you?"

He shook his head. "Nothing scares me now that you're back in my life," he said, though that wasn't entirely true. He was afraid of something. He was terribly fearful that she'd never love him like she'd loved her husband. That was why he wouldn't go to her home. He was afraid she only had so much to give, and that he would get the crumbs of her broken heart and always long for more of her.

"I don't want us to fall apart. I don't want us to lose touch," she said, gripping his shirt. "I want a chance with you. A real chance."

His fears evaporated into the night. Her words were a blanket wrapped around him. "We'll make this work. You'll come see me, I'll come see you, and we'll meet in the middle."

She grinned, her bright smile lighting up her emerald eyes. "We will meet in the middle," she repeated.

They resumed their pace. As they neared his hotel, she stopped and pointed. "That's my favorite passage. I just want to grab a coffee," she said, and they headed into the covered shopping arcade, still open in the evening. They strolled past a map shop, and he glanced in the window. "Cool maps," he remarked.

"We used to love that store," she said casually, then cut her words off like they'd been sliced.

We.

He winced. The reminder that she'd been a "we." That she was still, somehow, part of that we.

"I'm sorry."

"Don't be," he said, trying to let it go.

"I didn't mean anything by it."

That was the thing. She probably didn't. It was simply her baseline, her norm, her *we*.

And it was his hurdle. His Achilles' heel. His wish that they could be her *we*.

36

A glass display case stacked with chocolate tartes, rasp-berry cakes, and flaky croissants beckoned to him. Across from the hotel, the Roussillon bakery had long lines, but boasted the arrondissement's speediest bakers, or so Annalise had told him. "The line moves quickly."

"Good. Because I'm hungry. You keep me working hard all night long," he said with a wink.

She nudged him. "And you love my workouts."

"I do. And right now, I'd love breakfast," he said, his mouth watering as he surveyed the shelves of baked goods, from baguettes and rolls, to éclairs and strawberry pastries.

When they reached the cashier, Annalise ordered a baguette and a coffee éclair. The woman stuffed a loaf into a white paper bag, then wrapped an éclair in paper and twisted the ends.

"Pour vous?" she asked him.

In painful, deliberately prolonged, Americanized French, he said, *"Je voudrais un abricot tarte."*

Annalise rolled her eyes at his bastardized pronunciation, especially how he made tarte sound precisely like the French word for yogurt. On purpose. The woman behind the counter bent down, reached into the register case, and grabbed a small jar of yogurt. She thrust it at him.

"Wait, wait. I would also like an apricot tarte," he said, in his best French. He was rewarded with a grin and the treat.

Outside, they parked themselves at a small wooden table.

"Now the test. You hate coffee, but do you like coffee éclairs?"

"Let's find out."

As a cool breeze blew by, and a hint of gray swelled the sky, she slid the éclair to him. He bit into it, savoring the sweetness. He hummed around the flaky pastry, and wiggled his eyebrows.

"So that's a yes?"

He nodded. "Big yes. You keeping a list of my favorite things?"

"Perhaps I am," she said, and his heart thumped harder, simply because she'd truly wanted to know. She'd followed through. She was curious about his everyday wishes and wants.

They traded bites of the tarte, shared the yogurt, and pulled off chunks of bread as Parisians strolled by on a Sunday morning. Soon the sky darkened, and raindrops splashed across the cobbled sidewalk.

They tossed the remnants of their late breakfast into a trash can, and he offered her a hand. "You know what's good to do in the rain?"

"I do," she said, cupping his cheeks and kissing him as the world around them turned gray and wet and cool.

He moved his lips to her ear. "You smell like falling rain."

"Do you like it?"

"I love it," he said, lacing his fingers through her hair and inhaling her, so glad he didn't have to rely on a letter to get his fix.

She pulled back to look at him as if she was searching his face, studying his eyes, uncovering new truths about him, and maybe herself, too. "I think this is more than falling."

His heart beat faster, soaring to the sky, and he could hardly believe that life could be so good, so sweet. It was even better when they returned to his room and spent the next few hours in bed, taking their time, discovering even more, falling even deeper.

———

A small fire blazed in a fireplace, warming the centuries-old building that housed the tiny restaurant not far from the Eiffel Tower. Framed artwork of eggs, asparagus, and tomatoes lined one white wall. Another wall was red brick. White cloths draped the tables.

It was Michael's last night here, and already she missed him. The empty ache had started before he even left. She wanted him here. Wanted him to stay. She'd loved every moment with him.

Right now she simply loved watching him talk to Patrick, Noelle's husband. With the dinner plates cleared away, and the dessert served, they were discussing French politics and world affairs. Admittedly, it was kind of sexy to hear him so deep in conversation, a glass of red wine in his hand, his blue button-down shirt revealing a small patch of skin at his throat that she wanted to kiss.

Her lips longed to press against his chest. Her fingers itched to undress him. Her heart ached to have him close.

Especially since he fit so well with her family.

She understood even better why he'd learned French— to be able to talk like this, to be a part of her life. It was such a heady thing, such a romantic endeavor. She'd marveled at what he'd done, and now she witnessed it. This meal with her sister, her mother, and Patrick was one of the first times she'd heard him speak her language for this long. He was flawless, and kind of crazy sexy with his American accent. He didn't have the sloppy pronunciation of those who'd grown up knowing French. Every word was articulated.

He'd talked to her mother, too, during the meal, catching up first on some of her favorite French news from the radio she loved, and then she'd plied him with questions about Las Vegas. Was the Strip larger than life? *Yes.* Were the hotels as big as they seemed? *Absolutely.* Was the city full of sin? He'd answered yes to that one, too, a sad smile on his face.

She was amazed how much he loved his home, in spite of all the pain he'd gone through there. But that was behind him now that the last man had been taken in. They hadn't spent much time diving into details of the final arrest. Michael seemed to want to move on, and she couldn't fault him for not lingering on the specifics. Perhaps that was part of why he appeared so carefree again, so much the man she'd known when she was younger, yet so much this new man, too. Strong, protective, and yet vulnerable. She'd never known someone to put his heart on the line the way Michael had for her.

"He's a good man."

Annalise turned to meet her mother's light green eyes. Her voice was soft, a whisper just for her.

She nodded. "He is."

Her mother's hand, wrinkled from years, pressed to her forearm. "I'm glad you're letting yourself be happy."

"Me, too."

Knowing eyes stared back at her. "Have you told him how you feel?"

"Sure. He knows how I feel," she said.

Her mother squeezed her arm. "No. Have you told him you're in love with him, too?"

She froze, with the glass of wine on the way to her lips. She was falling, yes. But in love? It couldn't happen that fast. Not for her. Not when love was such a dangerous thing? Not when being in love meant she could be cleaved in two again?

"You should tell him," her mother urged.

Annalise parted her lips, but words didn't come. She wasn't sure what to say, or if she could even give voice to all these questions stirring inside her. Was she ready to go into the fire once more?

"Tell him soon," her mother whispered, then she pressed a kiss to Annalise's cheek before continuing. "There are only two men you've ever brought to meet me. Julien and Michael. He loves you so. And I know it's not a one-way street. I see the way you look at him. I see how you lean close to him. How your world seems to be his world."

A lump rose in her throat. Her eyes welled with tears, but none fell.

After the check came and Michael insisted on paying,

Annalise's mother announced loudly that Patrick and Noelle would walk her home.

Noelle nodded vigorously. "Yes. We'll help her up the steps."

"Go," her mother said, shooing them along. "Your home is around the corner."

They said their good-byes, and Michael and Annalise turned the other direction. "They seem to want us to go to my house," she said, floating the idea.

He tensed.

"Would you want to?"

"I'm not sure."

She stopped on the street, reached for his hand, then looked him in the eyes. "We're doing this, right?"

"Of course we are."

"I want you to see where I live. You're not just some man I'm slinking away to a hotel room to be with. You've had dinner with my family. I want you in my home. You're part of my heart. Part of my life."

He pressed his forehead to hers. His breath ghosted across her skin. His arms looped around her. With him, she felt so much potential, so much possibility, so much future.

She took him to her home.

———

I can handle this.

As he walked up the curving, carpeted staircase, his palm running along the dark oak banister, he steeled himself.

He'd run military intelligence. He'd negotiated with some of the toughest motherfuckers in the security business. He'd helped his sister through tragedy. He'd survived the splintering of his family, making sure his younger siblings were cared for.

He could walk into the home Annalise had lived in with her husband. No problem whatsoever.

Inhaling quietly, he let the air fill his chest, imagined it transporting strength throughout his body—even though each step was leaden, each footfall heavier than the last.

Get your shit together, Sloan. Man up

Annalise unlocked the green door. It creaked open, and pride shimmered in her eyes. Her irises danced as she held out her arm and led him through the narrow foyer into the small kitchen.

"My home," she said, beaming.

He catalogued the room. Red espresso cups. Sky blue dishes in the dish rack, and a clean sink.

Piece of cake. This was so manageable.

They wandered into a tiny living room, and before he could look around, she gestured to French doors that opened into a small den.

"This is my office," she said proudly, and showed him some of the framed photos on the wall, shots she'd taken over the years. There were a few images from the Middle East that had won her awards, but mostly the photos were of simpler things.

A lemon yellow dresser.

A crowded street-side café.

A leaf blowing across the sidewalk. Even a few of her black and white boudoir shots.

"You really are talented," he said, and his voice was calm, steady. This was easier than he'd thought. He didn't know why he'd been such a wreck about seeing her home.

Until he spun around and drank in her living room for the first time.

Her husband was all he saw. A framed photo on her built-in bookcase of him holding a handful of maps under his arm. Wincing, Michael connected the dots. In the picture, Julien stood outside the map shop they'd passed last night.

Another image showed him drinking coffee, looking studious. Another everyday moment.

Michael's eyes roamed to the low table that held a frame of her husband riffling through postcards at a sidewalk dealer. Cringing, Michael realized he'd walked along the Seine with her yesterday, maybe even past that dealer.

Her hand ran up his arm. It was warm and comforting, but right now he didn't want it.

His reaction was emotional, not rational. It was passionate, not thoughtful. He could have devised a million logical explanations to settle his brain and cool his nerves. Instead, raw emotions pricked at him.

"There's nothing I can do with you that you haven't done," he bit out.

"Don't say that," she said gently.

He gestured broadly. "He's everywhere. His imprint is everywhere," he said, and he felt like an ass. He turned around, his eyes narrowed. "And I feel like a complete fucking schmuck for saying that and feeling that."

"You're not," she said, shaking her head, her voice soft. "But your imprint is everywhere too. I have an entire photo album of our year together in Las Vegas. I've held on to it. I took it to university. I even looked at it the other day before you came here, along with the photos I took of you at Caesars. One of those photos is on my desktop right now as I decide how I want to frame it or crop it."

He dragged a hand through his hair, and for the first time wondered if Julien had felt this way too. If he'd been crazed enough to want to have this woman all to himself, to erase her history, and mark her only with him. Michael would have wholly understood. Because this intense need to be her *only*, as selfish and single-minded as it was, gnawed at him.

"Doesn't that matter to you?" she asked, frustration in her rising voice. "Knowing how much you mattered to me? I carried you with me in the only way I could. But Michael, this is unfair. This is where I have lived for the last several years. Do you want me to pretend I didn't have a life when we were apart? Should I have hidden all the photos? Tucked them away in a drawer and whitewashed my home?" She tapped her chest. "This is me. This is who I am. I've been married, and I don't want to have to apologize for it over and over."

Ah hell. He was a complete fucking jerk for feeling this way. He lowered his gaze to the cranberry red carpet with geometric patterns, poised to grovel, embarrassed at his ragged jealousy. But then a thought crashed unbidden into his mind, and he couldn't help but wonder if Julien had fucked her on this carpet. A wave of self-loathing slammed into him. He was envious of a dead man. He was eaten up by the fact that she'd had a husband. Who. Had. Died.

Michael was alive.

What the fuck was wrong with him?

"I'm sorry," he muttered, though he knew that wasn't enough.

She placed a hand on his arm. "Just because I cared for him, doesn't mean I can't feel for you. You seem to forget that I was in love with you before I met him, and yet

I was still able to love him and be happy. So I wish you would stop thinking I'm incapable of this. That I can't feel so much for you. It's not fair."

Perhaps she was right. Perhaps he was too stubborn. Too narrow. But this woman – she was it for him. She was *all* for him. And that feeling inside him, of never wanting to be without her, made him rash.

"Do you still love him?" His throat was raw as he gave voice to his darkest fear.

"Michael," she said, "a part of me always will. But I'm falling in love with you now."

He swallowed, collecting himself. He drew a deep breath, trying to let it out while taking in what she'd just said. But his chest churned with black and white and gray emotions, and he didn't know how to wrestle them to the ground and have them make sense. Instead, he spoke carefully. "Your home is beautiful. But I can't be here."

"But this is where I live. I want to show it to you," she said, imploring.

He shut his eyes. "I know. But I need to go. And I would like to spend the night with you elsewhere."

At the hotel he made love to her deep into the evening, letting the sex blot out the blackness in his heart, the ugly jealousy in his soul. For so long he'd been defined by loving her. It was who he was. He didn't know how to take only half of her heart when she had all of his completely.

He didn't want to be her second best, and yet he felt like the runner-up. The whole truth of his love for her boiled down to this—she could have chosen him in Marseilles, and she didn't.

Maybe it was unfair to feel that way, but it was true. He'd put his heart on the line then, and if she'd wanted him, she could have called off the engagement and they could have run away together.

That was what gnawed at him.

And he wished that he could go home and ask his father's advice.

37

She supposed she could have put the photos away. She could have hidden them, tucked them into a cabinet, pretended they didn't exist.

But what would have been the point of that?

As she raced down the metro a few days later on the way to a photo shoot at a client's Montmartre flat, a poster in the station caught her eye. It was part of the new campaign to stop metro riders from talking on the subway —a chicken dressed as a businessman clucked on the phone while the other riders stared daggers at him. She felt a kinship with the other riders in the picture. Not over secondhand cell phone conversations, but because she was annoyed, too.

She was fucking annoyed, as her train rattled into the station and she stepped through the doors. She was frustrated as she gripped the pole, and the subway rumbled away. She didn't want to constantly justify her past to Michael. He'd have to accept it at some point if they were truly going to be together and pull off this transcontinental relationship. Wasn't it hard enough to manage a long-distance love without this added layer of...bullshit?

She huffed and stared off, searching the faces of the other people in the car, wondering if the woman clutching six shopping bags on her lap was irritated too, if the teenage girl with her earbuds and the skinny jeans was ticked at the world like her. If everyone on this train was as goddamn frustrated as she was.

Michael had tried to be cool about Julien after they'd left her home. But she wasn't a fool. She'd read his emotions and sensed his distance back at the hotel. He'd pulled away from her that last night, and everything since then had been bittersweet.

She wanted the sweet, hold the bitter, please.

And she didn't want to make apologies for having loved before.

She reached her destination, climbing the many stairs out of the station, and walked along the curving, hilly streets to find her client's home. All the while, she forced Michael out of her brain. There was no room for annoyance now.

She raised the iron knocker at the door of her client's house, and was greeted by a stunning forty-something woman with black hair.

"Come in, come in," the woman said in a smoky, sexy voice, excitement in her tone. "I've been counting down the hours until the shoot."

As Annalise captured images of the boudoir session, the woman told her that she'd been divorced and was remarrying. The photos were a gift for her soon-to-be-husband. In the images, she appeared both sultry and joyful. This woman had moved on. Hell, Michael had managed to press on after losing his father and, for all intents and purposes, his mother. He still loved his father, though. So why the hell was Annalise being judged for having a special place in her heart for Julien?

After she said good-bye, she held steadfast to the notion that she was no different than anyone else who'd loved before. My God, she'd been in love with Michael before she even met Julien. At some point, Michael would have to accept that she'd been in love with someone else before she fell for him a second time. End of story.

If he couldn't deal, she'd have to walk away. The thought churned her stomach, though. She was moving on. Why couldn't he let her?

Anger stormed through her as she rode the metro. She stopped at her mother's, helping her to a doctor's appointment.

"She's doing better," the doctor said. "Her hip is stronger."

Her mother nudged her and winked. "See? I'm tough."

"You are," Annalise said, the first real smile appearing on her face today.

"You come from a long line of tough women," her mother said after they left the appointment and headed to a café, Annalise's elbow hooked around her mom's arm, their strides slow.

"I do," she said as they found a table on the sidewalk and ordered coffees.

"What's wrong then? Why do you seem so upset?"

"You're too observant for your own good."

"That's where you get it from." Her mom tapped the edge of her eye. "So tell me..."

Annalise watched the crowds *click-clack* by on the sidewalk, the cool, crisp air surrounding them. She gave her mother the gist of how Michael seemed unable to deal with her past. The coffee arrived, and they both lifted their cups, lost in thought.

Her mother took a drink then set it down on the saucer, her lips curving in a knowing grin. "I knew you loved him."

Annalise knit her brow, shooting her mother a curious look.

"What did he say when you told him you loved him?" her mother asked.

"I didn't say that. I said I was falling."

"Ah," her mother said, nodding sagely. "Therein lies the problem."

"How is that a problem?"

Her mother locked her fingers together, forming a bridge. "Falling in love and being in love are bedfellows, but they aren't the same. We often think they are, but they're truly not. *Falling* is just a way to float the idea, like a test of *I love you*. If you love him, you should tell him. Reassure him. He loves you so. Michael wears his heart on his sleeve for you, and a man needs to know he's special. He knows he's not the only one you've loved, but he wants to feel like he is." She unlaced her fingers and stared at Annalise, her eyes holding her captive, softly demanding. "Does he feel like he is? The only one?"

Her gut twisted. He was the only one for her now, but perhaps she hadn't exactly made that clear. "I really don't know."

Her mother patted her hand. "Make sure he knows."

That night, she wrote to him. She wasn't entirely convinced she wanted to say those three words in a letter, but there were other things to say. Things that were as important.

The truth of all her fears.

When she was through, she dropped it in FedEx. He would receive it in two days.

38

Sometimes when you drive to a familiar home, you're not even sure how you got there. You stop at the lights when they're red, turn on the blinker when you take a left, and suddenly you're there, though you can't recall the drive. You know the route by heart. You've done it so many times it's a part of you.

As Michael walked across the grass with his sister, his feet guided him in that same fashion along the path they'd traveled many times—a winding stone walkway, over spongy grass, then through a row of headstones, guarded by oaks and elms.

Shannon clutched a bouquet of sunflowers.

She came here often, leaving these flowers on their father's grave each time. Today, he accompanied her. It wasn't the anniversary of their father's death, nor was it his birthday. It was just an average day, and that was why they came. To remember those who were gone. Both their father, and the baby Shannon had lost ten years ago.

"You hanging in there?" he asked, eyeing her belly.

She nodded. "I wish I could speed up time, though.

Fast forward four more months and have the baby in my arms, to know he or she is safe and healthy, and alive."

He draped an arm around her shoulder. "Yeah, me too," he said, rather than giving her a platitude. *Everything will be all right.* He hoped it would, but both he and his sister had seen enough to know those sorts of statements were pointless.

The morning sun rose in the sky, and soon they reached their father's resting place. Michael read the engraved words out loud, as he always did when he came here with Shan. *Thomas Darren Paige. Loving father.*

"He was," his sister said.

"He was."

Shannon set the flowers at the base of the headstone, then kissed the granite. Michael's throat hitched, watching his sister. He kneeled down briefly and wrapped his arms around her, holding her close as tears streamed down her cheeks. She'd always been emotional; she was even more so these days while pregnant. Michael couldn't fault her for it, either.

Soon she rose, wiped her hands across her cheeks, and plastered on a smile. "I'm all better now."

He smiled back and tucked her hair behind her ear. "Course you are, Shannon bean."

"So tell me about Paris..."

"Ah...the elephant in the room."

But he found he needed to talk about this black hole in his heart, and Shan was precisely the person who'd understand best. As they stood by the grave, arms crossed over chests, a cool fall breeze rustling the leaves, he shared the fears that had bubbled to the surface the last night in Paris.

"And I think I might be a total asshole who has no

perspective, since I'm jealous of a dead guy," he said, with a forced laugh as he finished the story.

She rubbed his arm reassuringly. "No, you're not. You're just in love, and it's hard, but I don't know why you're so worried she can never love anyone but her husband."

"How is it even possible for her to love like that?" He gripped his chest, as if grabbing at his heart. "I'm so fucking crazy for her I can't imagine ever feeling this way about anyone else. How can she do it? She is the great love of my life. How will I ever be anything to her that comes close?"

Shannon parked her hands on his shoulders. She was tiny, and he towered over her small frame, but in that moment, she was the strong one. "You are my big brother who I have always looked up to, leaned on, and relied on. You've been like a watchdog, looking out for all of us. But you've forgotten to take care of yourself."

He rolled his eyes. "Fine," he said, not denying it. "But what does that mean?"

"You've got it wrong, Michael. Because you understand love on this powerful, intense level. That's your strength, but it's also your weakness. To you, love is an all-or-nothing proposition." She moved her hand back and forth like a pendulum. "You love Dad; you don't love Mom."

He scoffed. "Of course I don't love her. How could I?"

She sighed and squeezed his arm. "All I'm saying is you feel everything in your bones, in your marrow. And it's not conceivable to you that love can be more than one person, more than one thing. Like how you felt about Brent and how angry you were with him."

Michael flashed back to his reaction when Shannon told him she was together again with Brent. He hadn't been happy, and he'd told Brent as much. But he'd soft-ened eventually. He'd welcomed Brent into the family because of the man's deep love for his sister. "But we're good now. Brent and I get along."

"And I am so, so glad. But my point is this—right now with Annalise, you're stuck in All-or-Nothing Michael Land. You're the Michael who hated Brent and only saw him one way."

"And what way am I seeing things?"

"You think it's either you or Julien. But the fact that Annalise loved her husband is actually a damn fine thing," Shannon said, staring pointedly at him. "It says something about her character that she never strayed from him, and had the strength to turn away from you and give him all she had during their marriage. But you've somehow twisted that positive into proof that her heart is finished, and she can't possibly care for you."

"Fine," he grumbled, flashing back to what she'd told him about the photos of him. The album of their days together long ago, and the new pictures too. And while Annalise had shared so many moments with her husband, she'd shared so much with him too. Michael had been her first love, her first kiss, the first person to make her soar in pleasure. "Maybe I have. But still..."

She raised a finger, stopping him. "You have, and what I hope you can start to see is that it's possible to love two people deeply, madly, and truly."

He narrowed his eyes. "How? How can you say that?"

Her next words came out in a soft breath. "I love two people deeply."

He arched an eyebrow in question. As far as he knew, Brent was it for her—her one and only. Her first love and her last love, and she hadn't fallen for anyone in between. "Who?"

"Brent," she said, raising her chin, saying his name matter-of-factly. "I loved Brent in college for who he was then—a goofball, a funny guy, my sunshine hero. He's the same man, and yet he's also completely different. And I fell in love with the man he is now. A strong man, the guy who makes me laugh, a soon-to-be great father, my biggest supporter. The one."

"But he's the same man," Michael said, trying to make sense of his sister's strange theory.

She nodded. "I know. Of course he's still the same person, and yet...he's also not. He's different now than he was the first time we were together, and I loved him then, and I also fell in love with him again. With the man he is today," she said, stopping for a beat.

In her silence, a bird chirped in a tree, and somewhere on the other side of the cemetery, footsteps crunched on stone, and he spotted others visiting headstones, too. These moments surrounding him—of life and death and love and memory—tugged at everything inside him, yanking on all his heartstrings. "Okay, so maybe that's similar to how I feel for her."

"And how *she* feels for you," Shannon added. "But you have to rethink your all-or-nothing view of her. Because she's falling in love with you now, too." She poked him in the chest for emphasis. "She loved you then, and she loves you now, and you're fixated on what came in between. You need to let it go, because it's foolish to think there's only one great love."

"There is for me," he protested, but it was fainter this time, and his words seemed to hold less weight than they had before. Was she right? Was he proving his own theory wrong by falling in love with her all over again, but with the woman she was today?

"The girl she was at sixteen and the woman she is today are the same, but they're different." She ran a hand across her round belly. "And look at me. I love both of my babies. I love the baby I lost and the baby inside me," she said in a broken whisper. Then she held his gaze. "We have so much more capacity for love than we let ourselves feel when we're grieving."

He exhaled, then inhaled, letting her words expand and dig roots inside him. He knew she was right. He knew she was onto something. And he knew he needed to get out of his own way and let this love take shape.

———

Later, he met Sophie and Ryan for a drink at the Chandelier Bar after a fundraiser for a children's charity.

"Did you ask Annalise to come to the wedding?" Sophie asked once they ordered.

Michael shook his head.

Sophie pouted. "You're going to ask her, though?"

He shrugged but chased it with a *probably*. He needed to figure out what to say to her about so many things.

"Well, when are you seeing her again?"

"I honestly don't know. She doesn't get away much, since she helps take care of her mother. Unless it's for work."

Sophie raised an eyebrow. "Is that so?"

Michael tilted his head, trying to figure out what she meant, then decided he was tired of decoding. "Yeah, that's so."

When he returned home from work the next day, there was a delivery waiting for him at his building—a slim lavender envelope. Gripping it tightly, he rode the elevator up to the twentieth floor. His nerves were tense, tight, in case this was bad news, in case it was the end. If it was, he needed to be alone as he read it.

As soon as he entered his home, he leaned back against the door, slid his finger under the seal, and ripped it open.

Dear Michael,

Sometimes, phone calls don't suffice, and email becomes insufficient for our hearts. But I worry I've been negligent with yours. That I've assumed too much, and said too little—that my fears of losing a love have held me back. Forgive me for not being as open as I wanted. Sometimes the possibility of losing someone I care deeply for is like a fist squeezing my voice, choking it.

So I turn to the written word. We've always been good with letters, haven't we? I can write down what is too hard to say at times. And that is this. You asked me something on your last night in Paris, and I gave you an answer you didn't like. But you need to know that a part of me also never stopped loving you. How could I? You were my first, and I wanted you to be my last. That part was quieter, of course, during the last decade, as it should be.

But now that part is an active part. And what I feel is so much more than a lingering fondness for a first love. It's an aching, hungry place in me, and a blissful, joyful one, too. I want you in my life, Michael. I want new experiences with you. I want pictures of you and of us, of the places we'll go, and the things we'll do. Together.

*I'm trying to give you all I can. I said it badly in Paris, so
I'll say it again and again.*

I'm falling in love with you.

Will you please let me fall in love with you?

xoxo

Annalise

His heart beat furiously, like it had a thousand wings, trying to carry him away to her. When he called, her phone went straight to voicemail. He called a few more times but she didn't answer. That was unlike her.

At some point, he crashed on his couch, the lights of Vegas flickering brightly through the windows, watching over him.

His phone bleated sometime well after midnight. Blinking, he rubbed his eyes and hunted for it. He must have knocked it off the couch, since it sounded from the floor. He grabbed it, a slow smile spreading across his face when he saw her name.

Sliding his thumb over the screen, he answered, his voice still gravelly from sleep. "Hey you."

"Hi. Is there any chance your bed fits two?"

39

Anticipation skated across her flesh as she walked down the hallway on the twentieth floor, as she raised her fist, as she rapped on his door.

In less than five seconds, he opened it, looking sleep-rumpled and impossibly sexy. His black hair was a mess, his jawline was thick with stubble, and his blue eyes twinkled.

He wore black pants and a striped button-down shirt. The top two buttons were undone, and the shirt was wrinkled. It was nearly one; her flight had been late. She was slated to have landed at nine, and while she'd toyed with emailing him from the plane, she'd opted for the surprise.

There was something both comforting and appealing in knowing the other person would like the surprise...of you.

A slow smile spread across his face as he drank her in, then before either one of them said a word, he tugged her inside, ran his fingers through her hair, and kissed her like crazy. She wanted to melt in his arms and spend the night like this.

When he broke the kiss, she nearly stumbled, woozy and drunk on him. He reached for her arm, steadying her, then he brushed a few loose strands of hair from her face, flashing a casual grin. "So what brings you to town?"

She collected her thoughts, shifting away from his kiss. "Your soon-to-be sister-in-law hired me for a boudoir session. And she asked if I'd want to photograph her wedding, too. Seems she heard I don't get away from France much unless it's for work, so she arranged two jobs for me here. I don't usually do weddings, but I find jobs in Vegas have a particular appeal," she said with a sly grin.

Michael smiled, too. "She's a clever one."

"I'm excited to meet her," she said, then cast her eyes to her suitcase. "Is it presumptuous for me to not book a hotel room for the next few days?"

He shook his head, taking the suitcase and shutting the door behind her. "It would be criminal for you to stay anywhere else."

She glanced around, drinking in his home for the first time ever. His was sparse and neat. A wide gray L-shaped couch overlooked a glittering view of the city. A metal coffee table was littered with magazines, papers, and a silver laptop. In a cabinet was a huge TV screen, and a stereo system perched beneath it. She suspected Michael listened to music more than he watched TV. On the walls were framed photos of his family. His brothers and sister, a black-and-white border collie, and a picture of Michael and his father from many years ago.

But her interest in the setting waned quickly. She had more important matters on her mind, and in her heart.

"Did you get my letter?"

"I did. I loved it," he said with a simple smile.

And that was all it took. She was unleashed. She was

free. She'd flown across an ocean to surprise him, she'd come to his home to tell him her heart, and she was no longer going to let her fear of losing rule the day.

"I love you," she blurted out, standing in the quiet entryway of his home.

The corners of his eyes crinkled. "You do?"

She nodded and couldn't stop the grin from bursting across her face. "I love you, Michael. I just do."

"You're not just falling in love with me?" he asked, his eyes sparkling with mischief.

"I'm. In. Love. With. You." She took her time enunciating every word, then she held his face in her hands. He sighed happily and closed his eyes. She tilted her chin to kiss him, brushing her lips on his. "I love you. Now answer the question."

He broke the kiss and scratched his head. "What was the question?"

"Will you let me?" she asked, playfully imploring.

He tapped his chin as if considering her request. Then he laughed and tugged her close. "Yes. God, yes. Hell yes. And I'm sorry if I handled things poorly in Paris. I'm sorry for being distant and pulling back. I'm just so consumed with you, and I don't want to be your second best. Your runner-up."

She shook her head. "You're not. I have a big heart. There is room in it to love again, fully and deeply. I don't want it to be a competition, Michael. All I know is this," she said, slowing her words, meeting his gaze. "I love you, and because of that now I'm terrified of losing you. Even so, I won't let that stop me from feeling everything with you. Because I do feel everything, and I want to keep on loving you. Just let me love you with all I have."

He swallowed, his Adam's apple bobbing as he

nodded. "Yes. It is always yes with you. You're all I want. Now and always."

"The same," she whispered. "It's the same for me with you."

She pressed a kiss to his chest then traveled up his neck, layering his throat with kisses, his jaw, his ear. She nibbled on his earlobe, and he groaned. Then he scooped her up in his arms, strode across the hardwood floors of his apartment, kicked open the door to his bedroom, and set her down. Whispering sweet, dirty words, he stripped off all her clothes as she took off his shirt.

"I missed you," he said, his voice soft and vulnerable as he pushed her red panties to the ground.

"I missed you, too."

He slid a finger between her legs, gliding across her aching pussy. "And I missed fucking you."

"God, I missed that so much, too."

"And making love to you. And hearing you come. It's my favorite thing in the world—making you come," he said, dipping his head to her neck, sucking on her flesh as he rubbed his finger across her hot center. "The sounds you make. How you say my name."

She gasped. "I love it all with you. I want it all with you."

"Now?" he asked in a sexy growl.

"Now, please now," she said, begging as she unzipped his pants and he kicked them off.

"Show me how wild you are for me," he said, rough and commanding as he sank down on the bed, patting his chest. "Here. Ride my face, my love. I need you to come on my lips before I fuck you."

Sparks zipped across her skin as she climbed over him, straddling his face. With strong arms, and a ravenous look in his eyes, he pulled her onto his mouth, and kissed her wet pussy.

"Oh God," she cried out, and in seconds, they found a rhythm. She rocked against his face, and he gripped her hips, his strong fingers digging into the flesh of her ass as he devoured her.

He wasn't teasing. He wasn't playful. He was a hungry man, and he was eating her. With each lick, a savage pleasure tore through her body, twisting and coiling inside her. She thrust against him, moaning and fucking his tongue. With her hands braced against the wall, her hips moved in a frenzy, and he devoured her pussy, sucking, kissing, licking until she was mindless with pleasure and aching to come.

Then a hot flush raced over her skin, and desire curled inside her, shattering in a white-hot, neon burst in her body. His name tumbled from her lips as she cried out.

She barely had time to come down from her high when he shifted her off him, tugged her down the bed, and spread her legs wide. He stroked his rock-hard dick, staring at her legs. "So beautiful. You taste so fucking good. I want to eat you all the time. I want to have you in every way," he said, then lowered himself between her legs and sank inside.

In one deliciously intense thrust.

Her eyes rolled closed and her back bowed. "God, it's so good."

He pushed, thrust deep, then lowered his chest to hers. "So fucking good. And do you know why?"

"Because I love you," she answered in a murmur.

"Because I fucking love you, too."

And that was it. That was why she was in another world with Michael Sloan, fucking, and falling, and loving, and living, and feeling. So much feeling. Every nerve snapped, every cell blazed, everything else faded as he fucked her with so much passion, so much need, and so much love that she nearly burst. She wanted him now, she wanted him always, and she wanted him to know that he was hers, and she was his, and she would give him everything. As the pleasure built inside her again, nearing another crest, she tugged him even closer, whispering in his ear. Nothing complicated. Nothing artful. Just the three simple words that she knew he'd longed to hear. She'd never known anyone to love so deeply, so intensely, and she wanted him to have everything he wanted.

Her.

She could finally give him herself.

"I love you," she gasped, as another orgasm crashed into her, and he fucked her through it, chasing his own release.

————

"Well, that was a helluva surprise," he said minutes later, flopping on his back next to her in bed.

She laughed. "Glad you liked it."

"My favorite surprise ever," he said, then rolled to his side, resting his head in his hand. He traced a line down to her waist. "So Sophie helped you plan this?"

Annalise nodded. "She's quite a romantic."

"She seems to be." He sighed. "Just wish I didn't have to work at all while you're here. I have so much exploring to do," he said, traveling across her stomach with his fingers, letting her know which terrain he meant. "I want to do everything with you," he whispered, squeezing her rear, letting his meaning register.

She met his gaze with wide, earnest eyes. "Anything," she said in her sexy vulnerable voice. "You can do anything with me." Then she stopped and raised a finger. "Well, maybe not pee on me or anything like that."

Cracking up, he tugged her close and planted a kiss on her collarbone. "Yeah, not that. Definitely not that."

"But as for you having to work…" She dragged a finger down his sternum.

"What about it?"

"I have this photo shoot, but Sophie talked to Ryan," she said, her tone conspiratorial, like she was sharing a secret in high school.

"And what did Ryan have to say?"

"Apparently," she said, running that finger across his abs now, "Ryan asked Mindy to help out so you could have a few days off."

"But Mindy has a job."

Annalise shrugged. "I guess she's moonlighting for Sloan Protection Resources to help a friend. Besides, she told them that you introduced her to the new man in her life, so she was happy to help you see the woman in yours."

A smile pulled at the corners of his mouth. Mindy was a good friend. Sophie was a fantastic soon-to-be sister-in-law. Ryan was a great brother. He was a lucky son-of-a-bitch to have so many good people in his life.

"Sounds like a lot of people like you," she said and then straddled him, pinning his wrists in her hands, the ends of her red hair tickling his chest.

"I'm a likeable guy. And look at you. You like me, too," he said, playfully.

"I do like you. I'm in love with you, Michael Sloan." Before he could respond, she tilted her head, as if considering what she'd just said. "Michael Sloan," she repeated, like his name was new to her. "Funny. The first boy I fell in love with was named Michael Paige-Prince. Now I'm in love with this Michael Sloan fella."

"Same guy?" he asked, arching an eyebrow.

"Same. But different, too," she said, and with a sharp burst of clarity, he understood completely what his sister had meant—understood it because he felt it deep within his bones, all the way through his blood, and right into his heart.

40

With the Thomas Paige investigation closed, and both T.J. Nelson and Luke Carlton headed for trial, John Winston had taken on a few new cases, digging into another complicated homicide that demanded his attention.

With a crack-of-dawn run behind him, he headed into the office before seven, ready to tackle the workload.

But as he studied the evidence folder at his desk and downed his cup of coffee, something nagged at the back of his mind. A little detail that he couldn't quite fit into a neat box. Not from the new case, but from the old one.

Something didn't entirely add up. As he hunted for his case file, his phone rang.

"Detective John Winston here," he answered.

"Hey, Winston. This is Special Agent Laura K. Reiss with the FBI, Las Vegas division. We've got a case we're working that might have hooks into one of yours."

John returned to his chair, spun around, and said, "Tell me more."

"I'm betting this place has amazing breakfast potatoes because the fries I had a few weeks ago were out of this world," Michael said as he held open the door to the diner where he'd met Morris recently. It seemed almost a lifetime ago.

"Can't wait. I'm famished," Annalise said after she told the hostess they needed a table for two. The woman in the pink dress showed them to a booth, and Annalise ordered a coffee.

After the waitress vanished, Annalise flashed him a smile. She was radiant this morning—freshly showered, barely any makeup on, and her hair swept into a clip on her head. Then she yawned. "Jet lag."

He nodded. "I think we'll both be dealing with that a lot these days."

"We definitely will."

Even though he wished it were possible to see her more, he would take what he could get. He would live off the little morsels of time they were able to carve out. Maybe someday they could find a way to be in the same city more regularly. For now, he at least had faith in the two of them, and that was a beautiful thing.

"So what brought you here a few weeks ago?" she asked, after they ordered eggs and the waitress brought coffee. "This diner isn't exactly down the block from your home."

"The private detective I hired wanted to meet here to share some leads. The info about the piano shop that helped break the case open."

"Ah," she said with a nod, reaching for her mug.

He picked up the tea he'd ordered. "And you were amazing in helping us put the final pieces together."

She shook her head, as if it were no big deal what

she'd remembered. "It was nothing. Just a tiny bit of memory. But I want to hear more about how it all went down. We didn't talk much about it in Paris. I sensed you didn't want to get into the details then, but you know me. I'm always curious."

He smiled. "I do know that about you."

And so he started the story.

———

As Michael spoke about the night of the last arrest, a memory tugged at the back of her mind. It was of her last conversation with his father.

The morning before she left Las Vegas, she'd gone out to breakfast with Michael and his dad. They'd discussed plans for how the two of them could see each other again. She'd always loved that about his father. He was so supportive of their young love. They'd ordered eggs and toast—standard diner fare. She didn't remember the name of the diner, but it wasn't this one.

It was so odd that a little more than twenty-four hours later, he was gone.

She shook her head briefly, chasing away the memory.

"And one of the gang members they'd already nabbed had tipped off the cops about where T.J. had been seen," Michael said, when a faint buzz sounded from his side of the booth.

"Is that your phone?"

He glanced downward, patting his back pocket. "Yeah. I'll get back to whoever it is," he said, then continued the tale, and she tried her best to focus on what he was saying, but her mind kept tripping back to that day in the past.

Conversation with Thomas had been easy, even when

Michael went out to the car to grab an umbrella. Rain had started to fall, and he said he didn't want her to get soaked when they left the restaurant after breakfast.

"He's so chivalrous," Annalise said to his father. "He takes after you."

Thomas smiled. "He's a gentleman. Makes me proud."

"How is everything going at work? Were you ever able to sort out the missing details you were looking into?"

He scratched his chin and shifted his hand like a seesaw. "Sort of. It seemed I was getting closer, and I was really hoping it would help me get the job, especially since the company was worried about being audited."

"What happened then?" she asked, catching sight of Michael yanking open the car door in the parking lot.

His phone buzzed again at the table.

Grabbing it from his back pocket, he hit *ignore* without looking at the screen. Worry prickled at the back of Annalise's neck. "What if it's important?"

He inhaled deeply and shot her a small smile. "I'm sure whatever it is can wait five more minutes," he said as the waitress returned with their plates.

"Eggs, and our famous breakfast potatoes," she said, depositing their meals as a bearded man in a black windbreaker passed behind her. When the waitress left, Michael finished his story. "So they set up a trap, basically, at the club. The gentlemen's club we do the security for."

She nodded, recalling this part of the tale.

She picked up her fork and dug into her eggs, taking a bite.

"And as soon as T.J. was there in the cigar lounge at White Box—"

She choked. Grabbing a napkin, she brought it to her mouth, coughing up the bit of egg she'd inhaled.

"Are you okay?" he asked, knitting his brow and thrusting a glass of water in her direction. She waved him off. Her blood had gone cold, and all her senses warned of danger. This was the same feeling she'd had as a photojournalist when situations in war zones became too dicey.

"What did you just say?" she whispered. The hair on her arms stood on end.

"About the cigar lounge?"

She nodded, fear racing over her skin. "The cigar lounge. Where was it?"

"White Box," he said slowly, his brow furrowed. "Why are you asking?"

Her palms turned clammy. "That name," she whispered, her voice sounding haunted even to her own ears. "Your father said something the last day I saw him, something about White Box."

Michael blinked, confusion in his blue eyes. "What did he say?"

Like a diver rising up in the sea, the memory broke through to the surface. "We were talking about work. His company. The missing rides. When you'd gone to the car to get an umbrella, I asked him how everything was going, and if he'd learned anything."

"And what did he say?" Michael asked, gripping the table, his jaw tight, his eyes wide with concern.

Something so simple. So offhand. So *nothing*. It had never seemed like more than a needle in the haystack. Until now.

Until it wasn't.

She hurtled back in time to that last conversation.

"But it didn't help you get the job?" she asked Michael's father as they chatted at the diner, having finished their eggs.

Thomas Paige shook his head. "Nope. But there will be

others, I'm sure. I'm thinking of maybe switching to another limo company. Once I tried to move up, it became like a white box of information."

She arched an eyebrow. She'd never heard those words used that way. Perhaps it was an American saying she wasn't familiar with. "What does that mean?"

"Stuff was just erased. Rides disappeared. That's what I heard some of the guys there calling it. They called it a white box, and then one of them said it was the white box of information. I guess the guy who ran the place used that term. I was going to ask Sanders about it, since he drove him around, but I've decided it doesn't matter in the end. I'm just going to let it go."

"What a funny little saying," she said with a small laugh.

Thomas chuckled too. "Yeah, don't worry about that one. It's not a common phrase you need to know."

The check arrived, and so did Michael. "Got the umbrella," he declared, joining them as the conversation shifted back to the future, to their plans.

———

The ground began to sway. The whole diner seemed unsteady. "Did he say who ran the company? I always thought it was a guy named Paul, but someone else owned it. West was his name," Michael said in a barren voice, while his world seemed to spin off its axis.

Annalise shook her head.

He wanted to believe it was a coincidence. He wanted to reassure her that those were just two words. *White box.* But when his phone buzzed again in his pocket, and the name flashing across the screen registered, all he could think was that it wasn't over.

He answered the call from Morris in a split second. "What's going on?"

"Hey, Michael. Need to give you a heads up. I've been hacked, and some of the online research I did into Luke Carlton was accessed. Someone put two and two together and figured out I was working for you. I got an anonymous call last night to keep my nose out of the case. Which is weird, since the case is over."

His blood chilled to sub-zero temperatures, and instinct kicked in. *Get the hell out of here.*

"Any idea who it was?" he asked as he fished in his wallet, tossed a twenty on the table, and reached for Annalise's hand. He pulled her up and walked away as he talked to Morris, scanning the diner from the booths to the foyer to the exit as they left.

"No clue," Morris said, as Michael raced with Annalise to his car. "But I think I was followed as I looked into the piano shop. I think that tipped someone off. I'm sorry."

"I gotta go," Michael said, ending the call as he put Annalise safely in his car. He ran to the driver's side, slid inside, locked the doors, and reversed out of his parking spot. In his rearview mirror, he spotted a bearded man in a silver sedan pulling out, too.

"Michael, what's going on?" Annalise asked, her voice quaking as he drove.

"Nothing good."

He placed his phone in the holder, clicked on missed calls, and his heart sank when he saw John Winston had rung him twice.

As he turned onto the highway, he returned the call, but Winston didn't answer.

"Shit, shit, shit."

He gripped the steering wheel, trying to drive and

connect the dots, but he couldn't fucking figure out how they were all tied together. The thing that kept nagging at him was why Sanders had been so goddamn evasive, and what, if anything, that man had to do with White Box.

Whether White Box was the club or something else entirely.

As he neared the exit for his home, his phone buzzed, and Michael wanted to thank all the stars above that Winston was calling back. He answered on speaker.

"What the hell is going on with the case?" he bit out.

"Seems we've got some new information. I got a call from a federal agent this morning about some RICO charges that might be connected to your father's case."

Michael's head swam with this news. "RICO? As in racketeering?" He glanced at Annalise, whose eyes were wide with shock and fear.

"Where are you?" John asked. "I'm leaving my colleague's office. I'll meet you."

"Heading home," he said, then rattled off the address.

"I'm heading down the elevator right now, so I should be there in twenty minutes."

"Wait," Michael said, as tension gripped him. "Who's behind it? Who's involved? I need to know. Is White Box part of this? How the hell could White Box be part of this?"

John started to answer as Michael reached his street, but the words came out choppy. His phone was cutting out. Fucking hell.

"What did you just say?"

John kept talking, but only words like *informant, protection, guns,* and *drugs* were clear enough to make out. The rest was garbled. Finally the line died, and a minute later, Michael pulled into the parking garage at his building.

His pulse pounded dangerously fast. As he cut the engine, he met the gaze of the woman he loved, and saw so much fear in her eyes, but a toughness, too.

"Let's get inside and wait for John," he said, and she nodded.

He slammed his door, walked to the passenger side, scanned the lot, and, when he was confident it was all clear, he opened her door. She stepped out and he tugged her close, wrapping an arm around his Annalise and scanning once more.

His breath fled his chest.

All the alarm bells in his head sounded. By the door to his building stood a man he was far too familiar with—waiting for him.

"It seems we have business to settle."

41

Normally, he liked to delegate—have his men handle petty tasks like shaking people down. But sometimes you had to clean up your own mess. Like Michael Sloan. He was a tough one. He was too close, he knew too much, and he had figured out more than he should.

He'd connected the dots, according to what his man eavesdropping at the diner this morning had told him. That was something no one else had ever done. Not since years ago, when Michael's father had veered way too close for comfort.

Since then he'd operated cleaner. Neater, under the radar. But with the case blasted open, he'd had to dart and dodge.

Now it was time to do his own dirty work. And Charlie Stravinsky *hated* doing his own dirty work.

"Your mother was easy to manipulate into doing what I needed her to do. I fear you might not be so pliable," he said, stepping away from the wall of the parking garage and walking closer to the blue-eyed son of the man he'd convinced Dora Prince to have killed nearly two decades ago.

"You're right on that count," Michael said crisply. "This won't be easy. There are people who know you're involved."

Charlie waved that concern away, stopping at a green Lexus as Sloan grabbed the auburn-haired beauty with him and pushed her behind him. Fucking redheads. They were nothing but trouble.

Charlie nodded and clucked his tongue. "You're right. There are people who know enough to be dangerous, like you and like her. But that's going to end soon, isn't it? Unless you want to come work for me? Your mother did, for all intents and purposes."

Michael's eyes narrowed, burning at him, his jaw set hard. He was like a fuse waiting to blow, and Charlie was going to enjoy every second of setting him off. The man was too good, too pure. Watching men like him shatter into animals was such a high.

"This isn't about her. This is about my father," he spat out, seething.

But Charlie wasn't scared of Michael. He wasn't scared of a thing. He'd let go of fear many years ago. After his brother was killed at age nine in a robbery back in his home country, he'd vowed to never let anyone fuck with his family again. He'd done a fine job providing for all his brothers and sisters. His businesses made money that had put them through school. Years ago he'd moved them to America to keep them safe, along with his mother and father, too. His parents had since passed on, but he still took care of all his siblings, thanks to his businesses and the way they turned money into more money.

So when someone tried to mess with his business, they might as well be screwing with his family.

And no one went after Charlie's family and got away with it.

Thomas Paige had tried to, sniffing around in his limo company, asking far too many questions. Curtis Paul Wollinsky, his best friend, his comrade in arms, and the manager of West Limos years ago, had alerted him to Paige's queries. They'd tried to shut him up through T.J., their chief intimidator with the Royal Sinners, but that hadn't worked.

Then opportunity had presented itself. Once Charlie had learned that Dora Prince was already making moves on her own to order a hit for money, Charlie had his iron-clad solution—provide the means for Dora to go through with it. That way she couldn't stop it even if she tried. Damn shame she went to prison. She would have made an excellent lieutenant in his operations. She was loyal to the core, cold-blooded, and willing to act, especially when he'd threatened her children that one time she tried to back out.

Oh, that woman was willing to protect them. He really should visit her one day and thank her. But he'd deal with that another time.

Right now he had her pesky oldest son to shut up.

He extended a hand in Michael's direction, even though he was twenty feet away. The nerve of him saying it was about his father; the boy didn't realize he still had so much left to lose. "Or perhaps it's about you, and the only chance you have before you," he said, scratching his chin. "As I see it, your only way out is to come work with me."

Michael shook his head.

"You can do it. Everyone is corruptible if you threaten their family. It worked for your mother," Charlie said, as Michael shifted his eyes to the woman behind him.

"I'm not working for you, Charlie," he bit out as the redhead cowered. She was tall, though, and Michael couldn't quite shield her completely.

"But you do work for me. I hired you. I knew who you were, and look what happened." Charlie flashed his winning smile. His plan had worked like a charm—ingratiating himself with the security brothers, making them think he cared deeply about doing the right thing. Donating to the community center. Playing the concerned citizen. "You wound up liking me. We got along so well, Michael. Cleaning up the city together. Ridding Vegas of those nasty Royal Sinners I wanted to eradicate. You helped me get rid of the bad apples from my street crew— like T.J. He was a good one, but he was giving me a belly- ache by the end, so turning him in was a joy, and you made it so easy for me to be helpful."

Michael clenched his fists, holding in all his rage. Ah, what an absolute delight to watch the carefully controlled Michael start to boil over. "What do you want?"

Charlie stared at him like he was insane. "What do I want?" he repeated. "Isn't it obvious?"

Charlie took a step closer. Michael moved back, the woman now sandwiched between him and the back of his car. "Use your brain, Sloan. I want you to stop asking questions. If you can't do that, you can go ahead and join your father." He reached behind his jacket and took his gun from his holster, his eyes on Sloan.

Who moved like a goddamn cheetah. Before Charlie even raised his weapon, Michael's gun was pointing at his face.

Charlie didn't flinch. He'd stared down more frightening men. He'd stared down death. Besides, Michael wasn't tough enough. "You're not your mother's son," he hissed. "You're your father's son. You don't have it in you to fire that thing. You're too good, like he was. So we have two options. You either work for me, or we say good-bye."

"I'll take option three," Michael said, his finger nearing the trigger.

42

The devil moved quickly, hissed even faster, waving his gun in the direction of Annalise. She was shielded behind Michael, but not completely, and when Charlie darted to his right to aim for her head, Michael's only thought was to protect her. In both slow motion and terrible fast-forward, he shoved her farther behind him with his free hand as he pulled the trigger.

The bullet barreled through the air, on a hunt for Charlie's brain. But, Michael's move to keep Annalise out of harm's way had the twin effect of shifting the target by inches, putting him in grave danger.

The last thing Michael saw was the bullet ripping through the devil's arm.

Then a feral yell tore from the man's throat.

Michael's world turned warped as his own gun clattered to the ground. Like thunder after a bolt of lightning, the pain came a few seconds later, cutting through every cell in his body.

With a bone-shattering *thunk*, Michael crashed to the concrete, his skull whacking the floor of the parking garage. Blood poured from him, leaking all over his shirt, turning it crimson.

Everywhere.

His chest bled absolutely everywhere. Terror dug roots into the corners of her body. Her throat burned with tears, and her lungs tried to escape from her as she cried.

Her head roared in protest, her mind shouting *no*, trying to deny the horror. She dropped to the ground next to Michael, grasping, desperately trying to do something, anything, as she fumbled for her phone.

Panic welled up inside her, spilling over, suffocating her as she grabbed it in her pocket.

Not again. This couldn't happen twice. She couldn't lose someone she loved again. But the blood...it was on her hands, her face, all over him. Her hand pressed against his chest. Oh thank God, his heart was beating still. But there was so much red. She couldn't see a thing through her tears, wasn't even sure she could hear past her own cries. Somehow she stabbed the numbers nine-one-one with blood-covered fingers on the keypad before she screamed out a sob, the phone clattering to the ground.

Then a long, low moan fell on her ears.

It didn't come from Michael.

The hair on the back of her neck stood up, and she jerked her head toward the sound.

Ten, perhaps fifteen feet away, the man who'd shot Michael dragged himself upright. He clutched his left arm as it bled on his jacket sleeve. With his right hand, he groped around for his gun on the ground.

In the distance, shouts burst through the late-morning

air—maybe from inside the building, maybe from somewhere else in parking garage.

She didn't know where they were coming from, or who was on the way.

She knew one thing and one thing only.

He'd found his weapon, and he was reaching for it.

43

Eighteen years ago

Dora Prince had decided. She was backing out. She told Luke at the fabric shop where they'd agree to meet that morning. There in the last row, amidst buttons and ribbons, she wrapped her arms around his neck and said, "I can't do it. I can't go through with it. But I can't be without you either. I'll leave him, and we can be together. I don't need money. I have you."

He smiled warmly, that smile she loved. "Of course, Dora. You just need to talk to Jerry Stefano and call it off."

She drew a sharp breath. The man she'd hired to kill her husband terrified her, with his cold eyes and his even colder heart. He wouldn't be happy. His eyes had glittered when she'd told him the price for the hit, and she was sure he wanted the money. "Can't you tell him?"

Luke shot her a sad smile and shook his head. "Oh honey, I want to. But you know how this works. I need to keep my distance. The only way I can run the street operations for Charlie is by keeping myself clean. The less people suspect me, the more I can do his bidding, and the better I can pay my men on the street. The more I earn in the next year, the better the chance we can get away. I promise, baby. Call it off. Give me one more year to close out my deals, and then we'll find a way to get out of town with all the kids." He pressed his hands to her belly. "Including ours. I wish I could feel the baby kicking," he whispered.

She smiled. "Soon. Another month or so."

But Stefano didn't take the news well when she tried to cancel the hit, nor did Charlie. The man in charge of a burgeoning drug operation in the city summoned her, picking her up for a drive one day when her kids were in school.

She got into Charlie's car, and he talked as he drove out of her neighborhood. "Good to see you again," he said. They'd met once before.

"Yes, you too," she said, even as nerves prickled down her backbone.

"I hear you want to back out."

She nodded. "I do. I can't go through with it."

He flipped on the blinker to turn right. "Ah, but therein lies the issue, Dora. You can, and you will."

She shook her head, holding her ground. "I thought I could, but I need to move on from all this."

He glanced at her, knitting his brow. "From what? You're my top dealer. You run a magnificent route. I have plans, Dora. Big plans. You can work with me."

She swallowed, sucking in all her fears. "I can't do it."

He slammed on the brakes and pulled over on the side of the road, then stared at her. "It's too late for you to make that choice," he said in a snake-like whisper.

"Why?" she asked, her voice quaking.

"You're in too deep. Your husband has gone too far. His questions threaten my business, and when my business is threatened, my family is too. I don't like having my family threatened. You understand that, right?"

She nodded, bile rising up in her throat. She reached for the door handle. Maybe she could escape. Run. Call the police. But what would she tell them? That she was a drug-dealing, cheating woman who'd ordered a hit gone wrong?

He laughed and pressed the lock button. "You're not leaving my car. And you're not backing out. Your husband is figuring things out. I can't have him knowing what I do."

What he did was launder money through West Limos from guns and drugs sold on the streets by the Royal Sinners, who managed their business in the back of a piano shop. Luke, Charlie's right-hand man in the Sinners, had set up that end of the operation to run so smoothly that no one could link Luke, Charlie, the Sinners, the piano shop, and the limo company. But Dora's husband had started to catch on, only Thomas didn't yet know that Charlie was involved.

Charlie clearly wanted to keep it that way. Oh the sheer bitter irony that she'd met the man of her dreams at a simple work party and had tumbled into this dark underworld of money, drugs, and power. A world her husband barely understood. A world she wanted to escape.

Her heart raced. "What if I leave? What if I leave town with my family?" Dora asked, casting out desperate ideas.

He scoffed. "What if? What if? What if?" He mimicked her like a parrot, then grabbed her chin in his hand. "I'll give you the only *what if* that matters," he said sharply. "What if you do as you planned? Then I won't hurt your children." His eyes roamed to her belly, and a fresh wave of fear rolled through her. "Are we clear? You don't cancel the hit, and you come out on the other side with a neat, clean robbery-gone-wrong, executed by one of the finest hit men in the Royal Sinners, and then you are free. That is your last debt to me from the drugs you sold."

"Why do you need me to order the hit? If you want him dead, you can call Stefano yourself," she said, clutching at straws.

He narrowed his icy eyes at her and spoke, low and menacing. "I don't order hits. I don't have to. I don't need a hit connected to me, because I haven't made the mistakes you have." He shrugged and fixed on a smile, his tone shifting to an easy one. "But if you pull this off, I will let you go. You can leave town and be free."

Later that night, as she lay awake in bed next to her husband, Dora imagined calling the police. Asking for help. Turning in Charlie. But how was she to say anything and be believed? She was a drug dealer. A former drug user. A woman who was conspiring to commit murder for hire. An adulteress. They wouldn't believe her—they'd lock her up, and her children would be in real danger then.

Thomas was better off dead than with Charlie hunting all of them.

She tiptoed out of bed, grabbed the cordless phone from the kitchen, opened the screen door, and closed it behind her. In her nightgown, she walked deep into her yard and called Stefano. "It's back on."

She hung up, closing her eyes, the ground swaying as she made her choice. This was the only way she could protect Michael, Colin, Ryan, Shannon, and the baby in her belly.

And she did protect them. Even when it all unraveled. Even when the police locked her up. Even when Stefano went to prison. Even when the jury convicted her to life, too. She never gave up the names of the others.

She wasn't innocent. Not by a long stretch. But her silence made sure no one else ever knew who was involved.

It was her last chance to do the right thing when she'd done so much wrong.

For the next eighteen years from her six-by-eight-foot prison cell, she'd pulled it off, her silence driving her mad. But at least her children were safe from men who killed without mercy.

44

Four months ago

Sanders glanced around the cluttered office of Special Agent Laura K. Reiss. Her desk towered with papers, mugs, and picture frames. The bulletin board behind her was stuffed with notices.

She handed him a mug of coffee and sighed sympathetically as she took a seat across from him.

"I need your help, Mr. Foxton," she said, and her voice was deceptively sweet. She was petite and had blond hair that bounced in a ponytail. A Reese Witherspoon lookalike.

"How so?" he asked, forcing his voice to stay steady even as his gut twisted with worry.

"Here's the thing," she said, in that soprano voice. "Some of those guns you were transporting were illegally obtained. Which makes *you* a gunrunner for illegally obtained guns." She spelled it out like he was five, then lowered her voice to a stage whisper. "That's kind of a no-no."

"I didn't know what I was transporting," he protested. "I swear to God. I've never known. They give me the packages, and I take them from point A to point B." That was the truth, the full truth, and nothing but the truth. He'd never asked questions.

Laura nodded sympathetically and took a pull of her coffee. "Oddly enough, that's not really a good answer," she said with a frown. Then she turned it upside-down, her cheery demeanor returning. "But I believe you. I believe you're telling the truth."

He sighed with relief. "Good. Can I get out of here?"

She laughed, then shook her head. "Not so fast."

"What do you need?"

"We have a few options. I can work up some charges against you for your role in transporting firearms as part of the illegal gun trade in Las Vegas, and you can face time behind bars. Or you can use what's in here," she said, tapping her head, "to help me catch some bigger fish."

"What sort of fish?" he asked skeptically.

"Let's just say I'm looking into organized crime in Las Vegas. And I would really like to find out if your guns are tied to something a helluva lot bigger."

"I don't know, Ms. Reiss. I guess I should think about it."

She pointed at him playfully and shot him a knowing grin. "Well, you think about it Mr. Foxton. And keep in mind, you'd be doing the city a huge service. Because the more we talk, and the more you share, the better chance I have of putting away the men who are really making Vegas a nasty place. So how about a deal? I keep you out of prison, and you become my informant?"

The only thing he'd ever done was skirt the law. He'd never hurt anyone. Never killed anyone. All he'd wanted was to make a few extra bucks to provide for his family.

He loved his wife, loved his kids, loved his freedom more than anything.

There was really one choice.

———

Present day

Goddamn cell phone towers.

As John peeled out of the garage of the federal building, he tapped his fingers on the steering wheel, stealing glances at his phone as he waited impatiently for the signal to return.

"C'mon, c'mon," he muttered as the wheels met the road, heading toward Michael Sloan's home.

Soon the bars returned, and the second they did he dialed Michael's number again. He had to warn the guy. Michael's White Box client had set him up. John was sure of it now. He'd had an inkling this morning that something didn't add up, but there was no way to know the specifics before Reiss called.

John's investigation into the murder of Thomas Paige and the fed's investigation into organized crime had moved on two separate tracks for the last few months. Over the summer, the murder case had been reopened, thanks to the tip-off John received from Jerry Stefano's ex-girlfriend about other men being involved. Meanwhile, as he'd just learned, Sanders Foxton had been arrested for speeding four months ago, and in return for not going to jail, he'd started sharing all he knew about the operations at what had turned out to be a very shady company.

The same company where Thomas Paige had worked years ago.

A company that had been washed so clean, it raised no flags in the murder, and showed no ties to White Box in the present day, either. There was no paper trail at all to link the drugs and guns to the limo service—or the murder, of course—but it turned out Sanders had over-heard a few conversations in his runs, and those clues had been enough for Reiss to tie Charlie, Curtis, and White Box back to West Limo.

Charlie knew how to operate like smoke, hiding his tracks, never leaving a trail. But at least there was evidence now to bring them in.

As he turned a corner, John tried Michael once more. The phone rang and rang and rang.

He kept dialing, but with each non-answer, John's senses told him something was dead wrong.

His suspicions were confirmed when a crackle came over the radio. Paramedics were hauling ass to the same building that he was. Words like *multiple gunshot wounds* and *critical* pierced his ears.

Oh God. He was too late.

When he arrived, an ambulance was racing away, sirens blaring, speeding faster than he swore he'd ever seen one go.

45

Colin burst through the doors of the emergency room, his pulse hammering in his throat as he raced to the information desk, Elle by his side. The past and the present slammed into him in punishing jolts with each football—memories of his father's murder mixed cruelly with *this*. His oldest brother, the one who'd looked out for him, helped him stay sober when he first got clean, helped raise him...Michael had been shot in the chest and rushed to the hospital. They had no clue what his condition was, or if he was even alive.

Colin choked back that horrific thought as he stopped short at the desk, words tumbling out in a traffic jam. "Michael Sloan. He was just brought in. I'm his brother. How is he?"

The brunette in pink scrubs and wireframe glasses looked up and nodded. "Give me just a minute."

He turned to Elle, taking deep, sharp breaths, but they barely seemed enough to fill his mouth, let alone his lungs. "Elle," he said in a whisper. He couldn't say anything else. If he did, he would break.

Her lower lip quivered, and she looked like she was trying to form the words *he'll be okay*, but instead, tears slid down her cheeks and she clasped her hand to her mouth. They'd been in bed asleep when Sophie called fifteen minutes ago, hysterical with the news. Elle's son Alex was at a friend's house, and they'd uncharacteristically slept in until nine a.m., when they were greeted by a screeching phone and sobs on the other end.

Sophie and Ryan were on their way. Shannon and Brent, too, and their grandparents as well. But Elle lived closest, so they'd arrived first. Colin dragged a hand through his hair, trying to breathe, to ignore the beeping of machines, the clatter of equipment, the hushed conversations between nurses and doctors circling nearby, and the faces of all the other people waiting in the emergency room.

"Elle," he croaked out again, as the woman at the desk toggled through her computer screen.

She wrapped her arms around him. "He's going to be okay."

But she didn't sound like she believed it.

Resting his chin atop her head, because he felt like he might topple over if he let go, he turned back to the woman at the desk. "Do you know where he is? Is he in surgery? What's going on?"

The woman held up a finger. "One minute."

"Goddammit," he muttered. "Elle, is your mom working?" Colin asked, desperation coloring his tone. "Can she find out something?"

Elle shook her head. "She's not an ER nurse, but I can try to find her."

"Wait." Colin snapped his gaze in the direction of the woman in pink scrubs. "Sloan, you said?"

Colin let go of Elle and gripped the counter. "Yes. Michael Sloan. What's going on?"

She opened her mouth to speak, when Colin spotted John Winston rounding the corner. His eyes were downcast, his arm was wrapped around Annalise, and he looked like someone had died.

Colin's ears rang, and he heard nothing but the screaming in his own head.

46

Thirty minutes ago

Silver gleamed on concrete—two, maybe three feet away from her next to the wheel of a car—like a beacon.

A harsh pant came from Charlie, then the dragging sound of unsteady feet across pavement.

Her hands were covered in Michael's blood, her vision was blurred from her own torrential tears, and her pulse thundered in her brain.

But Michael's heart still beat, and in an instant, her choices crystallized into just one.

She lunged across Michael for the gun, rose to her feet, and spun around.

"I'm not done," the man seethed, as he rose to his full height, his gun in his uninjured right hand. "You and your white box comment this morning at the diner," he snarled. "You know nothing about my brother. Nothing about how he was buried."

She had no clue what he meant, and she didn't care.

She was nothing but nerves. She'd never held a gun and had certainly never fired one. She didn't know how to hit the side of a barn, let alone the heart of a man. But as he lifted his arm, her focus narrowed, and her mind sharpened.

Adrenaline bathed her brain in pinpoint clarity. She was alive, she was unhurt, and she was going to be faster than the man who wanted to kill her then finish off Michael.

As she raised her weapon, she realized she knew precisely what to do.

Like taking a picture.

Point. Aim.

Shoot.

The bullet flew.

And she prayed. And hoped. And wished.

Charlie crumpled over, grabbing his belly where she'd hit him.

Seconds later, the ambulance screeched to a stop, the medics poured out, and she was on the way to the hospital with her love losing his hold on life.

Now

He'd died in the emergency room twenty minutes later. Annalise had shot him in the stomach, the bullet nicking an artery and tearing through his intestines, the doctors had said. No time to question Charlie Stravinsky —no chance for a deathbed confession, but one was hardly needed.

His confession had been made when he'd arrived at Michael's building, ready to kill.

John had already put most of the pieces together that morning with the federal agent, and he needed to talk to Annalise to learn what had gone down in the parking garage. She could barely speak, though. Her hands were still shaking, and all she'd managed to say were the barest of details. There would be time enough for that later. After she'd been checked over and cleaned up, he walked her to the ER waiting room where he was rushed by family members—Colin and Elle first.

"What's going on?" Colin asked, grabbing his arm.

"He's in surgery. That's all I know," John said, wishing he had more news. The doctors didn't know. The nurses hadn't supplied any more details. That was standard practice for this kind of trauma. Get the patient in the OR and try to save a life if they could.

Colin's shoulders rose and fell as he took a deep breath. "Okay. But how does it look? Can't we get any more information?" Colin implored, his eyes wide with the plea.

John shook his head. "They don't have any other details to give. As soon as he arrived, he was rushed to the OR. They're probably trying to figure out the extent of the damage. If—"

"If they can save him?" Colin cut in.

John nodded. "Yes. That's what they're trying to do."

Then an animalistic cry ripped from the throat of the woman next to him, and Annalise slipped from his arms, crumbling to the floor. In an instant, Elle gripped her, wrapped her arms around her, and ushered her away.

Eighteen years ago

He lay on the driveway, his eyes fluttering closed, and Thomas knew this was the end. He could no longer move his lips to utter the word *help*. The night seemed to wink on and off, the stars in the sky coming in and out of focus and then fading. His body felt light, as if it were floating away from him.

The agonizing pain had ebbed, and as he lay on the asphalt by his home, his last thoughts were of his children. How much he loved them. How much he could continue to love them for the rest of time...here in this world, or in the next one.

And as the earth turned dark, he hoped he wouldn't see them again for a long, long time...

47

Her head was in her hands.

"I killed a man," she whispered barrenly. "And the man I love is dying."

Doubled over in shock and consumed with the sharp, cold sensation of impending grief, Annalise sat on the hard wooden bench in the hospital's chapel.

Elle, who she'd just met today, stroked her hair, trying to comfort her. Annalise thought she must be the one who'd brought her here from the emergency room an hour ago. Or was it minutes ago? She hardly knew anything anymore, except that all her fears were on the cusp of turning true. The prospect of Michael dying hurt so much—an ache in her bones that would never depart.

"You did what you had to do," Elle said, her voice strong as she ran her fingers through Annalise's hair.

"I did," she choked out, needing the reassurance. She had no regrets over picking up the gun and firing. She only hoped it had been enough to save Michael. But he'd been barely hanging on during the ride to the hospital. She'd hardly even been able to hear the words the paramedics barked when they gave him an IV and fought to keep him alive as he bled, and bled, and bled. The ambulance had seemed to fly at the speed of light, confirmation of how tenuous his hold on life was.

Oh God.

She couldn't imagine losing him. Couldn't conceive of burying him. Her chest heaved, and she coughed, choking on the pain.

Now, he was in the operating room and no one knew if the doctors could even save him. There was a bullet in his body. Near his heart.

The door creaked, and Annalise lifted her gaze as a platinum blonde rushed toward them—Sophie, the one who'd arranged for her to come to Vegas for a photo shoot.

"Hi. I'll be ready for your shoot tomorrow," Annalise said, her voice flat. She wasn't sure why she'd said that. Maybe because anything else would hollow her out.

Sophie gave her a look like she was crazy as she kneeled by her side and placed a hand on her thigh. "I'm not here to ask about work. Are you okay, sweetie?"

Annalise shook her head. "No. I don't know. I killed a man and Michael is dying," she repeated, because those twin moments of her life felt like *everything*. Her before, her after, her now.

"You saved a life," Sophie said, reaching for her hand. "Come on, now. You need to be strong for Michael. You need to be as strong as you can be."

Strong? What was that? Did she even know what strength was anymore? Did she know anything? Her world had been twisted inside out, shaken cruelly by the hand of Fate, and now Michael was—

She squeezed her eyes shut, blocking out the

word *dying*.

"Annalise," Sophie said, her voice gentle but firm. "You're allowed to be sad. You're allowed to be terrified. But you're not allowed to think negative thoughts right now. Michael is in surgery, and they are fighting to save his life. We need to be there in the OR waiting room for whenever the doctors come out. Not here." Sophie glanced around the chapel. It was warm and comforting, but it was a hiding place in some ways. "Come now. You can do this."

Sophie held one hand, and Elle took the other. Annalise was keenly aware that the three women in this chapel were in love with three brothers, and the other two were there to help her be tough for the brother that needed her. The man she loved.

She took a breath, inhaling hope and letting go of all else.

There was no room for thoughts of that killer. There was no room for hate, for vengeance, or for cold, heartless enemies.

There was only room for love. She would do everything to send her love to Michael, and her strength to the doctors working on him. She left the chapel, Elle and Sophie leading her to join the rest of the family in the OR waiting room.

They waited and they waited and they waited.

For an hour.

Then another.

Then for nearly one more.

Until at last, a woman in green scrubs pushed open the door, and surveyed the scene. She had lines around her blue eyes, and strong cheekbones. "I'm Doctor Brooks. Are you the family of Michael Sloan?"

48

Everyone stood.

Annalise, Elle, Sophie. Ryan, Colin, Shannon, and Brent, his arm protectively around his pregnant wife. The grandparents. Even the detective had stayed, and Michael's friend Mindy had joined the vigil.

Collectively holding their breath, crossing their fingers, and praying to whoever listened, they waited for the surgeon to speak again.

"It was touch-and-go there for a while. We didn't know where the bullet hit him until we opened up his chest. And he lost a lot of blood," the doctor said, her tone measured and even. Annalise was poised on the balls of her feet, every muscle strung tight, waiting, wanting, aching for answers. "Turns out he was shot in the spleen. We got lucky."

Lucky.

Oh God, never had a word been more beautiful.

Never had anyone said such a perfect word. Lucky was good.

"We were able to remove his spleen, and he'll be able to live a normal life without it."

"Oh my God. He's really alive?" Annalise asked in a breathless rush, desperately needing a second confirmation.

The surgeon smiled and nodded. "Yes. Very much so."

"Can we see him?" The question came from Michael's grandmother.

The doctor shook her head. "He's in recovery now. He hasn't even woken up yet."

Two hours later, a nurse said he was asking for Annalise. She brought her hand to her heart, then turned and embraced Elle and Sophie. "Thank God," she whispered, her voice breaking as it had in the chapel with them, but this time for a much happier reason.

———

Sanders set down the phone and breathed a huge sigh of relief. Becky wrapped her arms around his neck and kissed his cheek.

"He's going to be okay," he said, so damn grateful for the news his best friend's mother—Victoria Paige—had just given him. Her grandson Michael was going to be okay.

When Sanders was pulled over for speeding, he'd never expected his role as an informant would curl around and hook into the murder of his best friend from years ago. He'd had no notion that the bastards who ran the company had pressured Dora to commit murder. He'd thought for years, as nearly everyone did, that it was *her* crime. Her choice and hers alone. He never knew the men he worked for had wanted Thomas dead and had used Dora to make that happen.

It didn't mean he forgave her. Just meant that she didn't act alone.

But he could breathe easier, knowing that all her accomplices at last had been rounded up.

Becky sank onto his lap, her arms still looped around his neck, and he stayed there in her embrace for a long time.

———

John stepped through the ER doors and paced in front of the hospital, talking to Special Agent Reiss on the phone.

"And with the information obtained from Mr. Foxton, that's how we were able to focus in on West Limos," she said, and rattled off the details.

Agent Reiss had been looking into local racketeering activity for some time, and when Sanders Foxton had been brought in for transporting illegal firearms, he'd become the linchpin in the feds' investigation into the local crime ring that ran guns and drugs across Nevada. Evidently Sanders hadn't known what he was transporting, but the details of the runs he'd made over the years had bit by bit helped the FBI narrow in on one company.

A company that had appeared squeaky clean.

That company owned by a supposed West Strass. But as it turned out, West had been dead a long, long time. West Strass was an alias for West Stravinksy, the brother of Charlie Stravinsky who'd been killed by an unknown assailant in a poor neighborhood in his native country more than four decades ago. Since then, Charlie had moved to America and had been laundering his money through companies he set up with a fake identity in his brother's name. Apparently West Strass had many assets around the United States—a carwash in Texas, a dry cleaner in San Diego, a limo company in Las Vegas, and for a while he'd been the owner of a limo company in San Francisco when Charlie had relocated there, working as a loan shark and running rigged poker games.

But Charlie had returned to Las Vegas and established White Box with his friend and business partner Curtis Paul Wollinsky, who he'd taken under his wing decades ago when Curtis—who went by his middle name then—managed the limo company. Seemed all the questions Paige had asked about missing rides had tipped off Paul, who'd tipped off Charlie, who'd decided he wanted Thomas dead.

That task was all the easier because Thomas's wife was in love with the man who ran Charlie's army on the street—the Royal Sinners. There was a reason they were one of the most powerful street gangs in the country. They had access to criminal masterminds, to men adept at both violent and white-collar crime. Luke was the head, giving orders on behalf of Charlie and paying the Sinners better than average money for selling and dealing.

"Did he offer health insurance, too?" John asked Reiss with a derisive scoff.

"I wouldn't be surprised," she said, then added that they'd nabbed Curtis that morning, bringing him in on racketeering charges.

Funny that their investigations had been on parallel paths for a few months, never meeting until, all of a sudden, the paths collided.

That occurred when Annalise had remembered the term that Thomas heard used years ago, which was still a favorite of Charlie's today. *White Box.* While waiting for Michael to wake up, Annalise had told John what happened at the diner, how someone had overheard her conversation with Michael as they'd pieced the two paths together courtesy of that term.

White Box. Supposedly, according to what Annalise had said, it meant something related to Charlie's dead brother. Everything Charlie did circled back to his brother.

John stopped in his tracks when he realized what its meaning could be. Because Annalise had told him Charlie's last words. *You know nothing about my brother. Nothing about how he was buried.*

John's blood chilled as he realized Charlie's brother, at age nine, must have been buried in a white coffin. And so Charlie named his businesses for him, and for the way he left this earth.

It was oddly commemorative and terribly twisted at the same time. Which described the man who'd built, raised, and run the Royal Sinners. Terribly twisted.

The ways in which people remembered the dead could turn them into killers or into lovers.

John chased away the philosophical thoughts, pushing his sunglasses up the bridge of his nose as he refocused on the call. "Crazy to think this all started from a speeding ticket," he remarked as he paced the other direction.

"Right? But that's how it goes. Nothing happens for a long time and then one misstep and all the dominoes fall."

They were falling indeed. In the last few weeks, the most notorious street gang in the city's history had been effectively dismantled. John would never have been able to do his part without the help of the Sloan family—each of them had played a role.

That was fitting.

As he finished the call, he stared briefly at the sky, the sun poking through clouds.

Today was something like justice, and that was all he could ask for in this line of work.

49

Gently Annalise pushed open the door to Michael's room, nerves thrumming through her body. Instantly, his eyes swung to her, the blue irises sparkling as he lay in the hospital bed.

"Hey," he said, his voice scratchy from the anesthesia.

"Hi," she said, unable to contain a crazy grin, or the relief that flooded her heart. She crossed the few feet to his bed and drank in the sight of him. An IV drip snaked out of his arm, and his chest was bandaged. His face was tired, but a gorgeous smile tugged at his lips.

"You look beautiful," she said.

"I'd laugh, but it would hurt too much."

"Are you okay?" she asked, wonder in her voice, still amazed, still overjoyed that he was here.

"Yes, and that's what they tell me, too. But I suspect the morphine helps that feeling."

She smiled once more and raised a hand, wanting to touch his face, his arm...him.

"You can touch me," he rasped, answering her unspoken question.

She bent forward, touching him first with her lips, brushing them across his cheek. A quiet sigh escaped him. "I thought you were going to die," she whispered, the words spilling out with a fresh round of tears that fell on his cheek. She'd hoped to be strong. She'd told the other women she would be. But it was hard, so damn hard, and now all the relief and happiness bubbled up and poured out of her in these salty streaks along her face and his.

"Evidently, a lot of people did," he said wryly, his sense of humor as robust as ever. "The doctor said she wasn't sure if I was going to make it through, either. Can't say I'm bummed that I don't remember a thing that happened after I hit the parking garage floor."

"Do you want me to tell you?"

He nodded, and she pulled back. He patted the side of the bed that wasn't tangled up with his IV. "Sit with me, and tell me about the last six hours of my life."

She didn't need to be asked twice. She perched on the side of his bed and held his hand in hers. She cleared her throat, took a breath, and met his gaze.

Then she told him everything that had happened.

———

His mouth fell open as he took in the enormity of what happened after Charlie had shot him. But that moment when Charlie's gun had aimed at Annalise still played before his eyes. He gripped her hand tighter. "He was aiming at you. My only thought was to protect you."

"I know." She ran her finger across his hand.

"And then you...you finished it," he added, wonder in his voice.

She winced, her face squeezing as if in pain.

"Are you okay?"

She nodded. "Yes. Just processing it all still. But I'm more than okay."

"Wow." He shook his head, trying to make sense of everything. "You killed the man who tried to rip my family apart."

She nodded, tears slipping from her eyes. "You're the first man I loved, and the last man I'll ever love. I wasn't going to let anyone take you away from me."

Even though it hurt, even though he wasn't supposed to move, he lifted his arms, reached for her face, and held it in his palms. "I'd die to save you," he whispered softly, reverently.

With fierce eyes and a strong voice, she answered, "I wouldn't let you. Because I'd kill to protect you, and to protect us. I've got plans. I'm planning on loving you for a long, long time."

As she pressed her soft lips to his once more, he felt her love deep in his bones, all the way to his soul.

Love had once been an all-or-nothing thing to him, but with her, love was more than all. Deep and intense, it echoed across time, reverberating to the past, soaring to the future, and, vibrant and bright, love lived in the here and now.

50

Michael leaned against the bar, drinking a scotch and surveying the scene. The waterfalls at Mandalay Bay hummed, splashing down gently along the rocks, while a man at the black baby grand piano played Billie Holiday. The man was Sophie's ex-husband, who was still one of her closest friends, and Michael thought it was pretty damn cool that the guy was at her wedding.

What was also fantastic was that the piano player was just a piano player, not a camouflaged front man for crime.

Well, at least Michael was as sure as he could be that Holden was one of the good guys. Everyone here was, even Sanders, who was grabbing an appetizer from a waiter. He handed it to Becky, and she nibbled on it with a smile as he brushed a kiss to her cheek.

Michael turned to Colin, who nursed a Diet Coke next to him at the bar. "Think you'll be next down the aisle?"

His brother shrugged, but he had a sheepish look in his brown eyes. Michael stared at him. "That seems like a yes."

Colin laughed and set down his drink. "Maybe," he said evasively.

"C'mon," Michael teased. "I got myself shot. The least you could do is get married."

Colin frowned. "Wait. What does you getting shot have to do with me getting married?"

It was Michael's turn to laugh. "Nothing whatsoever. I just like milking this for all it's worth," he said, tapping his chest where the bullet had gotten acquainted with his body one fine day a month ago.

"Bastard," Colin muttered with a smile, as they scanned the crowd once more. Over in the corner, John snagged what looked like tuna sashimi on a fancy potato chip from a waiter's tray. He pretended to feed it to Mindy and then stuffed it in his own mouth as she laughed. Nearby, Ryan and Sophie chatted with a group of his hockey buddies from the league he played in. Sophie looked stunning, and Michael had no clue what kind of dress it was or anything like that, but she seemed like a 50s movie star, all Marilyn Monroe and radiant, while Ryan looked like the happiest guy on earth.

Nearby, Annalise snapped a photo of them. She'd taken the official wedding photos, and was also shooting candids throughout the day, from Sophie getting ready, to her arriving at the hotel, to the reception.

Michael nudged Colin with his elbow. "Seriously, though. Are you thinking about asking Elle? Or are you happy with how things are?"

"I'm happy with how things are, but I wouldn't mind marrying her, either."

"Is that so?"

Colin's eyes widened when he realized Elle had just

appeared by his side. Michael cracked up. He hadn't seen her coming, either.

Colin pulled her into an embrace. "I meant it in a good way."

She swatted his chest. "You better have meant it in a good way."

"Fine," Colin said. "Wanna marry me?"

Elle laughed, tossing her head back, her long hair spilling down her back. "Nice way to ask a girl."

"Well, would you say yes if I asked you?"

She narrowed her eyes. "You'll have to ask and find out."

Colin pressed a kiss to Elle's neck, then turned to Michael. "Thanks for getting me in trouble," he said.

"That hardly looks like trouble to me."

"Want me to go ask Annalise if she'll marry you?"

Michael gestured in the direction of the woman who'd saved his life, in more ways than one. "Be my guest."

He had no worries in that area. Maybe they'd get married. Maybe they wouldn't. But he didn't need a ring or a piece of paper to know she was his forever. He had the confidence in his heart, and the faith that he'd always find a way to take care of her, and give her everything she'd want and anything she'd need. "But hey, maybe our little bro will be next."

Michael cast his gaze to Marcus, who cleaned up well. The kid wore a gray suit and a tie and had brought along a date—a dancer named Cassidy, who worked for Shannon's Shay Productions. Marcus was heading back to Florida to go to school there, so this date might be a one-time thing, but judging from the way he looked at her, held her hand, and listened when she talked, maybe it would be more.

After all, sometimes long-distance relationships had a way of working out. When Cassidy pointed to the ladies' room and excused herself, Marcus scanned the tables until his eyes locked with Michael's, then he headed in his direction.

Michael clapped him on the back. "Hey there. Seems like you're having a good time."

"I am. First wedding I've ever been to."

Michael nodded toward Colin and Elle. "Probably won't be your last."

Colin rolled his eyes, and Elle slugged Michael on the shoulder.

"On that note, we're going to grab some of those stuffed mushrooms I see passing by," Colin said, pointing to a waiter with a fresh round of appetizers.

As they left, Michael dropped a hand on Marcus's shoulder. "You doing okay?" he asked, his tone one of concern.

"As much as I can be okay," Marcus said softly. "You know what it's like."

"That I do, man. That I do," he said, squeezing his brother's shoulder. Marcus's father, Luke, was headed for trial soon, and it seemed all but a given that the man would be locked up. Marcus would then have both his biological parents in prison. He had a stepmom and lots of siblings who loved him, though.

"But everything else in life is good," Marcus said, fixing on a smile. "And I am kicking ass in school."

"You get that from me," Michael said, deadpan.

Marcus scowled. "I thought Colin was the whiz kid."

Michael laughed. "Yeah, just pretend it's me, though. You gotta humor me. I took a bullet in my chest."

Marcus's eyes widened. "You're still milking that?"

He nodded. "And I will for a long, long time."

Later, Michael joined Sanders and Becky, who were chatting with his dad's old friends. "Retirement treating you well, old man?" Michael asked.

"Best thing I've ever done," Sanders said.

"Glad you got to see your dream come true," Michael said, and he meant it from the bottom of his heart. The man might have bent the rules, but his sins were small, and thoroughly forgivable, especially since they'd been instrumental in putting an end to so much pain and hurt in the city around them. Michael had learned in the last several months that the world was sometimes split into good and evil, into black and white. But more often than not, people were shades of gray, like Sanders. He was still one of the good guys, though.

Michael's attention wandered away from the two of them when a redhead in a slinky green dress and black heels winked at him from across the room. Her eyes seemed to sparkle, lighting up with mischief as she raised a finger to beckon him.

He excused himself, weaving through the crowds of friends and family, heeding the call of his woman.

"*Bon soir*," she said in a sexy, low voice.

"*Bon soir*."

"I found a broom closet."

He arched an eyebrow. "Did you now?"

She nodded. "Want to see?"

"In a hotel full of rooms, we need a broom closet?"

She pouted. "But our room is on the fourteenth floor," she said, since they'd booked one here for the night. "And that'll take five minutes, maybe ten, to get to since the elevator is so far away."

He looped his arm around her, brushing his fingers

along her back and down to the curve of her lovely ass. He squeezed it. "That your way of telling me you want me now?"

She inched closer, pressing her breasts to his chest. Her camera was slung over her shoulder. "I do. Apparently weddings make me even hotter for you."

"Can't argue with that," he said as she led him away from the reception and down the hall to the broom closet she'd unearthed for dirty deeds. She tugged him inside, shut the door, and set down her camera, then ran her hands along his chest.

She lingered on his scar, even through the fabric of his dress shirt. Three inches long and jagged, it rested under his pec. "It's one of my favorite parts of you," she whispered.

"Why is that?" he asked as he bent his head to her neck and kissed her throat, inhaling her scent.

She spread her fingers across the fabric. "Because it says you're alive."

He smiled against her skin, kissing her once more as his fingers found their way up the skirt of her dress. "So alive," he said, then dipped his hand inside her panties.

She gasped, and he groaned. Quickly, he unzipped his pants and in seconds he was inside her, making love to her against the wall in a broom closet at his brother's wedding. She looped her arms tightly around his neck, and he dug his fingers into her flesh, thrusting hard, taking her deep.

"Mark me with your words," she said in a breathy whisper. "Like you wanted to that night in New York."

He'd held back then, keeping them inside. He no longer had to. He brought his mouth to her throat, and kissed her hard, breathing out, "I'm so in love with you."

He traveled along her neck, kissing and nipping, biting and sucking, each time giving voice to the words she wanted to hear, and the ones he wanted to say. They were one and the same.

"I'm so in love with you, too," she said, crying out as he rocked his hips against her, filling her, fucking her, loving her, until they both came together again.

She was returning to Paris in a few days, and he wasn't sure when he'd see her again, but he knew that he would, and that somehow they'd find a way to keep making their long-distance love work.

EPILOGUE

Two years later

With her arm linked around his elbow, Michael strolled with Annalise's mother along the pathway by the fountains at the Bellagio. They stopped at the thick, stone railing that surrounded the manmade lake, gazing at the placid waters and the crowds waiting for the aqua ballet.

"In about five minutes, the water show will begin," he said to her in French.

Marie narrowed her eyes, shooting him a sharp stare. "English, young man."

He laughed deeply, then repeated himself as per her request.

"I cannot wait to see the water show," she said slowly, answering him in English, too.

"You'll love it. It's spectacular."

Marie was learning the local language. She'd insisted on a crash course in all things American, since she was living here now five months a year. Michael had bought her a condo in a nearby building, and he spent time with her a few days a week, helping her around the city, and working on her language skills. Marie saw her daughter nearly every day, since that was the point of this arrangement. Marie's health was improving, but she still needed assistance from her family, so Michael had devised a solution.

He'd moved her to America five months a year, and Annalise stayed in his home—now theirs—during those five months. They'd spend the next five months in Paris, and while there he worked remotely as much as he could, but mostly he enjoyed his days wandering around the city, eating the occasional coffee éclair and apricot tarte, and spending as much time as he could with his beautiful wife.

The other two months? Sometimes they travelled together. Sometimes they lived apart. But they always came back together, and truth be told, the time apart made some things even hotter.

With the new schedule, his workload had lessened, and that was fine with everyone involved. He'd once thought he couldn't give up work, but it turned out nearly dying changed your perspective. Work didn't matter as much as family. He had two families now—his own and his wife's—and he loved them both dearly. Besides, Sloan Protection Resources had a new partner. Mindy was a part owner, and she and Ryan had become the main forces at the company. Seemed to work well, since Ryan and Mindy had both married into the same family. Mindy was Mindy Winston now.

Colin and Elle had tied the knot a year ago. They'd decided to make it official since they found themselves—rather quickly—adopting a two-year-old girl from foster care who'd lost both her parents. She was one of Michael's truly adorable nieces. Shannon had a baby boy, and then a girl joined them soon after. Another girl would be coming into the family soon, since Sophie was ready to pop any day.

As for Michael and Annalise, well, maybe someday they'd have kids. For now, he was happy with the way things were. He'd be happy, too, if they changed. As long as he had her, it was all good.

"How was your visit to Hawthorne?" Marie asked.

He didn't answer right away. He inhaled deeply, lingering on the question. Seeing his mother was hard. It was tough. It challenged him like nothing else had. But he'd made the decision two years ago to let go of his all-or-nothing attitude toward her. He didn't call it forgiveness. Though he understood more of why she'd made her choices, he could never abide by them.

He didn't have to, though. He could choose to be the man his father had raised. A man who lived a life full of love, compassion, and hope.

And that was why he'd decided to visit her, now and then. To honor the lessons his father had taught him— lessons in mercy. Lessons in grace.

Today his mother had been chatty, talking about a new soap opera she'd started watching. When she was through, he'd updated her on everyone, telling her about how cute Shannon's babies were and showing her pictures. Then he told her about Marcus. Turned out the kid was a chip off the old block. He'd kept up the long-distance relationship with the dancer and that devotion had paid off. Cassidy had moved to Tampa recently, having landed a ballet gig there, near his college. He'd graduate with his business degree in one more year.

On prior visits Michael had updated his mother on the other news over the last few years. Luke Carlton had been sentenced to life in prison for conspiracy to commit murder, as well as multiple counts of racketeering. Curtis Paul Wollinsky had received forty years on RICO charges, and T.J. Nelson was in the big house for life, too. There had been no rumblings, nor even any whispers, of gang activity in a long time. And White Box had been shut down. The four Sloan siblings bought the shuttered property and donated it to the city to turn into something else —the Thomas Paige Library.

"It was a good visit," he said to Marie, shooting her a smile as the sun dipped lower and the music began, signaling the start of the show. "It was good to have Annalise with me."

A few minutes later, he felt Annalise's breath on his neck, then a kiss from her lips. "Hi, handsome," she said softly. She was freshly showered after the long drive back.

She gave her mother cheek kisses, and wedged herself between them, an arm around each. "My two favorite people," she said, and then they watched the fountains at the Bellagio spray water high into the sunset sky.

"We finally made it to the Bellagio," she whispered, for him only.

"We finally made it."

———

Later that night, they gazed out the floor-to-ceiling windows in their Las Vegas home, watching the lights of the city, one of her favorite pastimes. It was something they also loved to do from their home in Paris. Her flat had become his home as well, and was now full of pictures of the two of them.

She pressed her hand on his torso. "You're still the sexiest guy I know, even if you don't have a spleen."

He laughed. "Amazing that I work without it."

"You have all the parts that matter," she said, tapping his head then dropping her hand to the front of his jeans, squeezing him. She travelled up his chest and stopped at his heart. "But this one works best of all."

"Yes. It works pretty damn well, if I do say so myself," he said and then took her to bed.

Both outside their home and between these walls, there was peace, and hope, and so much love that she knew it would carry them far into happily-ever after, and then some.

THE END

Sign up for my newsletter to receive an alert when these sexy new books are available! If you enjoyed this series, please check out my Seductive Nights series, or my sexy sports romance MOST LIKELY TO SCORE!

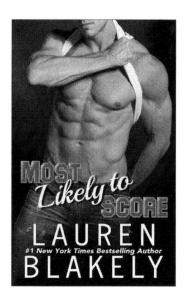

Jillian

I won't look down.

I repeat my mantra over and over, till it's branded on my brain.

This might very well be my biggest challenge, and I mastered the skill of *eyes up* many years ago.

But now? As I stand in the corner of the photo studio, I'm being tested to my limits.

I'm dying here. Simply dying.

The temptation to ogle Jones is overwhelming, and if there was ever a time to write myself a permission slip to stare now would be it. An excuse, if you will. For a second or two. That's all.

The man is posing, for crying out loud. He's the center of attention. The lights shine on his statue-of-David physique. Michelangelo would chomp at the bit to sculpt him. His body should be on display as the perfect specimen of the ideal form—carved abs with definition so fine you could scrub your sheets on his washboard; arms that could lift a woman easily and carry her up a flight of stairs before he took her; powerful thighs that suggest unparalleled stamina; and an ass that defies gravity.

I know because I've looked at his photos on many occasions. In the office. Out of the office. On my phone. On the computer.

In every freaking magazine the guy's been in.

It's my job to be aware of the press the players generate.

But it's not my job to check out his photos after hours, and I partake of that little hobby regularly. He gives my search bar quite a workout.

Still, I won't let myself stare at him in person, not in his current state of undress. My tongue would imitate a cartoon character's and slam to the floor.

If I gawk at him, I'll start crossing lines.

Lines I've mastered as a publicist for an NFL team.

It's something my mentor taught me when I began as an intern at the Renegades seven years ago, straight out of college. Lily Eckles escorted me through the locker room my first day on the job, and said, "The best piece of advice I can give you about managing your job is this: don't ever look down."

I'd furrowed my brow, trying to understand what she meant. Was it some wise, old adage, perhaps an inspirational saying about reaching for the stars?

When she opened the door to the locker room, the true meaning hit me.

Everywhere, there were dicks.

It was a parade of appendages, and swinging parts, sticks and balls as far as the eye could see.

The truth of pro ballers is simple—they let it all hang out all the time, and they love it.

So much so that the running joke among the female reporters who cover the team is that with the amount of swagger going on in the locker room when ladies are present, the TV networks should all be renamed the C&B networks.

But when you work with men who train their bodies for hours a day, and then use those same physiques to win championships, you can't be a woman who ogles them in the locker room.

MOST LIKELY TO SCORE can be ordered everywhere!

ALSO BY LAUREN BLAKELY

FULL PACKAGE, the #1 New York Times Bestselling romantic comedy!

BIG ROCK, the hit New York Times Bestselling standalone romantic comedy!

MISTER O, also a New York Times Bestselling standalone romantic comedy!

WELL HUNG, a New York Times Bestselling standalone romantic comedy!

JOY RIDE, a USA Today Bestselling standalone romantic comedy!

HARD WOOD, a USA Today Bestselling standalone romantic comedy!

THE SEXY ONE, a New York Times Bestselling bestselling standalone romance!

THE HOT ONE, a USA Today Bestselling bestselling standalone romance!

THE KNOCKED UP PLAN, a multi-week USA Today and Amazon Charts Bestselling bestselling standalone romance!

MOST VALUABLE PLAYBOY, a sexy multi-week USA Today Bestselling sports romance!

The New York Times and USA Today Bestselling Seductive Nights series including *Night After Night*, *After This Night*, and *One More Night*

And the two standalone romance novels, *Nights With Him* and Forbidden Nights, both New York Times and USA Today Bestsellers!

Sweet Sinful Nights, Sinful Desire, Sinful Longing and Sinful Love, the complete New York Times Bestselling high-heat romantic suspense series that spins off from Seductive Nights!

Playing With Her Heart, a USA Today bestseller, and a sexy Seductive Nights spin-off standalone! (Davis and Jill's romance)

21 Stolen Kisses, the USA Today Bestselling forbidden new adult romance!

Caught Up In Us, a New York Times and USA Today Bestseller! (Kat and Bryan's romance!)

Pretending He's Mine, a Barnes & Noble and iBooks Bestseller! (Reeve & Sutton's romance)

Trophy Husband, a New York Times and USA Today Bestseller! (Chris & McKenna's romance)

Far Too Tempting, the USA Today Bestselling standalone romance! (Matthew and Jane's romance)

Stars in Their Eyes, an iBooks bestseller! (William and Jess' romance)

My USA Today bestselling No Regrets series that includes
The Thrill of It (Meet Harley and Trey)
and its sequel
Every Second With You

My New York Times and USA Today Bestselling Fighting Fire series that includes
Burn For Me (Smith and Jamie's romance!)
Melt for Him (Megan and Becker's romance!)
and *Consumed by You* (Travis and Cara's romance!)

The Sapphire Affair series...
The Sapphire Affair
The Sapphire Heist

Out of Bounds
A New York Times Bestselling sexy sports romance

The Only One
A second chance love story!

Stud Finder
A sexy, flirty romance!

ACKNOWLEDGMENTS

Thank you so much for reading Sinful Nights and for loving the Sloan family. I am so very grateful to each and every reader for making it possible for me to keep writing books. I am grateful to so many people for bringing this series to your hands. They include KP Simmon, Helen Williams, Sarah Hansen, Kelley Jefferson, Jen McCoy, Kim Bias, Lauren McKellar, Kara Hildebrand, Candi Kane, Michelle Wolfson, and many more. I would not be able to make it through each day without my writer buds – Lili Valente, Laurelin Paige, CD Reiss, K Bromberg, Sawyer Bennett, Monica Murphy, Lexi Ryan, Adriana Locke, Corinne Michaels, Melanie Harlow, and many more. Thank you to all the bloggers who have helped spread the word and the readers who have loved this family!

As always, thank you to my husband, my children and my dogs for being my loves!

Contact

I love hearing from readers! You can find me on Twitter at LaurenBlakely3, Instagram, or Facebook at LaurenBlakelyBooks, or online at LaurenBlakely.com. You can also email me at laurenblakelybooks@gmail.com

Made in the USA
Middletown, DE
27 January 2019